THE HUNTER OF MAUTHAUSEN

Daley had been a young GI marching through the idyllic countryside. Five miles off, he could smell the sickening stench. He hadn't known then what it was. None of them had. Hearing the whispers passed down the line did nothing to prepare him for the reality of that camp. The bodies piled like cordwood. And even worse than the dead, the living. Emaciated, haunted faces that stared dazedly at the liberating army. Nothing he'd seen since had equaled that experience for sheer horror.

And now, as if it were a frame in a film suddenly frozen, Daley's mind focused on a single moment in front of his Tel Aviv hotel. The wind had lifted the man's white hair for one split second, and in that moment Daley had seen and known.

"Mother of God!" Daley said aloud. He'd looked right into the aging face of Rudolf Lobel, the man who'd once been known as "The Hunter of Mauthausen."

Also by Fran Yariv

LEAVING
THE HALLOWING
LAST EXIT

SAFE HAVEN

Fran Yariv

A DELL BOOK

Published by
Dell Publishing Co., Inc.
1 Dag Hammarskjold Plaza
New York, New York 10017

Dell ® TM 681510, Dell Publishing Co., Inc.

ISBN: 0-440-17527-5

Printed in the United States of America

November 1986

10 9 8 7 6 5 4 3 2 1

WFH

For two special people:
Gabriela Yariv, my daughter,
and
Daisy Cohen, my aunt

ACKNOWLEDGMENTS

Many thanks to the following people:

Paul Maslansky for the idea and his confidence, Gary Salt and Harvey Klinger for the moral support every writer needs, Paul McCarthy, the sort of editor a writer dreams of. To my Israeli friends Carmela and Eli Warshavsky who know so much and share so generously, Yael and Abraham Katzir, and Joan Gover.

I am grateful to the following individuals and institutions:

The Department of the Army Military History Institute, Emory University's Witness to the Holocaust, and the Center of Holocaust Studies in New York. The Public Relations Department of the Tel Aviv Sheraton Hotel. Guy Ben-Moshe of Kibbutz Hammat Gader, Ziv Rothem of the Jerusalem Police, Rivka Wientrob of the Israeli Police, M. Russek, the Division of Nazi Crimes in Jaffa, Professor Daniel Karpi of The Diaspora Museum, Dr. Alex Grobman, former Director of Holocaust Studies, Simon Wiesenthal Center, Los Angeles, and Aron Breitbart, Wiesenthal Center in Los Angeles, Detective John T. Maguire of the NYPD, and my modest plastic surgeon friend, Dr. W.S. In addition, I wish to thank my mother, Mildred Pokras, a first-class reader. Pete Anderson, who first educated me on the aesthetics of hunting, and Yitzhak Ben Yaacov, who allowed me to witness his skill firsthand. And Gary and Harry of Burger Continental who provided a haven I often needed and the baklava which I didn't need! And finally, to Amnon, for assistance above and beyond the call of duty.

"And the Lord spoke unto Moses, saying: Speak unto the children of Israel, and say unto them: When ye pass over the Jordan into the land of Canaan, then ye shall appoint you cities to be cities of refuge for you . . . and for the stranger . . . that every one that killeth any person through error may flee thither."

PROLOGUE

On a Friday in October, Detective John I. Daley, as was the custom in the Nineteenth Precinct, hosted a party in honor of his retirement from the NYPD. It was held in the lunchroom in two shifts to accommodate all the well-wishers. Daley ordered deluxe platters of cold cuts and salads from the deli, good booze, and even white wine for the younger cops. Thirty years was nothing to sneeze at, and he was going to go out in style. To Daley's amazement, his co-workers presented him with a gift that far exceeded his wildest dreams and that, although he had no way of knowing it at the time, would turn out to be a nightmare . . . for Daley and for at least two other human beings, none of whom knew the others . . . and that only the inscrutable hand of fate would throw together.

That same day an Ohio physician left his office earlier than usual and drove to a nearby hospital to visit his wife. She told him the bad news. Her leg, broken in a fall from a stepladder in the kitchen, was not healing as well as expected. The December trip was out of the question for her, she sadly informed him. Dr. John Dailey, a dutiful, devoted family man, insisted he would remain at home too. He could afford to miss one professional meeting. But his wife refused to hear of it. After some discussion, he kissed her good-bye, left the hospital, and stopped by the travel office where he was expected to finalize his plans. He sat in the car for several minutes reflecting. He didn't feel right going so far away, especially during the holidays, while his wife was not well. On the other hand, he was to present an invited paper. An honor, to be sure. He debated with himself, then tossed a coin. Heads, he would go. Tails, he would cancel his reservation. The quarter came up heads. Tragically, he would never know what that flip of a coin was to cost him.

On the other side of the world, in a fashionable Jerusalem suburb, an elderly gentleman was also deciding upon travel arrangements. Impeccably dressed as always, he sipped his first morning coffee and sighed as he reread the letter he'd received the day before. Clearly, he was faced with a dilemma. He looked forward to his vacations abroad. They were, Ruven Levi liked to tell himself, his one luxury. Yet, the letter put his trip in jeopardy.

Shlomo was going to the States to attend his son's wedding. He was sorry to miss the Tel Aviv conference but felt certain, he stated in his letter, "you will make an excellent substitute. Your reputation will enhance the entire proceedings." He supposed he would have to postpone the trip. Duty before pleasure. He was a man who, as his many friends would testify, took responsibility seriously. Perhaps in the spring he would visit Holland and see the tulips.

Just as he'd decided, his housekeeper entered with a shopping bag containing fresh bread and the morning newspaper. He opened the paper while she set about slicing thick slices of the heavy-textured rye and preparing his breakfast. His mouth curled in distaste as he read of the old Bolivian citizen who was to be brought to a long-overdue justice. The photograph showed a wizened, haunted face, yet the man was not much older than he. Clearly, the man's days were numbered and the end, whether by man's hand or God's, was in sight.

Levi set the newspaper aside. All their days were numbered.

12

He was past the stage of life when he could safely postpone pleasure. He would keep his vacation plans as they were but cut them a bit short. He spread a spoonful of jam on the bread, pleased with himself. There were solutions to every problem if one were only willing to examine all the possibilities and make the necessary compromises.

ONE

In a funny way, Daley thought, he'd miss it all. The dilapidated old stone precinct house that should have been torn down or fixed up years ago, the noises of the dingy, high-ceilinged rooms and hallways, the musty, stale cigarette smells. Even the long, boring ride from Queens. It suddenly hit him, as he drove out of the underground garage, that this really was the last time he'd be making that drive. That realization, plus the thought of the envelope in his pocket, brought him down abruptly from the high of the retirement party.

As he neared the Queens Midtown Tunnel, his mind on that damn envelope, Daley impulsively turned down Broadway toward Little Italy. He spotted a parking place almost in front of Vince's on Mulberry Street. The new sign, VILLA CAPRI, made him realize it had been over a month since he'd dropped in to see Vince.

The sign was the only new thing about the place. The inside of the restaurant was the same as it'd been for over thirty years. Dark walls with posters of Italy. Tables covered with red- and white-checked cloths, candles stuck in Chianti bottles. And the same pungent garlic and Parmesan aromas wafting from the kitchen.

Suddenly he was starving. Daley slid into a booth against the wall as Vince waddled out of the kitchen, talking to a waiter.

Daley watched him affectionately. Vince had put on even more weight. He looked like a panda with that head of curly black and white hair and those big, soulful Italian eyes. Funny what happened to people. Back in the Army, Vince had been a skinny little runt. He'd put on a few pounds himself since then, too, but on his six-foot, hard-muscled frame it didn't show.

As the waiter headed for the bar Vince turned and saw him. He hurried over with his hands out, a big grin on his face.

"Daley!" Vince lowered himself into the booth and signaled to the waiter. "How you been? You look great!"

"Feel great. You're looking prosperous."

Vince laughed, patting his pot. "I know what you mean."

The waiter stood at attention.

"Mario, a couple bourbons."

"I like the new sign," Daley commented.

Vince beamed. "I been talking to an architect about remodeling the inside. What do you think? You think the place looks old-fashioned?"

"What do I look like, a decorator? You ask me, people come to eat, not to look."

Vince sighed. "All these new places opening up around Columbus Avenue, they have this light, clean look. Plants and white walls and chrome tables. Look almost like museums or something. Maybe that's what people like now. I don't wanna be out of touch."

The waiter set drinks on the table.

"How about some cannelloni? Mario, an antipasto and a cannelloni."

"So where you been?" Vince went on when the waiter left. "Angie was asking the other night, 'Where's John? How come we don't hear from him?' She told me to have you over. I was gonna call you this week. How about it? Sunday?"

"Sounds good."

"Hey, you haven't seen the new addition." Shifting his bulk in the booth, Vince reached for his wallet and produced a snapshot. Daley studied the chubby infant.

"Theresa's newest. A boy," Vince said. "That makes four boys for her, and Cathy's expecting in March."

Daley passed the photograph back. "Cute. What're you trying for, your own basketball team?"

"Not me, them." Vince laughed proudly. "It's outta my hands. So what's new?"

"I packed it in today. You're looking at a retired NYPD detective."

"Hey, no kidding! Congratulations!" Vince's moon face looked ready to split from the grin.

The waiter brought the antipasto. Daley speared a pepper and tore a hunk of bread from the loaf in the basket.

"Yeah, thirty years. Seems like yesterday."

"I know what you mean. Seems like yesterday I bought this place. Hey, remember the night we tried to think of a name for it?" He laughed. "It was you came up with Villa Capri. You said it was the closest I'd get to Capri. You were right."

"Yeah." Daley laughed. "Weird how I was the one who got to Italy while you got shipped to England. What the hell were you doing there, anyway? I never did figure it out."

Vince shrugged. "Pushing papers. Not only boring but lousy food. I could've been a millionaire if I'd opened this place over there."

The war was the one experience that had bound them together for nearly forty years, yet, strangely enough, one they never discussed except for indirect references. That generally suited him fine. Talking about feelings went against his nature. It was the way he'd been brought up, Daley supposed. His family expected everybody to keep his personal business to himself. They weren't a family of gabbers like Vince's, where you could hardly get a word in. Yet the infrequent times over the years when he'd brought up the subject of the war, usually when he'd had the dream, the normally garrulous Vince seemed to turn off.

"You ever think about the war?" Daley asked.

"Not much. You?"

"You know when I thought about it? The other night I was

16

watching the news and I saw that old Nazi they caught up with in Bolivia. You see that?"

"Otto Mueller. Yeah. They're making a big deal out of it. What about him?"

"They're going to extradite him to Holland for trial."

"My grandson, Tommy's boy, was watching that. He says to me, 'Gramps, why don't they just forget it? He's so old he's gonna die any day, anyway.' I don't know, Daley, maybe the kid's right. Let bygones be bygones."

Daley was caught off guard. Back in the Army, Vince had been a softie, the stereotypical GI giving candy to kids. He'd even talked about adopting a war orphan until Angie had the sense to talk him out of it.

"Come on, Vince, you think they should let the bastard go?"

"They don't even know for sure Mueller's guilty. Hell, most of the witnesses are dead. Anyway, it doesn't matter."

"Doesn't matter! Christ, Vince, don't tell me you forgot those camps!"

"Maybe it's better to forget some things. You been a cop too long, Daley, that's your problem."

"You don't have to be a cop to recognize scum, and Mueller's scum."

"How many murders go unsolved here in New York every year, huh?" Vince challenged. "You better worry about the punks and psychos walking around here instead of a half-dead old Nazi!"

Daley'd decided long ago, the only way to be a cop and not go crazy was to harden himself so nothing touched or shocked him. He was surprised at his own emotional response.

"What the hell's with you!" he demanded. "You were there. We were there together. We saw it!"

Vince's face flushed angrily. His dark brows drew together as he belligerently pointed a pudgy finger at Daley. Daley was startled by the hard, almost savage expression that suddenly replaced his friend's normal placidity. Vince could have been a total stranger.

"Listen, Sir Galahad, it doesn't matter one goddamned bit what that bastard Mueller did, how many women or kids he gassed, because he'll never come to trial!"

"What're you talking about?"

Vince slumped back in the booth. He shrugged and his cheerful expression returned. Once again he looked like an overgrown choirboy.

"Well, hell, you're a cop, Daley. It's common sense. No way they can protect him now, with all that publicity. Somebody'll get him."

Vince suddenly became animated. "How's the antipasto, huh? You want some more bread?" He raised his glass. "Here's to you, Daley. So what're you going to do now?"

Although they were back on familiar ground, Daley still felt unsettled by Vince's uncharacteristic outburst.

"Go hunting, soon as the season opens."

"Some sport. The bird always loses."

"Not necessarily." Daley found himself getting wound up like he always did when he talked about hunting. "They got their tricks and you gotta be smarter than them. They take cover and then if you do flush them out so they take off, they come out with this flapping sound and it doesn't matter how long you've been hunting, it still startles you and throws you off. You don't know where they are or where they're going. You just know something's happening and you react. You can react wrong. Shoot over or under. Funny thing is, you think that's when they're most vulnerable, but it's one of their defense mechanisms."

He's spent all his life in a city, but when he was stalking quail Daley felt it was somehow natural. Uncivilized but natural, the way men were at the beginning. Hunting, he felt really alive.

"Sounds like being a cop," Vince remarked. "Going after somebody who's trying just as hard to get away."

"Yeah, but with hunting, even on days when I don't get a bird, when the bird outsmarts me, I still feel good. You oughta give it a try, Vince. Do you good to get out there in the woods early in the morning with the sun just coming up. Clean air. Trees, real trees. Come with me one time."

"I see all the nature I want, mowing my lawn," Vince laughed. "So what else besides hunting? What're you going to do now?"

"Maybe some part-time security work, maybe give talks.

18

You know, to civic groups, schools, neighborhoods out on the Island or in Connecticut, telling them how to keep from getting their jewelry ripped off."

"See how the other half lives."

"Yeah, or I might do some work with kids. I always liked kids. At least the way they used to be," he amended.

"I know what you mean. Knock on wood, my grandkids are okay so far."

Now that Vince had given him the opening he wanted, the reason he'd stopped by in the first place, Daley pulled the envelope with the Emerald Isle Travel logo out of his pocket.

"Vince, take a look at what the guys gave me. Can you believe this? Of all the goddamned things!"

Vince put on his glasses and studied the ticket and tour information as the waiter brought the cannelloni.

"St. Columbine Tour of the Holy Land." Vince let out a long whistle. "Jeez! That's some gift! That's terrific."

Daley pushed the food aside and lit a cigarette.

"They thought they were doing something nice, but there's no way I'm going over there. Colleen wants to see me, she knows where I live."

Vince sighed. "Daley, don't be a goddamn fool."

Daley took the ticket and shoved it in his pocket, anger returning at the old argument.

"What do you know? You got your whole family here. Christmas comes, you got a house full of grandchildren. You get sick, one of your girls comes running to see what's wrong. People ask 'How's the family?' you don't have to bullshit around it. You pull out the pictures. What do you know?"

"So if you're lonely—"

"Who the hell said anything about lonely?"

"If you're lonely," Vince persisted, "it's your own goddamn fault. Listen to me, you stubborn mick, who says you gotta sit alone in that house every night, huh? Since Mary Helen died, it's like a mausoleum, for Christ sake. Jeez, Daley, you live in New York, not some Kansas farm. There's movies and plays and restaurants besides this one. You're still a good-looking man. What about women?"

"Women!" Daley snorted.

"Yeah, women. You know how many times Angie told me

19

she knows this woman and that she wants to introduce you two?"

"Don't do me any favors. Nothing against Angie, but she and my sister, Peg . . . their idea of a great time is playing bingo in some church social hall with a widow whose big mouth's only topped by her fat—"

"Hey, now you're hitting below the belt." Vince laughed, pointing to his spreading paunch.

Daley leaned back in the booth and grinned despite himself. He and Vince went back too far for him to stay angry. When he stopped to think about it, he was closer to Vince than to his own sister, or to the guys he'd worked side by side with for thirty years. Vince knew things about him no one else did.

"What was so terrible, huh? That she married a Jew? That it?"

Vince was jabbing at him like some punch-drunk fighter.

"It wasn't my choice, but I could live with that. Hell," he said bitterly, "it was me introduced her to Ilan, remember?"

"So if not that, what?"

He wasn't going to let go, Daley thought. He'd keep digging at that unhealed wound until he drew blood.

"Lay off, Vince."

"I wanna know what was so terrible you haven't talked to your own daughter for twelve years."

Daley felt the ball of rage he'd carried around for all those years explode. His fist crashed down on the table. A fork sprang into the air and clattered to the floor. A couple at the next booth threw alarmed glances his way.

"Daley, let go of it," Vince said gently.

Daley lit a cigarette, surprised to see his hands shaking.

"Listen to me, what are you, sixty?"

"Fifty-nine," Daley muttered.

"Okay. How much time you think either of us got? Twenty, if we're lucky, me with the pasta and you with the booze and cigarettes, maybe not even that long. How many kids you got? One, that's all. How many grandchildren? One, that's all. Me, I got four kids and eight grandchildren and let me tell you, that's what it's all about."

Vince didn't have to tell him that, Daley thought. His only

grandchild was living halfway around the world, even named after him, and he'd never even laid eyes on him.

"A kid oughta have the chance to meet his own grandfather," Vince said.

It'd been a mistake to come by. He'd thought if anyone would understand, it'd be Vince, but here he was taking Colleen's side.

"Must be really something spending Christmas Eve in Bethlehem," Vince said, changing the subject again. "Angie'd give her eye teeth for that."

"You want the ticket, I'll give you a real bargain."

He ground out his cigarette and turned back to the cannelloni.

"Daley, no reason you can't take that trip. Don't see them. See Bethlehem, Jerusalem. The holy places. Have a good time and come home. Colleen'd never have to know you were there."

The restaurant was starting to fill up. Vince finished his drink and hoisted himself up out of the booth with a grunt.

"So what do you say? Sunday, four o'clock? How's the cannelloni?"

"Great."

Vince beamed. "On me. For the retirement. Listen, Daley, you got anything better to do in December? Take the trip and send me a postcard. It'll keep you outta trouble. Keep you from worrying about senile old Nazis!"

Daley laughed. "See you Sunday, but give me a break . . . no widows!"

He watched Vince making his ponderous way to the kitchen.

You got anything better to do?

Daley pondered the question.

TWO

It had been an unusually good vacation. Dr. Ruven Levi reflected upon the trip as he presented his passport to the clean-cut young man at the Swissair counter. Perfect weather—Europe was experiencing an exceptionally mild winter, luckily for him. He smiled, thinking how all his years in Israel had thinned his blood. To think that as a boy he'd enjoyed sledding and playing in the snow! He doubted if he could stand a European winter now, not that he would ever consider such a thing. When he'd immigrated to Eretz Y'srael he'd said goodbye forever to that bloodstained continent and all it stood for. But a visit was something else. The crisp European weather had invigorated him, bringing color into his cheeks. He'd indulged his weakness for fine food, bemoaning as always the lack of gourmet cuisine in Israel. He'd never developed a taste for the North African or oriental, as it was called, dishes, and the outstanding continental restaurants were pitifully few and far between, even if one did not mind paying the scandalous prices.

The airline official stamped his passport. Levi took out his wallet to pay the Zurich airport tax, his mind far off on the glorious scenery he feasted his eyes on for the last two weeks. He'd gone hiking in Garmisch-Partenkirchen, and then rented a car to drive south to Innsbruck. From there he'd gone west to the Aarlberg region of Austria, south through the Resia Pass, stopping for the night in the northern Italian spa town of Merano in the Adige Valley. And then sentiment had taken him to Venice, where he'd taken Frieda on their first vacation. Although Frieda had been gone for so many years, he'd not had the heart to return before. At this stage of life, he felt the desire for closure. To come full circle with the joys and pains of the past. He'd stopped on the way in Verona, that jewel town, and thought of Frieda and the past as he sat in a side-walk cafe staring at the lovely old Roman amphitheater.

Handing him a boarding pass, the airline clerk motioned him to passport control. Dr. Levi picked up his hand luggage and the bottle of Napoleon brandy he'd bought in the duty-free shop and proceeded. Yes, it had been a refreshing trip in every sense of the word. Yet, he wasn't entirely sorry to be cutting it short this year, for he admitted grudgingly to himself that he was tired. If the truth be known, each passing year made slight inroads into his energy and stamina and Ruven Levi hated to make allowances to age. He was, if anything, the ultimate survivor.

Even to survivors who had found a safe haven in Eretz, the insularity and confining feeling of a tiny country at times became difficult to bear. Most educated Israelis felt similarly. Hence, their passion for travel at every opportunity, despite the spiraling costs. That and, he mused as he entered the waiting lounge, the desire to buy the latest major appliances, which cost a fortune at home and which could be brought into the country for less. He smiled, thinking of his sister-in-law, Rivka. Thank God he'd managed to find the blender she wanted or he'd never have heard the end of it!

Settling down in the lounge, he opened his paper. More bad news everywhere. The world was crazy. A terrorist group was claiming responsibility for the bombing of a kosher restaurant in Paris. An American college freshman admitted killing twenty-three coeds over a six-month period. There was no law enforcement anymore, he thought sadly. Even in Israel the

23

police had their hands full. Two of his neighbors recently had their homes broken into. He felt safe with Buzz and encouraged Rivka to get a dog, but she turned up her nose at the idea of having an animal in the house. He turned back to his paper. The Iranians and the Iraqis were again making war noises; the Muslims and Christians were killing each other in Lebanon. The U.N. was once more trying to pass a resolution expelling Israel. And to top off all the insanity, the press was becoming hysterical over the Otto Mueller case, determined to make of it another Eichmann.

"Ruven, is that you?"

Levi looked up. A portly, middle-aged couple was standing in front of him, broad smiles on their faces.

Levi jumped to his feet. "Josef! How nice! And Gerte."

"We're on the same flight, I see," the other man said.

"And I see I have finally succeeded in getting you to Israel," Levi joked, shaking hands with them in turn.

"It should be a good meeting, and of course Christmas in the Holy Land will be exciting."

Levi laughed. "I wouldn't know."

"No, of course not. But just the same, it should be memorable. Well, Ruven, it's been a long time."

"Last year's meeting, I believe."

The woman smiled and playfully nudged her husband. "Yes, I missed that one in Rio, but this year I told Josef there was no way I would be left at home. I am so interested in seeing your country, Ruven, and getting some sun."

"You must let me give you some good advice," Levi said. "I will be most happy to do anything I can to make your stay more pleasant."

"It looks as though they've planned some interesting excursions between meetings," Josef said.

"Perhaps I'll join you on one or two," Levi offered.

"That would be wonderful!" Gerte exclaimed.

"The pleasure is mine. It's not often one gets to play tourist in one's own country."

Aboard the 747, Levi stowed his packages, took his seat, and buckled his seat belt. Running into Josef turned his thoughts to the days ahead. It promised to be a good meeting. His own paper on the latest techniques in tissue expanders was one he was proud of. He felt proud, also, that at last his country would be the host for this important international conference. God knows, he thought wryly, the economy could benefit.

Dr. Levi glanced out the window at the airport and surrounding wooded countryside. How often he thought of the lush forests of Europe, the grand architecture, the fine museums and concert halls. At those times a stab of nostalgia would pierce him, a feeling he knew was commonly shared by Israel's many immigrants, even the Russians. One never completely left one's roots, even if those roots contained poison.

"Ladies and gentlemen, welcome aboard Swissair Flight 671 to Tel Aviv," the steward announced over the plane's loudspeaker. Levi felt a quickening pulse. He really was getting sentimental in his old age, he thought, but he could not contain the rush of emotion at the very mention of his adopted land. He was, he told himself, as always upon returning home, a fortunate man.

THREE

"When we land at Charles de Gaulle we will deplane in the rear area for security reasons. A bus will take you to the terminal. Please proceed directly to the connecting plane."

Daley stretched cramped legs in the crowded aisle and reached up to the overhead rack for his jacket. He wondered if the guys back at the precinct had any idea when they bought his ticket just what kind of strange mix of humanity would be thrown together on the flight. Gabby St. Columbine parish widows, bearded and hatted Hasidic Jews, college kids in grubby jeans and sweatshirts. Where the hell did kids get the money to traipse all over the world, he wondered. Old Jewish couples making the once-in-a-lifetime pilgrimage to the Holy Land mingled with a fashionably dressed group, the men sporting red and white badges proclaiming "International Congress of Reconstructive Plastic Surgeons." And, in the middle of them all, John I. Daley, retired Irish cop. Who would've thought, he chuckled to himself.

"Security reasons. What do you think that means? Do you think something's wrong?"

The voice belonged to a plump, middle-aged woman with a green paper shamrock, identical to his, reading "Emerald Isle Tours" pasted on her fur coat.

"I've been so nervous ever since I got on this plane," she continued. "You read such horrible things about . . . well, you know." She glanced around, then lowered her voice to a whisper. "Terrorists."

Instinctively, Daley reached to his jacket to touch his weapon. He still felt naked, vulnerable, without it. Couldn't get used to not having it.

"When I told my family I was taking this trip," she went on, "they said, 'Mother, why there? Why the Middle East? Go to Europe or the Caribbean. It's too dangerous over there. A war could break out anytime.' Look what happened in Iran when those poor hostages were taken and innocent people were thrown in jail with them. I mean, what good is a government if they can't protect citizens? But I told my family, I have three daughters, all married, I said to them, 'I want to see Jerusalem before I die,' not that I'm ready to go." She batted her eyelashes. "Not by a long shot. There's life in this old girl yet, but even so . . ."

Already wondering how he was going to shake her, Daley eyed the exit where the doctors were massing.

"Maureen, I really don't think you need worry."

Daley turned. The clipped Boston accent belonged to an attractive woman who might have been the same age as Maureen but whose trim figure and smartly cut short dark hair let her pass for mid-forties. As she looked from the woman to Daley he thought he saw a conspiratorial glint of amusement in her brown eyes.

"The strictest security measures are taken on these flights just because of all the potential trouble," the Boston accent continued smoothly. "Now if you were flying into Rome or Athens, you'd have more cause to worry."

Impressed by her confident manner, Daley fell into line behind her. The heavier woman seemed unconvinced. She looked up at Daley.

"What do you think?"

"Seems to make sense."

The Bostonian smiled. Daley trailed the two down the steps

and into the small bus that transported them to the terminal. Remembering the reports of the Lod Airport massacre some years back, Daley silently credited the airline for the extra security precaution. It made him think back to the years when he'd been involved in security. All the headaches, the plans, the contingency plans, the trying to anticipate problems before there were any, knowing all the while that one dangerous nut, an Oswald or Hinkley or Moore, could find a way to slip through.

"Oh, isn't this grand!" the nervous woman exclaimed to Daley as the stewardess directed her to her seat on the connecting plane. "We're sitting together! I'm Maureen Flanagan." She offered a ringed hand. "You weren't at the slide presentation at St. Columbine's, were you? I don't remember seeing you there and I'm sure I'd remember you. I never forget a handsome man."

"John Daley." He saw with relief that the Bostonian was putting her purse on the aisle seat next to him, and he began to think how he might switch seats and put the two ladies together.

"A pleasure," Flanagan was saying. "Are you any relation to Pat and Mike Daley? He's in insurance and—"

"Here, let me help you with that," Daley said as the Bostonian opened the overhead compartment and started to lift up an overnight case. He noticed how agile and compact she was, her tanned arms firm, as though she were used to exercise.

"Thank you, but I can manage." She swung the case easily into the rack, then slid into her seat.

"John Daley," he said, holding out his hand.

"Rose Malloy."

Daley noted her hand. Well-kept but not pampered. Flanagan, he'd pegged for a widow. In the money, too, judging by the jewelry and manicure. Flanagan didn't spend her time doing dishes. Most likely spent the day gabbing on the phone to the three daughters and hunting eligible men at church socials.

Now, Boston, he thought, watching her out of the corner of his eye as she took a book from her bag, didn't do dishes either. And no husband. She handled herself with the easy

28

confidence of a younger woman used to being out in the world. Secretary or teacher, he guessed.

Once airborne, Daley settled back with a bourbon and water and looked at the copy of the itinerary Denny O'Hara, the tour director, had distributed. Two days in Tel Aviv. Knowing his daughter, Colleen, and he would be in the same city for the first time in twelve years gave him a strange feeling. But he told himself he wasn't going to see her anyway, so what difference did it make. Still, it was unsettling.

Boston was reading a travel book, underlining with a red pen. A teacher, he concluded. On his left, Maureen Flanagan listened to music, lacquered fingernails tapping along on the pull-down plastic tray.

"Will those passengers who ordered kosher meals please raise your hands?" the stewardess asked over the loudspeaker.

A sprinkling of hands went up.

"Your first trip to Israel?" Rose Malloy asked.

He nodded. "And you?"

She was one of the only ones on the tour who called it Israel. The others referred to it as the Holy Land, which made him think he might find himself riding a donkey in some biblical-looking place. He wasn't sure what he'd find—that, a Miami Beach, or some kind of military base. And, had he known at that moment what he would find in that land he'd never seen, he would not have believed it.

"Mine, too," Rose replied. "I was close two years ago. I was on a cruise around the Greek Isles and would have continued to Israel but there just wasn't time."

"Sounds like you get around."

"I'm a teacher, and those vacations are tailor-made for travel."

Daley grinned. "I knew it." He pointed to the underlined book. "Only a teacher reads like that."

"You're very observant. I teach history, and it's invaluable to actually see the places I talk about."

"Travel is broadening, as they say."

"Indeed. Ever try a kosher meal?"

He did a double take as she raised her hand to catch the stewardess's attention.

"I never have," she continued, "but seeing and trying new things is what I love most about travel."

The attendant stopped by her seat.

"I didn't order a kosher meal," Rose said pleasantly, "but if you happen to have an extra, I'd like to take it."

Daley laughed. He'd figured her for a teacher, but not a good Catholic on St. Columbine's Holy Land Tour who'd request a kosher meal.

"Of course, you could eat that stuff in New York," he pointed out.

He liked the way the skin around her eyes crinkled when she smiled. And she had nice eyes. A warm, amber brown.

"But it wouldn't taste quite the same, would it?"

"You mean what you said before about the security on these flights?" Daley asked.

"I did read it somewhere, and from what I've seen, it's true. They do take extra precautions on flights to Israel. Remember how long it took us to board? And I understand there are security agents on every flight, although I'd never be able to pick them out."

"I could."

"Really?"

Daley looked around the cabin. He spotted them immediately. Three casually dressed young men sitting separately toward the rear of the plane.

"Over there," he said softly to Rose, and nodded toward one of the men, who got up from his seat and strolled up the aisle. Daley watched the young man as he took a drink of water and paused to say something to the stewardess, who threw back her head and laughed.

"He's one."

"How in the world could you tell?"

"I'm a cop. Ex-cop, that is. Just retired a couple of months ago. We're used to looking at people, figuring them out, seeing things other people don't notice. Like this." He picked up her underlined book.

Maureen had removed her earphones in preparation for lunch.

"You're a policeman, Mr. Daley! How exciting! I feel safer already."

30

"I'm retired," he said.

With a pang of envy, Daley eyed the young security man. He was smoking a cigarette in the galley, joking with the stewardess.

Another stewardess slid the meals from the serving cart onto the seat trays. Daley peered curiously at Rose's tray. Chicken and rice. His own had some kind of beef stew. He was glad he hadn't tried for a new experience.

"How did you spot the security man?" Rose asked.

Daley was about to say he had the same look about him that Ilan had when Daley'd first met him in New York. That wariness underneath the deceptive air of relaxation. A cobra ready to spring. But any mention of Ilan and he'd be talking about Colleen next. He'd always distrusted people who unloaded their life stories on strangers. He wasn't about to dump his past history on Rose Malloy. As nice and interested as she seemed, she'd probably blab it all over the group. He was going to forget about Colleen and enjoy the trip, like Vince had said.

"Cop's instinct," he replied. "A few years back I used to be involved in coordinating security when bigwigs like the Pope or the Queen came to New York. You get to know the type."

"Well, I am impressed." She laughed. "You see the wonderful thing about travel? You learn something new every day."

Daley laughed with her. "How's the kosher meal?"

"I didn't say all the experiences were good, did I?"

FOUR

It was late afternoon when the plane touched down at Tel Aviv's Ben-Gurion Airport. As in Paris, the plane taxied to a halt a distance from the terminal. Daley noticed several vehicles—small buses, a yellow Mercedes, a Subaru, and an army Jeep—parked in a semicircle around the steps. The man he'd picked as a security agent was one of the first to deplane, joining a small group of blue-suited men lounging around the Mercedes. A handful of Israeli soldiers milled around the Jeep. Daley wasn't fooled by their relaxed attitude. The Israelis had the best security in the world, and he knew that at a moment's notice those young men joking with one another so casually could spring into action, guns flashing, with the same deadly professionalism as their brothers who had rescued hostages from Entebbe.

"The first step on foreign soil is so exciting." Rose rummaged in a large canvas purse and pulled out a camera. "I'm a compulsive photographer, but the slides come in handy in class. Especially on rainy days."

"Emerald Isle group, stay together inside the terminal!" Denny shouted.

"It just gives me the chills seeing soldiers with those big guns," Maureen Flanagan said excitedly as they rode in the minibus to the airport building.

To Daley the sight served as an abrupt reminder that he was in a land where anything could happen anytime.

Inside the terminal a smiling young girl greeted passengers with a tray of jelly doughnuts.

"Happy Hanukkah and welcome to Israel."

Daley helped himself to a doughnut. He was instantly struck by the total absence of Christmas as he stared at the huge electrically lit candelabra used at Hanukkah.

"What a lovely idea," Rose said, finishing her doughnut, "although ordinarily I stay away from sweets. . . ."

He was about to reply when she was suddenly swallowed up by a group of the blue-suited security officers. Daley saw one of them take her by the arm. He instinctively moved closer to intercede as Rose's alarmed eyes flew to him for help.

"May I ask, please, why you took that photograph?" one of the young men said politely.

Daley picked up on the tension underlying his courteous tone.

"May I see your camera, please?" A second man held out his hand.

Rose quickly turned over her camera.

"Why did you take that photograph?" the first one repeated.

"I wanted a picture of my first impression of Israel. The Jeeps and the soldiers by the plane. Why? Was there anything wrong with that?"

"For what purpose?" the first man asked as the second examined her camera.

"I'm a history teacher. I take slides of all my trips for my students in the United States."

The men exchanged a few words in Hebrew. The first one returned the camera.

"Sorry." He smiled. "Have a pleasant stay."

They seemed to melt into the crowd.

33

* * *

Once through passport control, Daley found himself in a large room with yellow and orange walls. The PA system was blaring announcements in Hebrew. He told himself this was no different from Kennedy or La Guardia, but he felt as if he'd stepped into another world. The terse exchange with the security men over the camera, the boys and girls in army khaki, Uzi submachine guns casually slung over their shoulders were tangible proof of the intangible tension he'd picked up on. Instead of unsettling him, it got his adrenaline going.

"Do you want to change some money, John?" Rose interrupted his thoughts. "We have time before the luggage arrives, and I'd like to get it out of the way."

Daley took a pack of traveler's checks from his pocket. Details he'd never thought about before now loomed large. He didn't know how much cash he needed, how much was safe to carry around. And he didn't want to ask Rose Malloy. But seeming to read his mind, she leaned over.

"It's so much easier to have fifty dollars or so on hand for shopping, and I want to look at some olive-wood things. They make wonderful gifts."

Daley headed with her to the Bank Leumi counter, where a line had already formed. He wondered if there would be enough time. He looked back at the luggage carousels, where the bags from their flight were just beginning to appear.

"Sliha, pardon me."

A white-haired man cut in front of Daley as he and Rose took their places in the bank line. Daley stepped back, allowing the man to cut through. He watched the man, a sprightly gentleman in his seventies, make his way to an adjoining counter. And as he watched he was gripped by a gut response. The man had an unusual, bouncing gait, rolling on the balls of his feet. Something vaguely familiar registered, clicked in Daley's mind.

After changing money, and with the unfamiliar Israeli shekels in his hand, Daley turned back to where Denny O'Hara was directing a porter to the baggage. To his right, at a counter with an INFORMATION sign over it, he noticed the white-haired tourist handing some coins to the girl behind the

34

counter and taking from her what looked like very different coins . . . thicker, with an indentation across the center.

"Excuse me, but what are those you just bought?" Daley asked, more interested in getting a closer look at the man than in the nature of his transaction.

The man turned. For a fraction of a second, his face was in profile.

"Tokens for the public telephone," he said pleasantly, "but if you ask for them, you should use the Hebrew word *asimonim.*"

"Don't I know you . . ." Daley began, but Rose's voice made him turn from the man.

"Smile, John!" She had her camera aimed. The flash went off. "I'll make a copy for you to remember your landing in Israel."

"I see I'm going to have to watch out if you're into candids," he joked. He turned back to ask the man with the tokens where it was they might have met, but he had disappeared. Daley scanned the terminal. Another flight had arrived. French-speaking tourists streamed through passport control and congregated around the luggage carousels. Daley caught a fleeting glimpse of the man's white head bobbing over the sea of humanity as he strode through the customs area. It was a walk he had seen somewhere before. And for some reason, it disturbed him.

Daley stepped up to the counter and took out a handful of change. He weeded out two dimes and a quarter, sticking them back in his pocket. He plunked down a handful of shekels and bought a half dozen tokens.

Although he couldn't have said why, he mentally filed away the face of the other tourist. Suddenly it seemed important.

FIVE

"It makes you think, doesn't it?" Rose pointed out the bus window to a group of miniskirted, hitchhiking Israeli soldiers toting their Uzis as casually as handbags. "So young. They look like my students."

Daley saw a VW pull to a stop by the roadside. One of the young girls leaned over to talk to the driver, then climbed in. The bus driver shook his head and made a clucking noise of disapproval.

"See that?" He nodded in the direction of the VW. "Always the soldiers hitchhiked home. Never any problems. Now it's very bad."

"Why's that?" Daley asked.

"We have kidnappings starting two weeks ago. A boy in Haifa, thirteen years old. And a nine-year-old girl in Tel Aviv, and last night two students from the Hebrew University in Jerusalem. Very bad. We never had such things before. Now it's like America."

"Do they know who's responsible?" Rose asked. "Were there ransom notes?"

Daley thought back to the Manzone case. His big one. The kidnapping of the eight-year-old son of a liquor tycoon had sent shock waves of fear through the city.

"We think maybe terrorists," the driver answered grimly. "Some new way they make their recruits prove loyalty."

He watched the VW pull away and shook his head again in disgust. "Stupid girl."

Nothing seemed to touch nerves like crimes involving kids, Daley thought. There could be a murder a minute in New York and nobody gave a damn. Let a child be kidnapped or killed or raped and suddenly the public went berserk. It even touched the most callous, proof being the high risk a child killer ran of being killed himself by fellow inmates. New York had its gangs and psychos and punks, he thought. Israel had its terrorists.

He turned his attention back to the coastal highway, the flat, brown countryside. As they neared the city, boxlike, beige concrete apartment buildings began to appear. The bus slowed to a near crawl inside the city limits, and Daley peered curiously at the crowded bus stands along the highway and the passing traffic. Women carrying net shopping bags and green paper cones of fresh flowers thronged the sidewalks.

The bus stopped at the light in front of a candy shop. Daley's mouth went dry as he strained toward the window to stare at the slim redhead who came out of the shop. He'd never seen that copper-colored hair on anyone but Colleen. The woman looked up, evidently saw a friend, and with a wave hurried across the street. Daley sank back in his seat. The woman couldn't have been more than twenty. Colleen, he reminded himself grimly, was past thirty.

WELCOME ST. COLUMBINE GROUP. The large green and white banner greeted them in the modern Sheraton hotel lobby. Denny O'Hara assembled them at a cluster of black couches in the center. In another corner of the lobby Daley saw a blue banner reading WELCOME RECONSTRUCTIVE PLASTIC SURGEONS next to a long table where drinks of fresh orange and grapefruit juice were set out.

An attractive young woman with a British accent passed out envelopes with hotel information and room keys. His was

832. He glanced surreptitiously over at Rose. Her key was 826.

He couldn't remember the last time he'd been even vaguely interested in a woman. Most relationships he'd seen, including his parents', were no damn good. He always figured it'd been luck with Mary Helen, but you couldn't trust to luck more than once. Still, he knew Vince had been right. He was lonely.

He fingered his room key as he watched Rose listening to the hotel representative explain the various restaurants. No doubt about it, Rose Malloy interested him. He'd felt the attraction the minute he saw her, but he didn't want any kind of long-term relationship. Not that she was likely to be interested in him, he thought. What would a well-traveled, educated woman like her want with a retired cop? The thought both cheered and depressed him. If Rose Malloy wasn't interested in him, it made the whole thing easy. Nothing to worry about. But on the other hand, if that was the case, he had the feeling he'd be missing out on something special.

"We've tried to keep your group as close together as we could, and most of you will find that your rooms are on the eighth and ninth floors," the hotel woman was saying.

From the corner of his eye Daley saw the doctors from the plane troop in. He watched them checking in as the girl went on to describe the hotel's special services.

"Your luggage is being delivered to your rooms," she concluded. "Once again, we wish you a very pleasant stay in Israel."

"A shower's going to feel like a million dollars," Rose sighed as the group straggled wearily toward the elevators.

Daley paused at the gift shop to buy a newspaper. He picked up a copy of the Jerusalem *Post* and stood in line behind an American teenager in a UCLA sweatshirt.

"Excuse me," he heard Rose saying, "but do you know if this is the same as aspirin?"

"Let me see. Yes, that would do. You're not well?"

"Only a headache. We just arrived from New York. Probably a combination of jet lag and fatigue."

Daley turned to see who it was Rose was talking to. The man from the airport stood not three feet away. White-haired, impeccably dressed in a conservative dark suit. Their eyes met for the briefest of seconds.

The man tucked a newspaper under his arm, then waved in greeting to someone standing outside the shop. Daley watched the white-haired man join his friend, walking with that distinctive, bobbing gait. A jolt of recognition shot through Daley. Certainly he'd seen that walk before. The two paused in the lobby as a third gentleman, wearing the International Plastic Surgeons badge, stopped to exchange a few words.

Daley quickly groped for the association, slipping back in time, lighting upon and then discarding the obvious possible connections: school, work, church, family, hunting.

"John?"

Rose's voice snapped him back to the present. She was watching him curiously. "What's wrong?"

"I know that man."

"What man?"

"The one you were talking to."

"Who is he?"

"I can't remember, but I know we've met each other before. Did he tell you his name or where he's from?"

"Why, no." Rose was puzzled. "We chatted only a minute. He was helpful and polite. I needed some aspirin and he was—"

"Did you notice anything about him?"

"Nothing unusual. Well, he spoke perfect English, but with a slight accent."

"Anything else? Think hard!"

"John, please! You're frightening me. What is it?"

His brain was spinning, trying to place that face, but he was drawing blanks. With Rose close behind, Daley strode out of the shop and across the busy lobby, where the man was entering the revolving door with his companions. Daley followed. A gusty wind was blowing in from the sea as Daley joined the three men on the sidewalk.

Daley tapped the man on the shoulder. He turned. Again those pale blue eyes behind plain-rimmed glasses met his.

"Sorry to bother you," Daley said. "I'm John Daley from New York. We talked at the airport. I'm sure we've met somewhere."

The man's eyes flickered over him without the slightest sign of recognition.

"I think not," he replied courteously.

"But . . ." Daley began, more certain than before that they had met somewhere, had some connection in the past.

A taxi pulled up and stopped. One of the men opened the door. The second climbed in.

As the man turned to enter the taxi a burst of wind lifted his longish white hair, blowing it back from his face. He quickly reached up to smooth it back in place, but not before Daley glimpsed his left ear. Noticeably smaller than a normal ear, its top was turned back on itself.

The taxi door slammed shut. The car pulled away.

Over the years Daley had come to trust his cop's instinct, that second sight that saw things others didn't. The inner voice that was always suspicious, always vigilant, was screaming an alarm. Something was wrong. Very wrong.

SIX

Daley was not the only one who believed in instinct. Although his formal education had been in the sciences, Ruven Levi was a firm believer in intuition. To be sure, man had come a long way since the cave, but Levi was convinced the distance seemed greater than it was. There was no situation in which he felt this more deeply than hunting, whether for *houglot,* or partridges, in the Negev, or *dorban,* porcupine, and rabbits in the fields not far from his home.

Levi knew himself to be an educated, cultured individual. He loved music and read books in three languages. Yet it was in hunting rather than in intellectual pursuits that he found his relaxation, feeling as if he were tapping into the very core of his being, the part of him that responded to a kill-or-be-killed tension. He had experienced that visceral response as a young boy hunting deer in the forests of Europe, and felt it still, ambushing wild boar in the Galilee. It was in hunting that Levi felt himself shedding the veneer of civilization and reverting to the more basic creature, which depended entirely upon instinct and intuition.

Many were the discussions he'd had with friends about the nature of man. Shlomo, for example, unlike himself, was a devotee of humanism. Not one of the religious fanatics who he believed were destroying the country, but religious enough to believe in the basic goodness of man. On that matter, although neither man could have any way of knowing it, both John Daley and Dr. Ruven Levi were more alike than different. To their way of thinking, it was only the repressive force of society, of law, that kept the instinctive animal nature of man in check. Each of them—Daley in the war and in his work, and Levi in the war—had seen firsthand the barbaric nature of man. Instinct, Levi believed, was the crucial part of man's primitive nature that had not been shed in the evolutionary process.

But as he sipped his tea in the small Hungarian restaurant on Dizengoff, he was less interested in philosophy than in the encounter he'd had with the American. What was it he said his name was? An Irish-sounding name. Dooley. That was it. Dooley. Two encounters, actually, counting the airport.

He barely heard Josef and Gerte. Fortunately they were being entertained by the others, and his preoccupation went unnoticed. The more he thought about it, the more it seemed that in some way the American posed a threat to him. Yet he could not for the life of him pinpoint their connection.

He tried telling himself that their chance meetings had no significance, were no more important than countless other such incidents of mistaken identity. How many times had he spotted a face in a crowd that seemed to call to him from the past? A common enough occurrence. But still Levi could not put the tall stranger out of his mind. There was a sense of power, an indefinable "aura," that Levi sensed in the other man. But it was more than that. It was something in the way the American, Dooley, had stared at him in the gift shop. And again outside the hotel, when the wind had blown his hair up. Levi knew that, in a reflexive gesture born of years of habit, he'd smoothed his long hair back in place, but he thought he'd seen the other man take note of his bad ear. The memory of that moment stirred something in him. While he'd made his adjustments, Levi had never lost his awareness of the deformity. That the other man had seen it disturbed him, as though the sight now gave the American an advantage over him, making him vulnerable. Vulnerability was a feeling Levi despised.

"Cigarette, Ruven?" Katz, a chain-smoker, offered a pack. Levi shook his head. "No, thank you."

"What an example you are, Avram," Gerte chided. "You should take a lesson from the Americans. Why, we were in the States last year and hardly anyone we met there smoked."

Katz was unruffled. He shrugged his hefty shoulders. "It is a way of life here. We are a nervous and a tense people."

"One can see that in our drivers." His wife laughed.

"Well, I see Ruven has given it up," Josef said. "As for me, I am still struggling with the other battle." He patted his ample stomach.

The waiter brought more tea. Levi allowed himself to retreat into his thoughts of the tall American.

It seemed improbable they had met. He knew few Americans . . . several physicians and two cousins of Frieda who lived in California.

"What do you say to a stroll after dinner?" Katz asked. "There is a new cafe not far from here that has a jazz combo. I've wanted to try it."

"For the jazz or the pastries?" Rubenstein joked.

They laughed comfortably.

The check came. Katz quickly tallied the total, and Ruven Levi reached for his wallet to pay his share. He could feel fatigue in his body . . . a slight ache in his calves, tension in his shoulders and neck. Perhaps a walk would relax him.

They left the restaurant and strolled down Dizengoff, stopping to peer into shop windows, Gerte and Josef commenting on the styles of shoes and clothing displayed. The street was teeming with life, as always. People sat in sidewalk cafes and filled the sidewalks. Lighthearted chatter filled the air. The ever-present ice-cream and falafel stands were doing good business with groups of young people.

Dizengoff was a part of Tel Aviv that Levi particularly enjoyed, the spirit and life reminding him of the European capitals . . . Paris, Vienna, Rome. A sophistication he missed in Jerusalem.

But tonight he was unable to join in the carefree mood of his companions. He was bothered. It was that American.

Suddenly, Levi was seized by the certainty that he should have gone home to Jerusalem after the first-day ceremonies. He'd decided only at the last minute to spend the night in Tel Aviv with friends, thus sparing himself the early morning drive back that going home would have necessitated. And as Katz led them to a small, brightly lit cafe, from which the sounds of Dixieland jazz floated, Ruven Levi, no less than did John Daley, paid heed to a little inner voice that warned him. Ruven Levi, like John Daley, could not ignore the instinct. And instinct told him he should have gone home, that something dangerous was to come from that innocent change of plans.

Levi was more than bothered. The cold feeling working its way into the very innermost core of his body was something he had not felt for a long time. Fear.

SEVEN

Daley tossed his jacket on the bed and stepped out on the balcony overlooking the water. He could feel the fatigue of the trip dropping away as he inhaled the brisk air. The sun was setting and the beach nearly deserted except for a scattering of boys kicking a soccer ball. The cabanas and yellow- and orange-striped umbrellas had a forlorn look. Several elderly couples walked slowly along the mosaic-patterned boardwalk. He watched a couple ambling toward the shore, their arms around each other. Their intimacy intensified his own sense of isolation.

What he needed, he told himself, was a shower and then a stiff drink. When he came out of the shower Daley saw that the new brown Samsonite he'd treated himself to had been delivered. When he tried to unlock it the key refused to turn. Then he saw the name on the luggage tag: Dr. John Dailey, 47 Oakwood Lane, Akron, Ohio.

He pulled on his pants and shirt, picked up the phone, and dialed zero. He waited impatiently for an answer, but after a dozen rings hung up. The long journey was finally catching up with him. He stretched out on the bed, thinking he'd rest for a few minutes before trying the desk again.

Bright blue sky. Fluffy white clouds like he'd never seen before. Postcard pretty. A small brown rabbit ran out of the woods and stood frozen in the road.

He heard the sound before he saw them . . . the thump, thump of marching feet. When they came into sight the line of men looked no more substantial than cheap plastic toys. Not real. Only the persistent thump of marching feet was real. One, two, one, two, in rhythm through the wooded countryside.

The rabbit stared stupidly at the advancing men, blinking for an instant in the brilliant sunlight before scampering off into the forest.

One, two, thump, thump.

The sounds grew louder. The men lost their doll-like look. The feeling was beginning in the pit of his stomach, and he knew now there was no way to stop the horror. Now another sound, a distant, unintelligible murmur, no more than the whisper of the wind starting at the front of the line, was working its way back. Growing, growing, it merged with the thump of marching feet. The feeling in his stomach was

46

becoming unbearable as the thump
and murmur grew to an insistent
explosion. . . .

His eyes snapped open. As always when he had the dream, Daley felt slightly nauseated. Mary Helen used to tell him he cried out in his sleep when it happened. He didn't know if he'd shouted now, but his shirt, damp with sweat, told him he probably had. He sat up, his heart pounding erratically in his chest as he looked around the unfamiliar room, trying to get his bearings. The face of the white-haired man flashed in front of him, those pale eyes behind the glasses, the deformed ear, which had been exposed for only a moment. The dream receded into the far reaches of his consciousness as he became aware for the first time of the knocking on his door.

A slight, pleasant-faced middle-aged man smiled at him.

"Mr. Daley, I hope?"

"That's me."

"I'm certainly glad to hear that!" The man held out his hand. "I'm Dr. John Dailey. Seems there's been a mix-up with our luggage. I hope you have mine, as I appear to have yours."

The doctor stepped aside and Daley saw his own suitcase.

"I was just going to call the desk about it."

The doctor came into the room and put Daley's suitcase by the bed as Daley handed him his own.

"Easy enough mistake," Dr. Dailey said. "Not only do we have the same name, but our room numbers are nearly identical. I'm 732. Just one floor below you. Your first trip to Israel?"

Daley nodded.

"Fascinating country. I was here three years ago, but things have changed in even that amount of time. I can see that already. Those kidnappings, for example. I just heard they found the body of that boy from Haifa. Horrible. He was evidently tortured." He shook his head sadly. "Tell me, are you here on your own or with a tour?"

"A church group from New York. You're part of that medical convention?"

Dr. Dailey nodded. "International meeting of plastic sur-

47

geons from all over the world. They'll most likely be scattered around various hotels, but most of the Americans are here and at the Hilton up the street. Well, I'm certainly relieved to get this back. I'm giving my talk tomorrow and all my slides and notes are in here."

"Don't think I'd have made a good stand-in," Daley joked. "I once delivered a baby in a car, but surgery's a little out of my league!"

As he closed the door behind the doctor Daley realized he should have asked him about the white-haired man. He opened the door. Dr. Dailey was making his way toward the elevator as Daley caught up with him.

"By the way," he said, "I ran into one of your group in the gift shop. At least I think he was one of them. I'm sure I've met him before but I can't remember his name. A man about seventy or so, tall, thin, longish white hair. Speaks English with an accent."

"There are over a hundred and fifty of us here from all over the world. I know only a few of the others. I do have a list of everyone at the conference, though, and I could give it to you if it'd help jog your memory."

"Thanks. It just might."

The elevator doors opened. The doctor stepped inside. The doors closed. Once he saw the man's name on the list, the association would come back. He would still that nagging little voice and begin to enjoy the trip. Daley glanced at his watch. First things first. A drink with Rose. Then dinner. The white-haired man could wait.

EIGHT

"I can't wait to take some pictures in the daytime," Rose said.

They were strolling along the beachfront walk with its curving mosaic pattern. "I imagine it's very colorful with people out on the beach."

"I didn't bring a camera," Daley admitted.

"I'll be glad to give you copies of my pictures if you'd like."

Rose was presenting him the perfect opportunity to stay in touch. It must mean she liked him, after all, he thought.

"Thanks."

"But you don't strike me as the sort who'd sit at home going through photo albums."

"Oh?"

It amused him, her trying to figure him out. They'd had drinks together, sat together at dinner along with a few of the couples on the tour. She'd laughed at his jokes, asked questions about his work. Still, he wondered what she really thought of him.

"You're a man used to activity."

"Is that good?"

"Oh, I should think so. You see, I'm observant, too, John. Am I right?"

"On the nose."

"Here's another observation. While I was waiting for you in the lobby before dinner, I saw your friend again."

"My friend?"

"You know, the man we saw in the gift shop."

Daley was instantly alert. "And?"

"And I can tell you this. Either he has a very poor memory or he's just plain rude."

Just the mention of the man unnerved him.

"Go on," he urged.

"Well, he'd been so pleasant in the gift shop, helping me with the aspirin. As I said, I saw him again in the lobby before dinner and I wanted to thank him for his help, but when I went up to him, why he passed by as if he'd never laid eyes on me before. I was left standing there with my mouth open."

Forgetful or rude. A third possibility pushed its way into his mind. Perhaps the man did recognize him but didn't want to acknowledge it. While he was convinced he knew the man from somewhere, the other's blank stare had been convincing. Ordinarily that would be enough for him to conclude he'd been mistaken. But something was wrong. He couldn't put his finger on what, but each time he thought about that white-haired man an uneasy feeling came over him. Why had he snubbed Rose? The only thing that made sense was that, associating Rose with him, the man wanted to avoid them both. It was the why that didn't make sense.

"What did you say to him?" he asked.

"Nothing. I didn't have a chance. He just sailed by. He's the opposite of you, I would say. I can't imagine your being either forgetful or rude to a lady. I can tell some other things about you too." She smiled. "I can tell you were married. Probably a widower."

"How did you know that?"

"I've known a few men in my time. There are definite signs. The divorced ones try too hard. The ones who never married don't try at all, and the widowed . . ." She stopped. "Well, I have to keep some secrets."

50

"Anybody ever tell you you'd have made a damn good cop, Rose?"

"No, thank you! Teaching is hard enough, although there are times I feel like a policeman!"

"And you, were you ever married?"

"I'm afraid I was my family's big disappointment in several respects. I was the youngest in a family of five. I was working as a secretary when my oldest sister died. She left three small children, and as the only single one, I was the logical choice of caretaker. Not that I didn't want to help. I did, and I loved my nieces and nephew, but after four years I realized that the family just assumed that would be my role in life. I'd always wanted to be a teacher, and I woke up one morning and said to myself, 'Rose, it's now or never.' "

"And?" Daley was fascinated, imagining Rose as a young woman bucking family pressure.

"And I went back to school against the wishes of the family. I know to them my need for independence was an abandonment. They could have understood it if I'd married, but as it was, there were very bad feelings on their part and some guilt on mine. As for the marriage, I never met the right man or the timing was wrong or whatever. But I consider myself very fortunate. I've had a career I enjoy, good friends, travel. If I have any regrets at all, it's never having had a child. Of course if I were a young woman today, who knows? I'd probably have a child like so many single women do."

"You're kidding!"

"That shocks you, doesn't it? Having a child would have been a very precious experience. Tell me about your children."

Daley felt his guard automatically go up. "Who said I had children?"

"A good Catholic like yourself!"

Rose was watching him with amused curiosity. He wondered if he could trust her, but to his surprise, found he wanted to talk.

"Actually, I have a daughter and a grandson here in Tel Aviv."

"How wonderful!" she exclaimed. "And how long since you've seen each other?"

"Twelve years."

"My goodness, it's going to be quite a reunion, then."

"No, it won't, because I don't plan to see them. My daughter, Colleen, and I are what you might call estranged."

"Oh, John." Rose's voice was compassionate. "How in the world did she end up here?"

"That's the ironic part. If it wasn't for me, she'd be in the States, where she belongs. About thirteen years ago some of the top Israeli brass came to New York. Dayan and a few others. I was coordinating security with the Israeli team. There was this one young guy I liked right off the bat. He'd been to school in the States, knew a lot, had a great sense of humor. So I invited him home to dinner. My wife, Mary Helen, had died. Colleen was in college then, studying history. She's a history teacher, like you. And she was going with this law student from NYU. We all figured they'd get married. Anyway, she and this Israeli took one look at each other and you didn't have to be an Einstein to figure out something was happening. So, next thing I know, Colleen wants to take a trip to Israel and work on a kibbutz for a summer. Suddenly she's switching her major from British history to the Crusades. She broke it off with the other boy, married Ilan, left the Church, became a Jew. And this from a girl who went to parochial schools, who wanted to be a nun when she was twelve! There wasn't anything she ever wanted she didn't get, and all I expected from her was a daughter nearby, grandchildren to enjoy. That she follow the faith she'd been raised in. Was that so much to ask? She turned her back on me, plain and simple."

"That's a strange way to put it," Rose said. "Turned her back. Seems to me she simply chose her own way of life, and from my own experience, I'm sure it wasn't an easy choice."

"Just like a woman," Daley said sharply.

"What does that mean?"

"Just that it's predictable. One female taking the side of another."

Rose's amber eyes flashed. "Do you really think so little of women?"

She turned and faced the beach and sea beyond. Daley studied her fine profile, the proud set of her shoulders, and knew he'd offended and hurt her. Yet her defense of Colleen after he'd opened up to her had stung.

"I guess you're a dyed-in-the-wool chauvinist, John Daley. It doesn't surprise me but it does disappoint me."

Rose had turned back, once more the proper Bostonian schoolteacher. She started back toward the hotel.

"Hey, wait a minute!" Daley caught up with her, grasping her arm.

"It's late, John, and I'm really quite tired."

"I'm tired, too, damnit, but I don't like being called names! Let me tell you something. When they first started all this women's lib and ERA business, I was for it. And Colleen had everything a son would've had. I never treated her differently, so don't go calling me a chauvinist!"

They walked in angry silence along the beachfront. Just as Daley was starting to feel foolish about his outburst, he felt the gentle pressure of her hand on his arm.

"I can imagine how it must hurt to feel you lost Colleen. I can see her side, John, because it reminds me so much of my own situation. I didn't follow the path my parents wanted for me, but I had to make my own life. And even now it hurts me terribly to know how I disappointed them. Colleen probably feels hurt too. I know you haven't asked for advice and I really don't want to step out of line, but why not see her and try to make it up?"

"We don't have anything to say to each other."

"I should think you'd have a lot to say after twelve years."

"I shouldn't have told you all this." Daley managed a self-conscious laugh. "Only my old friend Vince, back in New York, knows the whole story."

"I'm glad you told me. Sometimes you have to overcome pride and take a chance on trusting."

"Kind of goes against a cop's nature," he said lightly.

"You were a human being before you were a cop, John. Why don't you give your daughter a chance to explain?"

He shook his head. "One thing I learned in police work. Most explanations aren't worth a damn."

Daley took off his jacket and emptied the change from his pocket on the desktop. The telephone tokens were a silent rebuke. Why had he bought them if not to call Colleen?

He stripped down to his shorts and turned on the TV. A

53

shirt-sleeved interviewer was talking to an elderly man he kept calling Goldschmidt. Daley left the set on out of habit, although he couldn't understand a word.

He'd meant it when he told Rose most explanations weren't worth a damn, and while he told himself there was nothing Colleen could say to him after all these years, now that he was here the urge to see her and the boy was becoming strong.

He sat on the bed and lit a cigarette, wishing he had a drink. He thought maybe he'd call room service and order up a bottle of bourbon, then, looking down at his widening waist, resisted the temptation. He'd seen too many guys go to pot when they retired.

He stared at the TV, his thoughts on Colleen and his grandson, Yoni. The Hebrew from the TV interview filled the room with strange, guttural sounds. The interview ended. Daley caught the words *Dachau* and *Auschwitz* and suddenly he was staring at old news footage of concentration camps. For an instant he thought he would be sick.

The face of Otto Mueller appeared next, the same photograph that had been in all the papers. Now Daley was riveted to the set. There followed an old photograph of Mueller as an SS officer, a German shepherd by his side, then shots of the villa he'd resided in in Bolivia. Then the interviewer was back, talking to a woman. Daley got up and turned off the set. He picked up the newspaper he'd bought earlier. The headline stopped him cold: "Otto Mueller Dead."

He skimmed the story underneath the photograph of the old man. Mueller'd lived in an exclusive La Paz suburb for the last twenty-five years. Now justice was cheated, Daley thought, reading with disgust the curiously fatalistic, low-keyed words of Israeli officials. "God has tried him," one was quoted. "Bullshit," Daley muttered. And as he put the paper down and headed to the bathroom, he thought, Vince, that old son of a bitch, was right. Otto Mueller would never come to trial, only it wasn't a vengeful survivor who'd gotten him, but an old and weak heart.

As he was brushing his teeth his conversation with Vince came back to him, and with it an eerie feeling that it was more than idle speculation on Vince's part. It seemed as if Vince had actually known, but of course how could he have? Although he was bothered, Daley was too tired to think about it.

Without bothering to hang up his clothes or put on pajamas, Daley fell into bed, exhausted. He felt he could sleep forever.

> *Bright blue sky. Fluffy white clouds like he'd never seen before. Postcard pretty. A small brown rabbit ran out of the woods and stood frozen in the road.*
>
> *He heard the sound first. The thump, thump of marching feet. Then he saw them, the line of men, which from his vantage point looked no more substantial than cheap plastic toys. Not real. Only the persistent thump of marching feet was real. One, two. One, two in rhythm through the wooded countryside.*
>
> *The rabbit stared stupidly at the advancing men, blinking for an instant in the brilliant sunlight before scampering off into the forest.*
>
> *One, two, thump, thump.*
>
> *The sounds grew louder. Another sound was merging with the thump of marching feet. A distant, unintelligible murmur, no more than the whisper of the wind, starting at the front of the line, working its way back. Growing. Growing. The words began to sort themselves out. "You're not going to believe it." And then the smell washed over him. Not like anything he'd ever smelled*

before. Like the gates of hell
opened up, the putrid stench of
death was everywhere. . . .

Daley was awake. His heart was pounding so erratically, he was afraid he was having a coronary. The man!

As if it were a frame in a film suddenly frozen, Daley's mind focused on that moment in front of the hotel. The wind had lifted the other man's long white hair for one split second before he had reached up to smooth it back. And in that instant Daley had seen his ear. The small, odd, cup-shaped ear. An ear he'd never forget because he'd stared at it every day for three weeks nearly forty years before.

"Mother of God!" Daley said aloud.

NINE

His watch said 5:10. Although he'd slept only a few hours, and fitfully at that, Daley knew sleep was out of the question.

Rudolf Lobel. "The Hunter of Mauthausen" they'd called him. Now that the association had come back, there was no stopping the flood of memory. The first impression he'd had as a young GI marching through that idyllic countryside and smelling, five miles off, the sickening stench. He hadn't known then what it was. None of them did. Hearing the whispers passed down the line did nothing to prepare him for the reality of that camp. The rotting bodies piled like cordwood. And even worse than the dead, the living, who might as well have been dead. Emaciated, haunted faces that stared dazedly at the liberating army. Nothing he'd seen since had equaled that experience for sheer horror. Some of the men became physically sick, throwing up from the stench and shock.

Daley sat up in bed and reached for his cigarettes, even though his throat was raw from the half pack he'd smoked till two in the morning. Mother of God! Rudolf Lobel! He hadn't seen Lobel there at Mauthausen but he'd seen the results of his handiwork. The maimed and crippled survivors who'd described the experiments done on them by the Hunter—sterilization, castration, drug tests, heart injections, and the "special operations" done in the "hospital." He remembered listening with disbelief as a former prisoner described the daily procedures in which various organs were removed from living bodies to be bottled and stored on dissection-room shelves. And he remembered the evidence suggesting that Lobel and his staff had skinned the bodies of those prisoners with interesting tattoo marks, sending the skin to the Gusen pathology lab for processing into gloves, book covers, and lamp shades.

It was only later, as he stood guard at the U.S. trials in Landsberg, that Daley had come face to face with the monster. Lobel. He remembered his first sight of the man as he entered the courtroom, flanked by guards. Daley had noticed first his walk, that unusual bobbing gait. It caught his eye each time Lobel walked in and out of the room. He'd been struck by how ordinary-looking Lobel was, ordinary but for one thing. His ear. From where he stood guard Daley had had a clear view of the deformed ear, visible beneath the closely cropped dark hair. He'd stared at it for the three weeks of the trial, fascinated, trying to reconcile in his mind the man with the horror he had seen.

Daley inhaled a lungful of smoke and slowly let it out. He needed coffee badly, but the coffee shop wouldn't open for another forty minutes.

Rudolf Lobel. Incredible. But he was convinced that Rudolf Lobel and the white-haired man were the same. He stubbed out the cigarette and went to the bathroom. The bloodshot eyes and unshaven face staring back at him from the mirror looked more depraved than any war criminal's. He splashed cold water on his face and began to shave.

By the time he was ready to go down for breakfast, he had convinced himself it was impossible. It had to be. There was no way Rudolf Lobel could be in Israel. An obvious case of mistaken identity, a combination of the publicity surrounding Otto Mueller and being in Israel, where there were so many survivors of those camps. The dream had triggered something in his memory, he told himself, the white-haired man's walk was similar to Lobel's, causing his memory to play a trick on him. He couldn't even be certain, given the brief instant he'd seen it, that the ear deformity was the same. In the light of day, as Daley locked the door and set off toward the elevator, it did seem ridiculous.

Just a sprinkling of tourists was in the dining room at six-thirty. Daley crossed the red ceramic-tiled floor, past the neatly set tables with their coral tablecloths, to the buffet in the center of the room.

"Good morning," Dr. Dailey greeted him from the other side of the buffet. "Isn't this something? This is what's called an Israeli breakfast, and I must say it's impressive. In fact, I may skip lunch."

The table was laden with platters of sliced cheeses, smoked and pickled herrings and other fish, baskets of freshly baked rolls and breads, bowls of yogurt, finely chopped salads, marinated cucumbers, shredded carrots in orange juice. While a chef scrambled eggs in a copper-bottomed frying pan, guests poured their own grapefruit and orange juice.

"Where are you off to this morning?" the doctor asked as Daley took a plate and helped himself to a roll.

"We have a city tour later on."

"Fortunately my paper is one of the first. I can duck out of the later session and do a little sight-seeing myself."

"They give you time off for good behavior?"

Dr. Dailey grinned. "They plan conferences only in interesting places. They'd never get an international meeting going in Buffalo, say. And once people are here they certainly want to take advantage of the opportunity to see some of the country. So the organizers of the meeting have planned a trip to Jerusalem and Bethlehem. The wives are the lucky ones. They have something planned every day. I believe today the ladies are off to Caesarea."

"You fellows better be careful or Proxmire will give you the Golden Fleece Award," Daley joked.

The doctor took a cup of coffee. "We'll risk it. If you're alone, please join me."

"I'll do that."

Daley took his plate to the window seat next to the doctor. The beach, even at that early hour, was alive with activity. He saw twosomes playing a kind of netless Ping-Pong out on the sand. Old people were already strolling the promenade while joggers in sweatsuits and shorts ran along the water's edge. He spotted two middle-aged men in olive-drab uniform carrying Uzis and eating ice-cream cones as they sauntered along the boardwalk.

"Those guys look a little old to be soldiers," Daley commented to the doctor, "and more than a little out of shape."

"I'm told they're volunteers who patrol the boardwalk. Terrorists, you know."

"The NYPD could use them."

The doctor grinned. "Isn't it the truth! But strange as it seems, I feel safer here than in New York."

"Even with those kidnappings?"

"That appears to be rather an isolated thing, judging from the general panic. This morning's paper indicates they suspect a terrorist group."

Daley's eyes automatically sought out the two uniformed men mingling with the beachgoers.

"I guess people get used to living under constant stress," the doctor said. "Of course, having been in law enforcement, you'd know about that."

Daley nodded. "It's amazing what you can get used to."

"Oh, before I forget," the doctor said as he finished his coffee, "here's that list I promised you. I hope you find your friend's name on it."

"Thanks, but I think I made a mistake."

Nevertheless, he took the Xeroxed list.

"I've been meaning to ask you," the doctor said, getting up to leave. "I have an eleven-year-old son who's addicted to those TV police series. How accurate are they, anyway?"

Daley grinned. "About as accurate, I'd guess, as those doctor series my wife used to watch."

The doctor laughed. "Touché." He got to his feet and gathered his briefcase and newspaper. "It's been a pleasure. Have a pleasant day."

Daley helped himself to a refill of coffee, then, returning to the table, lit a cigarette and took out the list the doctor had given him. He started to read the names. Over two hundred. He began with Allen, Henry, New Rochelle, New York, and continued until he reached Zuckermann, Ernst, Munich. As expected, Rudolf Lobel was not included, nor was there any variation on the name, even though he paid particular attention to every Germanic-sounding name. None bore any similarity to the name Rudolf Lobel. But there were five names with the initials R.L. Ronald LaVine, Ralph Lee, Ruven Levi, Richard Lindell, and Ramona Lowenthall. With the obvious exception of Ramona Lowenthall, it was possible Rudolf Lobel was one of them. He would begin with those four names.

He wished there was someone around he could bounce the problem off of. Rose Malloy would think he'd lost his marbles. Vince was on the other side of the world and he was so touchy whenever the subject of the war came up. Then it came to him in a flash. Daley nearly laughed aloud. Ilan. Who better than his own son-in-law? Ilan would know if it was within the realm of possibility for Rudolf Lobel to be in Israel.

He found a telephone token and went to the lobby in search of a public phone. Halfway there he changed his mind. Better to go in person. See Colleen and the boy, get that over with, since it obviously would keep eating at him until he did. Once there, he would find the opportunity to ask Ilan about Lobel.

The drive through the heart of the city seemed to take forever. One-way streets were congested with rush-hour traffic. The sidewalks were massing with people headed for work. The taxi wound its way past the large Malkhei Hamedina Square, up Jabotinsky, and stopped at a traffic light in front of a high school. Daley watched the students congregating, dressed much like Americans, in jeans with backpacks slung over their shoulders. Across the street, business-suited men relaxed over newspapers and coffee at an outdoor cafe. Housewives marched purposefully with net shopping bags over their arms.

The driver pointed across the street as he drove past the cafe.

"Over there. Biltmore Street."

"I'll get out here," Daley said as they turned the corner and he saw that the tree-lined residential street was one-way.

He stood at the corner for a moment when he saw her

striding out of an apartment building two houses down. This time there was no mistaking that long-legged walk, the proud tilt of the chin, the copper hair. However, the striking figure in boots and long green skirt was no longer a coltish girl but a woman. Daley's heart was beating a tattoo. He wanted to sprint the short distance to see her close up but something kept him back.

Ilan, heavier than he remembered and unfamiliar-looking in suit and tie, hurried out behind her, the boy at his side. The three stood on the sidewalk. Daley felt like a voyeur, staring, unseen, at the intimate tableau. Colleen said something to the boy, then bent and kissed his cheek. For a moment Daley saw himself, twenty years younger, kissing Colleen good-bye as she left for school. The memory was a pain squeezing his heart. The boy waved and started down the street.

Here was his chance. He could call to them or hurry down the street and meet them face-to-face. He hesitated. Too long, for Colleen and Ilan climbed into a maroon Peugeot. The moment was lost. When the car was only a few feet away he saw Colleen laughing as she reached over to rumple Ilan's hair affectionately. The car turned the corner.

Angry with himself for not having gone to them, Daley told himself he'd only have made a fool of himself by confronting them unexpectedly after twelve years and telling them he'd spotted a Nazi war criminal. But his sweaty palms and dry mouth told him the real reason he'd held back had been fear.

He left a quarter of a block between himself and Yoni, following the boy as he rounded the corner, where he joined up with a companion, dressed as he was, in jeans, navy pullover sweater, and shirt. Their loud, boyish voices carried down the block. The fact that he couldn't understand a word his own grandson was saying intensified Daley's left-out feeling. He pushed on, not wanting to let the boy out of his sight, feeling an invisible cord holding them together.

The school, a small one-story stucco building fronted by a dusty playground and enclosed by an iron fence, sat at the end of a cul-de-sac. A cement structure, enclosed on three sides, stood inside the entrance and contained a bench where an old woman sat knitting.

Cars pulled up at the gate. Students scrambled out. Parents

drove off. Daley's eyes were riveted on the figure of his grandson. Yoni was the best of Colleen and Ilan, he thought proudly, with her light, slightly freckled skin, the Daley green eyes and fine features, and Ilan's dark curly hair and flashing smile. A charmer. Mary Helen, he thought wistfully, would have been crazy about him.

Yoni and his friends were kicking a ball around the play area as teachers sauntered in and out of the building bantering with the children. The informality was a far cry from the disciplined parochial schools he and Colleen had known, he thought. Daley stepped closer to the gate.

"You want something?"

He looked up. The old lady was standing by the gate looking at him from eyes sunk deep in a wrinkled face.

"You want something here?" she repeated.

She was staring at him suspiciously, and Daley saw that instead of the knitting, she now held a ledger book of some kind. Mother of God! Guards all around the damn country, he thought.

"I'm a tourist. Just looking around."

She shot him another penetrating look.

"American?"

He nodded. She took a pencil from her pocket and Daley saw the faint blue numbers on her skinny arm. He looked away, gripped by a revulsion as powerful as it was sudden.

A bell rang and the children raced to the door.

"You want something here?" she asked again.

What he wanted, Daley realized as Yoni disappeared into the school, was something he could never have. His grandson.

TEN

"You were either up very early or very late," Rose commented as they prepared to board the bus. "We missed you at breakfast."

"Early. I went for a walk," he replied curtly.

He was sorry he'd confided in her about Colleen. Now she probably felt entitled to know everything about him. It irked him to feel he'd misread her. She was just another nosy, possessive female, after all. He turned his attention from Rose to the Israeli guide, who introduced herself as Yael.

"First stop, the Shouk ha Carmel," she announced. "That's a wonderful, old open market."

"Did anybody leave this on my seat?" Maureen Flanagan called out.

Daley turned in time to see her reach down to where a square, brown paper-wrapped package lay on her seat. Instinctively, he lunged forward, pushing her back.

"Don't touch it!" he barked as the startled woman stared incredulously, holding her arm where it had banged against the metal armrest. Daley whirled around.

"Everybody off the bus, fast!" he commanded.

"Oh, my God! It's a bomb!" a shrill voice cried.

Daley felt panic sweeping through the bus as the group surged toward the door. Maureen Flanagan's voice could be heard over the hubbub. "It was just sitting there! Who put it there?"

Daley tried to suppress his own growing fear at the knowledge that the innocent-looking package could explode any second, ripping apart bus, bodies, and half the street.

A few years before, he'd been called to Little Italy to investigate a bombing. Three highly placed Mafiosi had been blown to bits, along with the restaurant they'd been eating in, a waiter, a couple celebrating a silver anniversary, and a wino who'd been passing by. He'd never forgotten the gore—bloody bits and pieces of human beings mixed on the sidewalk with shards of glass, plaster, and fettuccine. He hadn't seen anything so gruesome since the war. Those images came flooding back as he herded the last of the panicky passengers off the bus.

"Everybody back! Please stand back!" Yael cried.

Daley stood apart with the guide and Rose as the driver ran into the hotel. A crowd quickly gathered. Daley saw Dr. Dailey and several physicians by the revolving door. His eyes scanned the crowd for the Hunter. He caught a glimpse of white hair, but it could have been anyone.

"What do you think, John?" Rose asked fearfully. "Is it a bomb?"

"We'll find out."

"We must wait to see," Yael said. "This is a good lesson for all of you. Here in Israel you must be always on the alert for suspicious-looking packages like the one on the bus. Never, never touch them and never accept any package from a stranger. We all owe Mr. Daley our thanks for his quick reactions."

Snatches of excited conversation floated around him: ". . . PLO . . ." ". . . bus blown up in Hebron . . ." ". . . terrorists everywhere . . ." ". . . child murdered in Haifa. . . ."

Daley looked at his watch. Two minutes had passed. The crowd stood a respectable distance from the bus and its ominous cargo. They'd gotten off alive, but Daley felt the dry-mouthed, heart-pounding aftereffect. His shirt clung damply to his back, and he knew the sour smell he smelled on himself was fear. To get on a bus in this damn country required an act of faith, he thought darkly.

The minutes dragged. Traffic slowed as curious drivers gawked at the crowd. Sirens sliced through the air and two blue police vans careened around the corner, pulling to a halt with a screech of brakes. A uniformed man jumped out of the first and ordered the area around the bus cleared as two other men in flak suits and metal helmets emerged from the second vehicle and ran into the bus.

Daley glanced at his watch again. Exactly six minutes since the driver had run off.

While the bomb experts were on the bus the policemen from the second car questioned the passengers. No one had seen anyone or anything. Daley thought back to the old woman guarding his grandson's school. No matter how many precautions were taken or how alert the population was, the threat of danger remained. He pictured Yoni on a city bus innocently picking up a lethal package on a seat or nudging one unknowingly with his foot, and again saw the grisly scene in Little Italy before the men had come with the plastic bags to collect the human debris.

A burst of applause cut into his thoughts. The officers emerged from the bus holding the package aloft, broad smiles on their faces.

"Only a scare," Yael cried happily. "We can continue. Thank you again, Mr. Daley."

Daley watched the crowd disperse as quickly as it had formed. Yael followed his gaze.

"Business as usual," she said with a shrug. "A bomb or grenade or some other terrorist device is found somewhere in Israel every day. And almost as troublesome are the fakes."

"Oh?"

"You see, the terrorists' objective is to disrupt life here. You saw the confusion . . . the street cleared, traffic blocked." She frowned. "They achieved their goal, and if it's dynamite and a few people are killed, it's a bonus."

Giddy with relief, the group reboarded. As the bus pulled

66

away from the hotel Daley looked back. The crowd had thinned. The bomb experts were back in their specially fitted vans. He spotted Dr. Dailey and his companions, gesturing as they obviously described the incident to a group of people that included the Hunter.

A chill swept through him. He imagined Lobel's cold stare, his twisted smile. "This was for you, Mr. Daley," he imagined him saying in that accented English. Then as the bus turned the corner Daley jerked himself back to reality. He was getting paranoid for sure.

Daley wandered through the bustling, colorful Shouk ha Carmel, where vendors at open stalls provided a show in themselves in their noisy attempts to lure customers to their wares—everything from chickens to jogging suits. Fresh produce, Jaffa oranges, avocados, grapefruits, eggplants, huge radishes, nuts, and spices tempted shoppers as housewives mingled with tourists. Small boys pushing wheelbarrows of fragrant, freshly baked pita and Iraqi breads adroitly maneuvered through the crowds.

Daley noted it all absently. His mind kept flitting from the bomb scare to the frustrating sight of his grandson. The kidnapping and ever-present dangers of war and terrorism made him angrily protective. Colleen had no right to raise his grandchild here. It would be worth seeing her just to tell her that.

At lunch in a self-service restaurant on Dizengoff Street, Daley skeptically eyed the strange foods. Little pastry-looking things called *borekas,* meat and eggplant moussaka, stuffed cabbages and peppers, salads and falafels in pita.

"You didn't just take a walk this morning, did you?" Rose said as he joined her at a table. She was biting into a falafel with gusto. He took a tentative bite of a cutlet, the least objectionable thing he'd seen.

"Thought you were a teacher, not a detective."

"I guess we've both made a mistake then," she countered sharply. "Chauvinist wasn't the correct term. Curmudgeon is more like it."

Daley pushed his plate away and lit a cigarette. He knew he'd hurt her feelings again, but trying to rationalize his own caustic remark reminded him that most people were untrustworthy. Sure, there were exceptions, and maybe Rose Malloy was one of them, but for all he knew she wasn't. Nothing he'd seen in his experience as a cop had fostered a benign view of human nature, and even before, when he'd been a young kid in the Army, the gore and senseless brutality of battle had been only a preamble to the shock of Mauthausen. And he remembered the ordinary-looking men and women on trial at Landsberg, accused of atrocities. He'd been unable to reconcile those faces, faces like that of the Hunter, with the horrors he'd seen. He'd concluded long ago, people were seldom what they seemed. Still, looking at Rose Malloy's intent and intelligent face, he found himself wishing she were the exception, that she was the woman she first appeared to be, even though all his years of dealing with people convinced him it was unlikely.

As the bus drove through the modern, sprawling campus of Tel Aviv University and stopped in front of the Diaspora Museum, Daley told himself that even if Rose Malloy were the Virgin Mary herself, he'd probably already screwed it up. She'd taken another seat on the bus, far from his.

He dispiritedly followed Yael through the museum, aware of the distance Rose was putting between them. As they toured the models of synagogues from all over the world, most of which had been destroyed, Daley again thought back to Lobel. He told himself he'd probably never see him again. But Yoni. His grandson, Yoni, was another matter. Now that he'd seen him, Daley knew there was no way he could put Yoni out of his mind. The boy was his flesh and blood. Whatever had happened between Colleen and himself, he and Yoni had a right to meet.

Daley fingered the link between them, the telephone token. He would call the boy. But first he had another call to make.

ELEVEN

Dialing long-distance was easier than getting room service, Daley thought wryly. And the connection, amazingly enough, was perfect. Vince's voice, although thick with sleep, was clear as a bell.

"Daley! Where the hell are you?"

"Tel Aviv."

In the background Daley could hear Angie's anxious cry, "What's wrong? Is it Cathy?"

"It's Daley. . . . Daley, what's going on? You okay?"

"Yeah, great."

"Jesus, do you know what time it is? It's . . ."

Daley could picture Vince groping for his watch. He realized he hadn't given any thought to the time difference.

"Daley, it's six A.M.!"

"Sorry about that. Listen, Vince—"

"So how's it going? You see Colleen and Yoni?"

"Sort of."

"Sort of. Boy, oh, boy, I can imagine what that means. So what's going on? You miss my cannelloni or something?"

"Vince, something really weird happened. I mean, it's hard for me to believe but . . ." Daley hesitated. He felt foolish but compelled to plunge ahead. "Well, remember Rudolf Lobel? They called him the Hunter."

"How would I know him? I never went hunting."

"Listen, Vince, Rudolf Lobel. The name mean anything to you?"

There was a silence.

"No, should it?"

"Try this, then. The Hunter of Mauthausen."

"Is it a book, play, or movie?" Vince chuckled, fully awake and enjoying himself now. "Sounds like—"

"Vince, I'm serious."

"At these prices, I believe it. What the hell's this costing you, anyway?"

"Vince, Mauthausen. Remember Mauthausen."

The silence hung heavily. He thought he heard a sigh on the other end.

When he replied Vince's voice had lost its joviality. "What about it?"

"Remember the hospital? The experiments? Rudolf Lobel, Dr. Rudolf Lobel! Remember that poor son of a bitch who was castrated and the eighteen-year-old girl who—"

"Yeah." Vince was curt, cutting him off. "I remember. So what?"

"Well, I saw him. Here in Tel Aviv."

The stunned silence was followed by a burst of laughter.

"You spent a small fortune, woke me up in the middle of the night for this? I always suspected you had a perverted sense of humor, but jeez, Daley, this is too much!"

"It's no joke. I'm sure it's him."

"Shit, Daley, we never even saw the guy. Are you flipping out or something? How much did you have to drink?"

"I saw him. At his trial in Landsberg. Listen, Vince, Lobel had a strange walk. I watched him walking into that courtroom every day. I wouldn't forget that walk. And he had a—"

"Lemme tell you a true story," Vince cut in. "I went to my high school reunion a couple of years ago. I spent half an hour talking to a guy who I thought was the husband of one of the girls in our class. Turned out he had been one of my best

70

friends! The point is, I didn't recognize him and he didn't recognize me. That's what time does. And you're telling me you recognize somebody you saw only briefly almost forty years ago?"

"Well, I told you it was weird."

"More than weird. Impossible. Let me ask you this. If it was Lobel, ask yourself how come only you recognized him? That make sense to you?"

"No."

"Anyway, weren't all those guys put away or executed?"

"Yeah." Lobel, he knew, had received a life sentence.

"Okay. So that settles that. You know your problem? You can't stand retirement. You're looking for excitement, but this is going a little too far. So how's it going? What kind of a place is it?"

"Interesting. I'll tell you about it when I get back."

"Send me a postcard. And lay off the booze. Maybe you'll stop seeing Nazis." Vince laughed.

Daley hung up. He felt sheepish but relieved. Vince's arguments made sense. Reaching into his pocket for another token, he once more picked up the receiver.

At the other end of the world Vince lay in bed, wide awake.

"I don't understand what he wanted," Angie mumbled. "Is he okay?"

"Sure. You know Daley. Unpredictable. I think he had a little too much to drink. Go back to sleep."

Vince patted his wife's plump shoulder.

When he heard her breathing return to its sleep rhythm, Vince slipped out of bed, put on slippers and robe, and stealthily made his way downstairs to the kitchen.

When he was nervous he ate. Vince opened the refrigerator and surveyed the contents, his mind on the phone call and Daley. Leave it to Daley, he thought, admiration mixed with apprehension. He found some leftover ham, made himself a sandwich, and poured a glass of buttermilk. Then he sat at the kitchen table and asked himself what the hell he was going to do.

He felt his heart skip a beat. The doctor had told him not to get overly excited. With his weight, he was a prime candidate

71

for a coronary, but he couldn't contain the anxiety Daley's call had stirred. He told himself he could leave it alone, forget about it. Hopefully, he'd convinced Daley to forget it. But he knew Daley too well to believe it. Once Daley got an idea in his head, dynamite wouldn't budge him. And if Daley really believed he'd seen Rudolf Lobel, he'd follow through. And if he followed through . . . Vince felt the sweat breaking out on his forehead. Jesus! He thought back to the sixties, the chaos, the demoralization of the country in the wake of Kennedy's assassination, the Vietnam debacle. The country'd almost fallen apart. And then Watergate had further eroded the nation's spirit. It had hurt him. He'd taken it all personally, as if the America he'd believed in and loved all his life had been invaded by a foreign enemy. Now things were on an upswing. The country was back on the track. It was once more a country he felt his grandchildren could live in safely and with pride. And he knew if Daley were to persist, then once more national confidence would be shaken. Maybe this time enough so that recovery would be impossible. Yet, Daley was his friend. His closest friend. What would Daley do in his place? Daley would say there wasn't any choice.

Vince finished his sandwich. He rinsed his plate and glass and left them in the sink. With a heavy heart, he picked up the telephone.

He, like Daley, had a good memory. Not for faces but for numbers, and so he did not need to look in the locked desk drawer for the number he dialed.

It had been a long time. A very long time, yet he instantly recognized the voice that answered with a curt "Yes?"

"This is Leonardo," he said, "I just got a call from an ex-cop friend. He's spotted the Hunter."

TWELVE

The hubbub of excitement seemed to die as quickly as it had started once the spectators saw that the so-called bomb was simply another false alarm. Like all Israelis, Ruven Levi had responded initially with apprehension when word spread in the lobby where he'd been discussing the morning program with Yossi and Avraham. Now the crowd broke up. People continued about their business.

Levi stood on the sidewalk by the hotel door and shook his head. He felt the fear leave his body, but it was immediately replaced by anger. Anger at a world that would not let a country live in peace. And then the anger was replaced by still another emotion . . . a more familiar one. Resignation.

He glanced at the passersby. He saw on their faces a business-as-usual expression. This was, for better or worse, life in Israel.

The large Egged tourist bus was about to pull away. Levi could imagine how the scare would be magnified in their stories back home. For the group had appeared more than frightened. One or two of the women had seemed to be on the verge of hysteria.

"That's our quota of excitement for the day," Yossi said, standing next to him. "Might as well get back. They'll be starting any minute."

Levi started to turn back toward the hotel when he caught a glimpse of the tall American on the tourist bus. And he was staring straight at him.

Levi turned quickly away, irritated and bothered by that gnawing twinge of dread. He disliked strangers intruding into his life. He had always been such a private person. And now he feared that this American would become a nuisance. And to make matters worse, he still couldn't for the life of him place that man. Levi rarely forgot people. Unlike some of his colleagues, he even remembered patients he hadn't seen in years when running into them in a nonmedical setting. The disturbing thought flitted through his mind that perhaps age was really creeping up. The beginnings of senility. Then he dismissed it. He was far more alert and vigorous, mentally and physically, than men decades younger. Still, it disturbed him to be unable to dredge up the memory of that American. He wouldn't have cared except that the other man seemed so insistent, so certain they had met.

The tourist bus had pulled away from the curb.

"Ruven?" Yossi was looking at him curiously.

"I'll join you inside," Levi said. "I want to get something from the desk."

The desk clerk looked up from the stack of receipts she was marking.

"Yes?"

"I'm Dr. Levi with the medical conference. Are there any messages for me?"

"All messages for the conference are in the meeting hall."

"Ah, thank you. Oh, by the way, did you hear about the package on the bus outside?"

She shrugged. "More mishagash."

"Just what the Bureau of Tourism needs," he commented dryly. "By the way, what group was it?"

"A church group from America. Catholics."

Levi was puzzled. Surely there could be no connection. He

hadn't been to the States in over fifteen years. Of course if the man Dooley was a physician, they might have met at any number of international meetings, but it was unlikely. If he was a physician, he'd be attending the conference.

Levi glanced at his watch. He had twenty minutes before the interesting paper would be read. He walked through the lobby to the coffee shop. He ordered a coffee, then as the busboy set water and silver on the table, he spoke to him softly in his atrocious but understandable Arabic. An observer would have thought they were just conversing. Would have been unaware of money changing hands. As Levi sipped the coffee and watched the young Arab leave the restaurant, he smiled at his own deviousness. In the Middle East there were still two ways of doing business.

When the boy returned he had in his hand a Xeroxed page of names. Levi's eyes quickly sought the *D*'s on the St. Columbine Holy Land Tour sheet. Daley, John I. New York. Retired detective. Dolan, Katherine. New York. Housewife. Duffy, Jack. New York. Contractor. Dugan, Rosemary. New York. Court reporter.

Levi folded the paper and put it in his pocket. He took the last sip of coffee and reached in his pocket for change. The busboy nodded to him as he left the coffee shop.

Daley. John I. Daley. That was the name the man had given him in the gift shop. Daley. Levi thought. Daley. The name meant nothing. Retired detective. He didn't know any detectives, had never known any personally, and certainly no American detectives. The face, strong and craggy, with green eyes and jutting chin, was unfamiliar. Yet, the man had seemed so sure.

The doctor tried to still his intuitive nervousness by telling himself that cases of mistaken identity happened all the time. And, after all, aside from his ear, there was nothing unusual about his appearance. As a plastic surgeon, he knew better than most people that his face might have belonged to countless other men. There was no way of knowing for sure if Daley had noticed his ear, but he reassured himself with the thought that congenital disfigurations such as his were not uncommon.

No, you're not getting senile, Ruven, old boy, he told him-

self as he headed toward the meeting hall. Mr. Daley from
New York has simply made a mistake. And yet he could not
silence the voice that told him he should have gone directly
home.

THIRTEEN

It was only when he got out of the taxi that Daley thought of the boy. Hell, he should have brought a gift. Kids always expect presents. What kind of a grandfather was he? No kind, he reminded himself. Ilan's mother, he thought jealously, probably brought the kid presents all the time.

He heard the click of locks turning as he started up the second flight of stairs. The door opened as he rounded the landing on the third floor. A short, round woman in a print housedress stood smiling in the open doorway. Behind her Daley saw the curious face of his grandson.

"Shalom, Mr. Daley!" the woman cried. "I am Esther, Ilan's mother!"

Yoni stared at him shyly.

"Sabba? Grandfather?"

Daley stuck out a hand. The boy took it. The ice was broken.

"A wonderful surprise," Esther was saying. "Colleen will be very happy." She bustled in and out of the kitchen, plying Daley with coffee, snacks, despite his protests.

"She is shopping before the stores close for Shabbat."

"She's shopping for Egypt," Yoni said, helping himself to a piece of strudel. "They're going for vacation. I wanted to go too."

He had quickly lost his initial shyness and deluged Daley with questions.

"Tell me about the police," he begged. "I see *Columbo* on television and I tell all my friends my American sabba is a New York City detective, just like Columbo."

"You know about me?"

The boy laughed. "Come, Sabba!"

Pulling Daley out of his chair, he dragged him down a hallway to a back bedroom dominated by posters of America. The Statue of Liberty, the Grand Canyon, the Golden Gate Bridge. He took a scrapbook from his bookshelf and sat on the floor. Daley lowered himself next to the boy. Yoni turned the pages. Daley couldn't believe it. One after the other, they were filled with photographs of Colleen . . . as a child, as a girl, as a young woman, photographs of Mary Helen and photographs of himself.

"That's my other safta, isn't it?" Yoni said, pointing to a snapshot of Mary Helen. "And look, here's you, Sabba."

Interspersed among the photographs of Daley were newspaper clippings with his name underlined in red. Cases he'd solved, cases in which he was only mentioned, and even a clipping about a talk he'd given to the Catholic Youth Organization. He was stunned. Colleen had not let the boy forget.

"Ima said you would come to see me someday," Yoni said. "I asked her all the time. She told me how busy you are with detective work, solving murders. But I knew you'd come. I think maybe if I don't become a pilot, I'll be a detective, too, just like you."

Daley wanted to hug the boy.

"Maybe a pilot's better," he said. "You can see the world."

"But I want to be a famous detective, like you," Yoni sighed, "or in the Secret Service, like Abba used to be. Do you have a gun, Sabba? Can I see it?"

Daley laughed. "I stopped working last month. That's why I could come to see you now."

The boy's face fell. "Where is your gun?"

"Had to give it back."

Yoni's face brightened. "Sabba, come look."

He jumped to his feet and motioned to Daley to follow.

The other bedroom was larger. A double picture frame was displayed on the dresser top. Colleen and Ilan in what must have been a wedding photo, and in the other half, he saw with a start, a copy of his own wedding picture. His face and Mary Helen's, both so young, stared at him. But Yoni was pulling him to the closet.

"Look, Sabba," he said. "You can use this if you need it."

The boy pushed a row of dresses aside and, reaching behind a shoe box, pulled out a Colt .44.

"Hey, put that thing down," Daley said.

"It belongs to Abba."

"Does he know you play with it?"

"I don't play with it. I just know where it is. Don't tell him, Sabba. Please?"

Daley put the gun back behind the shoe box. Yoni was watching him anxiously. Daley grinned and tousled his curly head.

"I won't tell. Our secret."

They were deep into a game of checkers when they heard footsteps on the stairs. Yoni jumped up.

"Ima's home!"

Daley stiffened at the sound of the door opening. He heard her call out. Colleen's musical voice, only speaking Hebrew. He got to his feet and stared at his daughter.

Her face went white, then flushed almost the color of her hair. She looked from Daley to Yoni to her mother-in-law. Her arms were filled with packages. Esther took them from her. Colleen made a move toward him, then stopped herself. She uttered a nervous little laugh. Yoni was dancing around them, chattering rapidly as he switched effortlessly from Hebrew to English.

"It's Sabba, Ima! From New York. He came to see me and he told me all about New York!"

"John Daley in Tel Aviv," Colleen said. "Praise the saints, it must be a miracle!"

"Ima, can Sabba stay for supper?" Yoni cried.

Esther was smiling. "Tonight is Shabbat. Yes, stay for supper."

"Please, Sabba!" Yoni cried.

Colleen's eyes had a trapped look. Daley recognized it, because it was exactly the way he felt.

FOURTEEN

"Baruch atah adonai, elohenu melech ha'olam . . ."

Daley listened as Colleen, a white scarf over her copper hair, blessed the Sabbath candles. It was all Greek to him. But so what, he told himself. He used to celebrate Mass in Latin and what did he know about Latin? Still, it seemed unreal, his American daughter, product of parochial schools, speaking Hebrew. Celebrating Hanukkah! Even more unreal had been finding himself lighting a Hanukkah candle at Yoni's insistence. After the Hanukkiah was lit, there had been an exchange of gifts.

"I'm sorry I don't have a Hanukkah present for you, Sabba," Yoni apologized, "but you didn't tell us you were coming."

"Now we're even," Daley responded. "I owe you a present and you owe me one."

The Sabbath candles lit, Ilan pulled a chair out at the head of the table.

"John, you sit here, in the place of honor."

Daley watched Colleen set a large, braided loaf of bread

and a knife in front of Ilan. Mary Helen always joked that she took after him. "A great poker face," she used to tease. It was true. As Colleen sat down he didn't have a clue from her expression about what was going on in her head.

"Still can't believe you're here," Ilan said. "And you're lucky with the weather. This time of year we could easily have rain."

"Somebody must've put in a word upstairs," Daley responded.

"From here it's a local call," Ilan joked. "You look great, John. So, tell me, how're things in New York?"

Ilan's warmth pleased Daley. Whatever differences he had with Colleen, Ilan was okay. They had easily fallen into their former comradely relationship, reminiscing about the security problems they'd faced together in New York. Ilan had since left the Israeli Secret Service, gone to law school, and now, from the looks of the tastefully furnished apartment, was doing more than all right.

During dinner Yoni plied him with questions about detective work. When Daley wasn't entertaining the boy with some of his more interesting cases, he and Ilan were talking foreign policy. Even Esther joined in, wanting to know about the newest American food processor her neighbor had brought back from the States.

Halfway through the simple meal of cheeses, yogurts, fish, and diced vegetable salad, Daley realized he and Colleen had barely exchanged a word. She brought and cleared dishes, talked to her mother-in-law in Hebrew, to Yoni and Ilan in English. She picked at her food and, it seemed to Daley, pointedly avoided his eye. She appeared to relax a little only as the meal drew to a close and she served fruit and tea along with jelly doughnuts similar to those he'd tasted at the airport. "Suganiot, traditional at Hanukkah," Ilan explained before launching into a description of their planned trip to Egypt.

"We're still getting used to the novelty of being able to travel to an Arab country," he said. "Our friends who've gone to Egypt loved it. We've wanted to go for some time but I haven't been able to get away. You should try to see Egypt, too, John."

82

"Now that you're traveling, Dad," Colleen added, "you might as well see as much as you can."

Ilan's face brightened. "How about coming along with us? There's probably a space on the tour."

"Thanks, but I'm committed to my own tour. They've got something going every day. Tomorrow we're going to Jerusalem."

"Sabba, you'll like it there," Yoni broke in. "I went last month with Ima. You can ride on a camel by the Old City. When I have my bar mitzvah, maybe I'll have it by the Wall."

"We're going to visit all the holy places," Daley said with a sideways glance at Colleen, the words *bar mitzvah* burning into his brain. "The Via Dolorosa, the Church of the Holy Sepulcher. We'll be in Bethlehem on the twenty-fourth."

Colleen casually peeled an apple, ignoring the heavy-handed references.

"Bethlehem will be a mob scene Christmas Eve," Ilan said. "Can you imagine the security problems? They expect over twelve thousand people this year. We usually watch the midnight Mass on television."

"You must take a heavy coat, John," Esther warned. "It is very cold in Bethlehem. You mustn't catch cold."

"There's a Jewish mother for you." Ilan winked at Daley. "She still tells me what to wear!"

"You'll enjoy it in spite of the commercialism," Colleen said. "In fact, I'm sure you'll enjoy the entire trip. There's so much to see. Tell me, how are Aunt Peg and Cousin Trish? I haven't heard from them in a couple of months."

"You write to them?"

"We correspond. I write to them, they write to me."

The air was charged with unspoken accusations. Land mines . . . like the fact he hadn't known she and Peg were in touch . . . which they were carefully sidestepping. Daley brought her up on family news . . . which relatives had married, died, moved, who had had babies.

When supper was over Yoni dragged Daley to the other room for a game of checkers while Esther and Colleen cleared the table. Daley remembered Vince saying, "That's what it's all about." He knew now what Vince meant. Even though he hardly knew the boy, he felt an unfamiliar tenderness toward his grandson.

When Yoni won the game Ilan announced he was driving Esther home.

"Yoni, come with me. I want company," he said.

"But it's Friday, Abba," he protested. "I'm going to Ofer's house."

"You come with Grandma and me. I'll take you there after I drop her home."

"Why? We always go by ourselves on Friday. It's Ornit's birthday and I don't want to be late."

Esther said something in Hebrew. Daley didn't understand a word of what followed, but from the agitated expression on the older woman's face, and the pout on Yoni's, he knew the argument was continuing.

"Come, Yonaleh," Esther said at last, putting on her coat. "Go get your jacket. We'll give Sabba and Ima some time together."

Which was not something he was entirely ready for, Daley realized. But for the moment he found himself alone with his son-in-law as the boy went to get ready.

"What do you think about that Mueller case?" Daley asked him.

Ilan shrugged. "Too bad he never came to trial, but that's the way it goes."

"I had a very strange experience yesterday," Daley said casually. "I saw someone, a man I'm sure was a Nazi war criminal. You know I was an MP at the American war trials after the war. I'm sure the man I saw was one who was on trial."

"Here in Israel?" Ilan looked at him skeptically. "You mean you saw a Nazi here? Who is he?"

"Rudolf Lobel. He was the doctor at Mauthausen. What do you think?"

"Highly unlikely for many reasons. There have been cases of mistaken identity like that. Very similar, in fact. A couple of years ago a concentration camp survivor swore she saw an SS officer on a bus here in Tel Aviv. She started screaming, and before you knew it there was a mob around the guy ready to hang him. The police came, and it turned out he was totally innocent. The woman meant well, but it was a mistake."

"So you think it's impossible," Daley said.

"I'd say so. Collaborator, yes. There were some Jewish collaborators, you know, and I remember one of them being apprehended in Israel, pointed out by a survivor. The man was arrested and tried. But you're talking about a German Nazi." He shook his head. "I'd say no."

"What about the physical similarities? This man had the same unusual walk, and the same ear deformity."

"I don't know, John. It's been forty years. It's easy to make a mistake after all that time."

"He's part of an international medical conference at my hotel." Daley took out the list of names the Ohio physician had given him and gave it to Ilan.

Ilan was thoughtful. "Look, if it'll help, I've got a niece in the public relations department at the hotel. I'll give her a call and ask some questions. But there must be two hundred names."

Daley pointed to the four names he had circled.

"Start with those."

FIFTEEN

Colleen settled herself in a low beige chair, her long legs thrust out on an ottoman.

"Sorry about that little scene with Yoni," she apologized.

"What was it all about?"

She ran her fingers through her hair. The familiarity of the gesture caused a lump in his throat. He saw her as a young girl poring over a difficult homework assignment, running her fingers through unruly hair. And with that association came other memories he had to force back before he cried from the sheer force of the emotions flooding him.

"It's just that children here in Israel are so used to being independent. Every Friday, for instance, Yoni's class gets together for a party. The children go by themselves, either walking or on bikes."

"At night?"

"It's different here, Dad. Safe. In spite of all the wars and the threat of war, Israel is really a safe haven. Anyway, we used to feel so. You may have heard about the kidnappings. Well, tonight Ilan insisted on driving Yoni to his friend's house. Yoni didn't like that. I'm sure all the panic will die down, but we're all being extracautious right now. The kidnappings have shaken people up."

"I'd think with all the wars, Israelis would be used to that sort of thing."

"That's the funny part. An outsider would assume so, but we're talking about two different things. One is the external threat of war and sure, we live with it, but in the back of our minds. Our everyday lives go on like anywhere else except for certain precautions."

Daley remembered the bomb scare on the bus. In New York he probably wouldn't have reacted as he had.

Colleen frowned. "It took some getting used to, but now I accept it. My days of guard duty at Yoni's school, Ilan going to the reserves every year. But one thing we prided ourselves on was the warm and safe social structure of life, especially for the children. Israel is a wonderful place to raise a child."

Sure, he thought, with terrorist bombs, kidnappings.

"Didn't you ever think about coming home?"

Colleen gave him a long, sideways look. "This is home."

"You might think about your son," he countered.

"I am. I want him to grow up in a land where he can feel a real commitment, a sense of purpose. These are things we lost in America." She stood up and went to the bar. Then laughed as she turned back. "Oh, for God sakes, Dad, we've been together less than three hours and look at us! How about a brandy?"

"Gotta watch my weight."

"Come on, you look terrific."

"A few extra pounds." He shrugged, pleased by her compliment. "I'm going to start working out regularly when I get back home."

"You can carry it. I'm glad I got your height. That way I can hide a few extra pounds myself."

"You? You don't have to worry. You look great."

"I have a busy life."

Daley was aware of how cautious they were being with each other, like strangers on a blind date.

Colleen poured two drinks, handed him one, and held her glass up.

"L'chaim. To life."

"Cheers."

He took a sip, thinking how maybe it wasn't going to be so hard, after all. Some of the tension he'd felt all evening drained away. For the first time he began to think maybe they could be friends. He admitted to himself that that was what he really wanted, in spite of all the years he'd spent denying it to Vince and to himself. But he didn't have the faintest idea how to begin to heal the breach. He reminded himself it was a two-way street.

"I don't know why you didn't tell us you were coming, but whatever the reason, I'm glad you came. Really glad."

Colleen looked like she might cry, which was how he felt now that she'd made the opening move.

"You can't imagine how excited Yoni is. He brags to all his friends about you. You're a hero to him."

Daley leaned back, warmed by her words. All his anxieties about what might happen when he saw Colleen now seemed absurd. She was happy to see him. His grandson was happy. It seemed ridiculous to think he'd waited so long.

"Yoni showed me his scrapbook. You could've knocked me over. I was surprised he even knew about me."

"Come on, Dad, of course he knows about you. Did you think I wouldn't tell him?"

"Never sure with you. You were always full of surprises."

"I guess I was."

"Hey, remember that time you were about eleven. You wrote a letter to *Time* magazine? You never said a word. I go to the dentist and out of the blue he says to me, 'I saw that letter your little girl wrote!' " Daley laughed. "Your mother must've bought fifty copies. What was it about, anyway?"

"Civil rights."

"Yeah. Well, like I said, you were full of surprises."

"Mother always said I took after the Daley side." Colleen laughed. "Especially when we locked horns. I remember when I was fifteen, how badly I wanted a black dress and Mom said no, not until I was eighteen. Oh, was I furious with her!"

"I remember that," he said. "I guess she thought it was too grown-up. We didn't want you to grow up too fast."

"Or at all."

Daley knew, in the sudden silence, that his offhand comment had triggered sensitive areas. He had wanted to keep her young and with him and had failed. And for over twelve years he'd lived with the bitterness of that failure.

"But, Dad," Colleen said, breaking the silence, "how could you think I wouldn't tell my own child about his grandfather?"

"I just didn't think you cared too much about things like family."

Colleen's jaw tilted up in that defiant way he knew so well. "The Daley look," Mary Helen used to call it. The look that meant they were digging in for a fight, and Daley knew with a sinking feeling everything had suddenly changed.

"Do you want to explain that remark or should we just forget you said it?"

The way she said it, with such cool assurance, made his good intentions fly out the window.

"Damnit, no! I don't want to forget it, and in case you really need an explanation, try this. In our family, family feeling means caring about family and doing for them. Didn't seem to me you learned that lesson."

"You honestly think I don't care?"

"All I know is, other girls don't run halfway around the world. They find husbands near home. They stay near their family, if they have family feelings, that is. Maybe we just let you have your own way too much. Spoiled you. My old man laid down the law to us and we did what he said. That's family feeling."

Colleen tossed off the rest of her brandy. She was angry now and he was glad. Whatever pain she was feeling now was nothing compared to what he'd felt when she'd left.

"You can't stand the fact that I stood up to you when you couldn't stand up to your father. That's the bottom line." Colleen laughed bitterly. "Deep down, you really do think I ruined my life! Let me tell you something. I'm happy, which is more than I can say for you. But that's not something you'd know anything about." She stood up, her fists clenched so that the knuckles turned white. "Oh, you're a fine one to talk about family feelings! You never answered any of my letters, not even when Yoni was born! At first I was hurt, then furious. Then, finally, I just didn't give a damn."

Her letters had come weekly at first. Daley remembered the temptation to rip the air letters open and keep the tie, however distant, with her. But something kept him from giving himself that pleasure . . . the need to punish her, even if it meant punishing himself more. And so he'd forced himself to return the letters unread. And when he didn't answer, the letters came less often until they stopped.

"People asked me all the time, when was my father coming to visit, and I lied and told them you were too busy at work or in poor health. I was ashamed to tell the truth."

"And how do you think I felt going to Mass, with Father Flynn always asking about you with that little smile on his face, knowing he was feeling sorry for me. Well, nobody ever felt sorry for me in my life!"

"And when did you get so religious?"

"Let me tell you something, missy. Even a bad Catholic's a Catholic. And when a daughter of mine, my flesh and blood who was brought up in the Church, turns her back on it like it was dirt, that's to be ashamed! How do you think I felt not being able to talk to the guys I work with about my own kid! Them bragging all the time about their children and grandchildren and me making up stories. You know what those guys think? That you live here because you're a historian studying the Crusades! So don't go talking ashamed to me."

"So you're disgusted with me." Colleen sat back down. She no longer looked angry. Only tired. "I can understand it from your point of view, I guess, your generation and background. But, Dad, what about Yoni? He's my son. He's part of us. He's half Daley. Good Lord, he even looks like you!"

Seeing the tears in her eyes, Daley began to soften. He wanted to comfort her the way he used to when she was a child. But she was going on.

"Not one letter to that boy. I covered for you all these years so he'd think he had a loving grandfather. 'Grandpa's very busy. They need him at work, that's why he can't come to see you, that's why he doesn't remember your birthday!' And now you'll waltz out of here and I'll have to start lying again about his wonderful American sabba who's too busy and selfish to write. Some family feeling! You're a hypocrite!"

The compassion he'd felt a moment before disappeared.

"I'm glad your mother isn't alive to hear you now. You'd have broken her heart."

"You didn't know Mother any better than you know me," Colleen cried. "What would have broken her heart is your insane stubbornness."

She was crying, and for an instant Daley again felt himself weakening, tempted to try to repair the damage. But he made himself remember the names she'd called him. Liar, hypocrite. The unfair accusations. She could cry all night and he'd be damned if he'd make one move.

"If you want to talk about turning your back," she sobbed, "what about parents who turn their backs on their children! You were my idol, my idea of everything that was good and strong. I trusted you. Whatever I did, you used to back me up, so when I fell in love with Ilan, I naturally expected your support. Oh, I knew you'd be disappointed he wasn't a nice Catholic boy, but even so I didn't expect or deserve what I got. Maybe you were a cop so long, you just lost any real feelings you ever had. You abandoned me, not the other way around!"

Colleen swiped at her nose with the back of her hand. "And you want to hear the funny part? I was so happy when I saw you here. I really believed you'd changed. I said to myself, we'll have a chance to make it up. But you'll never change. We did just fine without you! Why did you have to come?"

Here he'd come halfway around the world to her and somehow she was turning it around to put him in the wrong. There was a bitter taste in his mouth as he shakily got to his feet.

"Anybody can make a mistake."

He'd been right all along. It was too late. There could never be anything but bitterness and anger between them.

SIXTEEN

Vince stirred a packet of sugar into his coffee as he studied the dignified man across the table. He felt a slight pang of envy. Time had treated the other man kindly. Better than him, for his companion didn't seem to have aged at all in the thirty years since they had seen each other. A sprinkling of gray in the dark hair, maybe a pound or two, a little flesh under the eyes. Otherwise, he looked the same as he had then . . . like a banker or college professor. Well-dressed, patrician WASP. The man probably never ate. Vince comforted himself with that thought as the waitress brought their breakfasts. Hotcakes and bacon for him. Poached egg on dry toast for the other man.

The man lightly salted his egg and smiled briefly.

"You haven't lost your taste for food, Leonardo. I remember how traumatic it was for you to be stuck in England, of all places."

Vince laughed. "My rotten luck! With France so near!"

"Sorry, this place isn't much better than England," the man

said, with a glance at the unimaginative coffee-shop decor, "but it's convenient."

He didn't say convenient to what and Vince didn't ask. He was still used to not asking questions.

The waitress warmed their coffee. Vince noted the other man took his black. He resolved to cut down on the sugar in his.

"Tell me about John Daley. What sort of man is he?"

Vince sighed. "Thing is about Daley, you could know him for twenty years and still not be able to answer that for sure. He's a private person, you know what I mean?"

The other man seemed unperturbed as he carefully cut into his toast. Vince knew he was waiting. How to describe Daley? He was complex, but Vince figured he knew him as well as anyone could.

"He's a stubborn s.o.b.," Vince said, "his own man. I think he probably could've been chief of police except that he rubbed a lot of people wrong. He never kissed anybody's ass. Once he makes his mind up, you might as well forget it. Like with his daughter. He's got only one child and the sun rose and set on her all the time she was growing up. So what happens? Daley got it into his head that when she married an Israeli she deserted him. He won't have anything to do with her or his grandchild, and I know it kills him. But that's how he is. But that same quality made him a first-rate detective. You know he's the one who cracked the Manzone kidnapping?"

The other man looked impressed for the first time.

"Yeah," Vince went on, "he had his picture all over the papers with that one. He's resourceful and he never gives up."

The other man took a sip of coffee. "How cooperative would you say he is?"

Vince felt suddenly wary.

"In what sense?"

"Let's say, what might be our chances of getting Mr. Daley to cooperate with us."

Vince couldn't contain a hoot of laughter.

"Chances about as good as my dropping fifty pounds by tomorrow morning." He shook his head. "Take my word for it, it would be the kiss of death as far as Daley's concerned. I can see it now!"

Vince turned back to his breakfast, almost amused at the thought.

"What makes you so sure?"

"Look, not only is the guy uncompromising but he's almost irrational when it comes to the subject of the war and war criminals. Every now and then he tries to get me into a discussion about it. Usually when he reads something in the paper about some old Nazi being located or fighting deportation, like Rauca in Canada, and that scientist who worked on the Saturn Five rocket, what's his name? Rudolf, that's it, and Artukovic, and Klaus Barbie, and Mengele having lived all those years in Brazil. You should have heard him when they arrested Otto Mueller! Daley was foaming at the mouth!"

Vince was silent for a moment, remembering that last discussion. He'd understood Daley's outrage, had shared it himself. Having to force himself to take the opposite position made him feel like a shit. But he told himself he'd long ago accepted the fact that the world wasn't always what you wanted it to be. Hell, the war was enough to prove that. And then, once you accepted that fact, pragmatism took over. Basically, countries were just extensions of individuals, and just as individuals looked out for number one, so did nations. How else was it that our best friends were our former enemies, Germany and Japan, and our former ally, the U.S.S.R., was the enemy? But Daley had never accepted the way the world was. And Vince was aware of the irony that the hard-muscled, hard-talking detective was a crusader in disguise, an idealist, while he, the pudgy, outgoing Italian, was the realist.

"I'm sorry to hear that," the other man said. "It makes things a little more complicated. But if anyone has influence on your friend, it would seem to be you. I don't have to tell you the importance of terminating his interest in this affair."

Vince recognized the order implied in the statement. He pushed aside the last bit of his pancakes, his appetite gone.

The other man had finished his breakfast. He wiped his lips with the paper napkin and signaled to the waitress for the check.

"Next time, come down to my place," Vince said. "I'll treat you to a real meal."

Again, a brief smile flickered over the other man's face.

"Let's hope there will be no need for a next time. It's up to you."

And that, Vince thought unhappily, was what he was afraid of.

SEVENTEEN

From the window of the bus the countryside looked like a vast checkerboard, the brown of plowed fields juxtaposed with green orchards. The road from Tel Aviv to Jerusalem was lined with eucalyptus trees, and beyond, framing the fields, stately cedars, which were planted, Yael informed the group, to break the wind around the orange groves. Daley was oblivious to the beauty of the changing scenery . . . flat, sandy coastal plains that gave way to orchards and farmland, industrial areas and sleepy villages. He'd barely slept, his mind replaying the painful episode with Colleen, and when he had managed to doze off he'd had the dream.

He was back in the camp, reliving that first shocking sight of Mauthausen, the skeletonlike prisoners, the rotting dead bodies piled like cordwood, the overwhelming stench that was everywhere. He'd forced himself to wake, and waited out the dawn on the balcony staring out at the sea, smoking and thinking. And at last, over breakfast in the empty dining room, Daley came to terms with the stranger who'd been plaguing his thoughts.

He began by telling himself he was most likely mistaken. Rudolf Lobel had been sentenced to prison at Landsberg. Secondly, nearly forty years had passed. Too much time for an identification of someone he'd only seen and never talked to. Thirdly, as Ilan had pointed out, the whole scenario was highly improbable. Even if Lobel were a free man, it was unlikely, inconceivable, he'd come to Israel, where there were so many survivors. Look at Mueller, Daley told himself; he'd holed up in Bolivia surrounded by guards. Whatever Lobel was, he was not a fool. And finally Daley told himself as he finished his third cup of coffee, it was none of his business, anyway. Better to leave Nazi hunting to the Simon Wiesenthals of the world . . . or to God. It was with a sense of relief that he'd put Rudolf Lobel, the Hunter of Mauthausen, out of his mind. He only wished he could do the same with his daughter.

Daley's foul mood began to disappear as the bus, nearing Jerusalem, climbed through steep and thickly forested hills, then, on the last leg of the trip, up a narrow corridor strewn with rusted and wrecked military vehicles.

"They were left here to remind us of the lives sacrificed in 1948 to keep this pass open," Yael said in response to his question. "If not for that sacrifice, the population of Jerusalem might have starved to death."

At the first glimpse of the pale gold stone walls of the Old City of Jerusalem, Daley felt an unexpected surge of excitement.

The group was ushered from the bus through the ancient Jaffa Gate. Once inside the Old City itself, Daley felt he'd stepped back centuries. Narrow alleys lined with shops and stalls, crowded with people, strange sounds, exotic smells of spices and foods assaulted his senses.

"It's history come alive!" he heard Rose exclaim.

He was conscious of her coolness to him since they'd boarded the bus. Relationships at the precinct or even with Vince had been uncomplicated. He knew where he stood and what to expect. Now, in the space of a couple of days, he found himself mired in misunderstandings, confused by new and conflicting emotions.

He watched Rose snapping away with her camera at the

Arabs, the men sitting outside shops drinking thimble-sized cups of coffee, heads covered with flowing kaffiyehs. The women covered from head to foot in embroidered dark dresses, bundles balanced on their heads, the small boys selling large round loaves of bread and spices. Christian priests in flowing black cassocks mingled with Hasidic Jews in fur hats and long coats, young Israeli soldiers, tourists speaking a babel of tongues.

"Just think of the history," Rose remarked to Maureen Flanagan. "The Acropolis, in Athens, is beautiful, but it's a museum. These same buildings and streets go back centuries, but people still live and work in them as they did then!"

Denny O'Hara and Yael bypassed the Armenian Quarter, leading the group down the bustling David Street to the Christian Quarter. They made their way through the Via Dolorosa, stopping at the unobtrusively marked nine Stations of the Cross, and then at last entering the old church itself, architecturally a disappointment to Daley but enclosing the area formed by the last five Stations of the Cross and supposedly built on the spot where Jesus was crucified.

Daley hadn't been to church more than a half dozen times since Mary Helen died, but as the monks and nuns showed them the various stations inside the church, he thought he'd have to be made of stone not to feel something. He remembered the old saying "Give me a child till he's five and I'll give you a Catholic for life." There was something to it. Even Colleen would feel something.

Outside the church, Denny gave them shopping time. Seeing Rose begin to gravitate toward a group of women, Daley impulsively pulled her aside.

"I need some help," he said. "I figure a teacher like you would know what would be a good present for a ten-year-old boy."

Rose eyed him over the rim of her sunglasses.

"Do I have to take a blood oath to behave myself? No questions?"

Daley grinned and thrust out a hand.

"Truce?"

"Truce . . . I think."

Yael sidled up to them.

"You look like you could use a snack after all that history and culture," she whispered to Daley with a conspiratorial wink. "Come with me and taste the best hummus in Jerusalem!"

"Hummus? Is that a food or a disease?"

The guide laughed. "Come and see!"

The Abu Shoukri looked like a tiny hole in the wall to Daley as he followed Rose and Yael inside. There the guide spoke to the waiter, who disappeared behind a curtain separating the eating area from the kitchen. A few minutes later he reappeared with bottles of cold beer, plates of a pale, pasty-looking dip, and large round pitas. Yael laughed at Daley's expression.

"Like this . . ." She broke off a piece of pita and scooped some of the dip in it. "This is hummus. Made of ground garbanzo beans and olive oil. Very healthy and delicious, yes?"

Rose quickly followed her example. "It *is* good. Come on, John, try it."

Daley dipped a piece of the warm bread in the dip. The beer would help it go down, he told himself. To his surprise, it wasn't bad.

"You have time for some shopping," Yael told them when they'd finished eating, "but only forty-five minutes. We'll meet back at the church at noon."

Rose's lively company buoyed his spirits. They wandered in and out of the tiny shops, looking at handwoven Bedouin rugs, copper and silver work, carved olive wood, Jerusalem pottery, Hebron glass, leather goods, comparing impressions as they went along. The narrow streets teemed with activity as they passed little coffee houses where Arab men sat playing sheshbesh. Daley laughed at the sight of a young European in tight jeans and a T-shirt sitting next to a huge-bellied Arab smoking a water pipe. The sweetish smell of hashish blended with the aroma of spices and coffee. Rose insisted on his posing by a donkey while she snapped a picture. Daley realized he was enjoying himself more than he had in years.

As noon approached Rose stopped in front of a souvenir shop and took an olive-wood cross on a chain from its hook.

"This is nice. How much?" she asked the old Arab who stood watching in the open doorway.

"Six hundred shekels. Very nice, very good quality."

Rose started to reach into her purse but Daley stepped in.

"Hold on, you're not going to pay it, are you?"

"But I love it!"

Daley took her aside, out of earshot of the old man.

"There's no price on it. You have to bargain with him, Rose. I'll show you."

"I thought you hadn't traveled."

"I've been to Orchard Street in New York." He grinned.

Rose stood aside, an amused look on her face. Daley picked up the cross and made an elaborate show of admiring it, turning it over in his hands. He slipped the chain over Rose's head and stood back. The proprietor was grinning and nodding.

"Beautiful, no?"

"Beautiful. How much?" Daley asked.

The Arab repeated the sum. Daley sighed regretfully.

"Very nice, but I can't pay so much. I'll give you five hundred twenty-five."

The man clicked his tongue disapprovingly and took the cross from Rose. He replaced it on the hook.

"Very fine quality," he repeated.

"I can see that," Daley said sadly. "Beautiful."

"For you, a special price. Five hundred seventy-five."

The Arab took a paper from behind the counter and began to wrap the cross in it.

"Five hundred fifty," Daley countered. "I think I saw the same one in another shop for five fifty."

The man rolled his eyes skyward and sighed.

"Five hundred seventy. My best price, for the lady."

Daley took Rose by the arm and started across the alley to another shop.

"Five hundred sixty," he flung over his shoulder.

"Okay. Five sixty. For the lady."

Daley counted out five hundred sixty shekels. Outside, with the cross in her purse, Rose laughed delightedly.

"You absolutely amaze me, John Daley!"

She reached for her wallet but Daley waved her off.

"My present."

She looked at him uncertainly, then smiled. "Thank you, John. It will always remind me of you and of this trip."

"The trick," he told her, "is to make them think you love it. You're dying to have it only it's more than you can pay. Let them think you're really going to walk out without it. If you have to, leave. You can always come back."

Rose slipped her arm through his. "I know you're supposed to bargain, but somehow I always feel sort of guilty. It's such a piddling amount, after all."

Daley laughed. "That guy could probably buy and sell us both ten times over. Anyway, they love it. It's the way to shop over here. I remember when I was in Italy during the war. It was the same thing. A big game."

"You were in the war?"

"In the Army from '43 to '47. In Europe."

"That must have been an experience. I'd like to hear about it sometime."

"No, you wouldn't." He looked at his watch. "Hey, we'd better get going if we're going to get some lunch."

The group was led through the Muslim Quarter to the Damascus Gate and to an Arab restaurant that looked to Daley like a pasha's tented palace, with polished brass tables, oriental rugs, and huge copper pots. As they waited for their tables to be readied, he saw Dr. Dailey standing at the head of the line.

"Dr. Dailey, we've got to stop meeting like this," Daley joked when he'd worked his way through the line.

"You've got a point." The doctor grinned. "People may talk."

"Tell me, is this place recommended by the AMA?"

"I don't know about that, but it certainly smells good. How do you find Jerusalem?"

"Very biblical."

They compared impressions briefly. "Where's your group staying?" the doctor asked as he was called to his table.

"The Intercontinental."

"At least I know I'll have my own luggage tonight. We're at the King David. Oh, by the way, did you find your friend's name on that list I gave you?"

"Nope. I must have made a mistake."

Once seated, waiters scurried around serving them the house specialty: small salads of mushrooms, of tomatoes and

101

onions, of eggplants prepared in various ways, spicy Turkish salad, hummus, and large, still-warm pitas, all followed by lamb kabobs and rice. They were lingering over baklava and tiny cups of strong Turkish coffee when a fragment of conversation made Daley snap to attention.

He almost laughed aloud. A group of men at an adjoining table were discussing hunting. Here he was, thousands of miles from home in a city as exotic as any he could imagine, and what did he find? A bunch of hunters just like him.

He turned to look at them. There were four, all speaking English, all over fifty, and all wearing those red and white International Plastic Surgeons badges.

Daley was about to butt in and ask them if there was any decent hunting in Israel when he found himself staring into the face of the white-haired man.

Their eyes met. Daley's body stiffened in an involuntary response. The man turned his head in what seemed to Daley to be a deliberate, almost defiant, gesture. All his resolutions of the morning disappeared. Rudolf Lobel had a passion for hunting, hence the name "The Hunter." That could apply to thousands of men, but Daley's inner voice told him otherwise. He had to see him close up. Talk to him. Try to see the profile. The ear.

Daley saw the waiter taking their money. He stood, but before he could make his way around the crowded table, the hunters were gone.

EIGHTEEN

"By all rights, I know I should be exhausted," Rose said as the waiter cleared the coffee cups and dessert plates, "but I'm just too keyed up to think about sleep. It's been such an exciting day. Nothing really prepares you for Jerusalem."

Across the table, Maureen Flanagan stifled a yawn.

"You may be keyed up, but I can't keep my eyes open one minute longer. And we have to be back on the bus at eight-thirty tomorrow!"

"Why so early? This is supposed to be a vacation," Jack Duffy, a retired contractor complained.

"What about you, Mr. Daley?" the Widow Flanagan asked. "You've been quiet tonight."

"Guess I'm beat too."

"Well, good night, all," Maureen chirped, getting to her feet. "I need my beauty sleep. See you all at breakfast."

Daley watched her waddle off with the others from their table.

"I did think the church was awfully small," he heard her saying to Mr. Duffy. "I mean compared to St. Patrick's in

New York, don't you think? Now, there's a church, not that size is everything."

"Poor Duffy doesn't stand a chance," Daley remarked wryly.

"Oh, John, be kind," Rose said with a glint of amusement. "She's really a good soul."

"You sure about that, are you?"

"No, but I like to give people the benefit of the doubt."

"Which is more than she'd give you. She's jealous of you."

"Oh, I doubt that."

They left the table and headed out of the dining room. Rose linked her arm through his as if it were the most natural thing in the world. It'd been a long time since Daley had felt a woman's arm in his like that. It felt companionable. Nice.

"I see the way she looks at you when she thinks you're not looking and the way she tries to keep center stage when you're around. She'd give one of her minks to look as good as you, to be like you. She's even started talking with a Boston accent!"

Rose laughed. "Well, I am flattered, although I think you're exaggerating."

"Just observant."

"Then you must see how interested she is in you."

Now it was Daley's turn to look surprised.

"John, really! It's so obvious it's almost a joke. Everyone on the tour can see it. The poor woman's had her eye on you since you stepped on the plane in New York, and when you reacted so quickly to the package on the bus, you became a hero! I'm convinced she'd kill to get a seat next to you on the bus and I'm afraid she's put out with me for monopolizing you."

"Is that what you call it? Monopolizing?"

"That's what she'd call it. I'm not sure what I call it."

"Why don't we try to define it over a drink?"

He was feeling almost light-headed, even though he'd had only some wine with dinner. He wasn't used to this kind of bantering, but he liked it. He could definitely get used to it and to Rose. Some man had really missed the boat with her.

One drink led to another. They talked about everything under the sun. She asked him about his work and then really listened, asking intelligent questions. They compared childhoods, and when, halfway through a story he was telling about getting lost in a department store when he was six, Daley took her hand in his, she didn't make a move to take it away. He knew then it was going to happen.

There was that one moment, as he unlocked the door to his room and stepped aside to let her in, when he suddenly panicked, wondering if he'd let himself go so much that he'd lost the hard-muscled body, that he'd disappoint them both, that maybe it was all a mistake, and that Rose Malloy wasn't a lady to screw once and forget. But the moment passed. The door closed, her arms wound around his neck more gently than any arms he ever remembered, and she kissed him.

"I like you, John Daley," she said, then stepped back. For the first time since they'd met, she appeared flustered. Her cheeks reddened. She gave an uncertain little laugh.

"I have to confess, I'm not accustomed to shipboard romances."

"Is that what this is?"

Rose's eyes gazed steadily into his, and there was no duplicity there.

"It can be whatever we want. As much or as little."

Daley felt the ball thrown back in his court.

"I don't know what I want," he admitted. "I know I liked you from the start. I'm not used to this either. I mean"—he paused, groping for the right words so that he wouldn't sound as unsure as he felt—"I haven't made any commitments since my wife . . ."

Rose's gaze never wavered. "And I never made any. Period. I suppose that makes us even. Or well-suited."

And they were.

After, as Rose slept beside him, Daley stretched out on his back, enjoying the warm presence of her body, the fresh perfume of her skin and hair. And the relaxed but alive feeling of his own body.

He'd almost forgotten how good sex could be. He and Mary Helen had been kids who taught each other and he'd never been interested in fooling around on the side. After Mary Helen died, though, he felt like he'd dried up. Yet, he knew women still found him attractive. And he took pride in his strong body, his full head of silver hair, his easy smile. He'd forced himself through the motions after Mary Helen but inevitably kept thinking about her and feeling as if he were doing something wrong. Almost like Father Flynn was peering over his shoulder.

Now he waited for that same guilty, disloyal feeling to come back, but all he felt was happy. He recognized the feeling because it was so long since he'd felt anything like it. The word made him think of Colleen, and his tranquility was spoiled. What was it she said? Something like happiness wasn't something he'd know anything about.

Daley slid out of bed and went for his cigarettes. He took the pack and matches and opened the curtains. The view from the hotel, Yael had told him, was the best in all Jerusalem. Situated on the Mount of Olives, a place sacred to Jews, Christians, and Muslims as the site of the oldest Jewish cemetery, the place where Jesus ascended to heaven, the tombs of Mary and Joseph, the hotel commanded a panoramic view of the Old City.

It was even more impressive at night, he thought, momentarily forgetting about Colleen as he stared out at the illuminated walls.

His mind was a jumble of impressions and feelings. Israel, a strange land no newspaper or TV program could prepare you for. Modern, bustling Tel Aviv, where people looked and acted like Americans except you kept running into kids in uniform carrying Uzis and every bus had signs warning of suspicious packages. Jerusalem, where Arabs in ancient garb mixed with modish European types. Donkeys trotted side by side with Fiats and VWs. A place that almost defied description, where with every step it seemed there was a Bible story, where a sense of energy and purpose overlaid a subtle tension.

He felt himself come full circle back to Colleen, now one of them, living her own life without him. Like she was an orphan, he thought, excluding him from her life. And Yoni. Bitterness welled up in him at Colleen for throwing in her lot with foreign people in a foreign land and depriving him of his grandson.

He stubbed out his cigarette, staring at the moonlit golden stone walls of the Old City. The last thing he'd expected to find was Rose. Maybe meeting Rose was worth the pain of Colleen.

Vince should see me now, he thought, almost laughing as he recalled the remark Vince made about his being lonely and living in a mausoleum. He wondered if Vince and Rose would like each other and realized with a start, he was already thinking of Rose as part of his life. A mistake, he cautioned himself. There was no room in his life for a permanent woman. He lit another cigarette. And besides, what did he and Rose Malloy have in common? Not much. She liked the theater. He couldn't remember the last play he'd seen. He loved hunting and they'd already had a heated discussion over the so-called morality of the sport. Rose read novels. Daley liked biographies. There obviously was no common future for them. Still, he'd have to see her again, if for nothing else than to get copies of the photographs of the trip.

Feeling the effects of the long day, he turned off the desk lamp and climbed into bed. Rose stirred beside him. He reached over to brush her arm gently.

*Bright blue sky. Fluffy
white clouds like he'd
never seen before.
Postcard pretty. A small
brown rabbit ran out of
the woods and stood frozen
in the road.*

*He heard the sound first.
The thump, thump of
marching feet. Then he
saw them, the line of men,
which from his vantage
point looked no more
substantial than cheap
plastic toys. Not real.
Only the persistent thump
of marching feet was
real. One, two. One, two,
in rhythm through the
wooded countryside.*

*The rabbit stared
stupidly at the advancing
men, blinking for an
instant in the brilliant
sunlight before scampering
off into the forest.*

One, two. Thump, thump.

*The sounds grew louder.
Another sound was merging
with the thump of marching
feet. A distant,
unintelligible murmur, no
more than the whisper of
the wind, starting at the
front of the line, working
its way back. Growing.
Growing. The words began
to sort themselves out.
"You're not going to
believe it. . . . You won't
believe it." And then the
smell washed over him.
Not like anything he'd
ever smelled before. Like
the gates of hell had opened
up. The putrid stench of
death was everywhere. . . .
He'd never get it out of
his nostrils, suffocating,
revolting, and then . . .*

"John! Are you all right? What is it?"

Rose was holding on to his arm, and even in the moonlit room he could see alarm in her face. His heart was pounding so erratically, he was afraid he was having a coronary. His mind did a quick flip back in time to the airport in Tel Aviv, to the gift shop in the Sheraton, to the restaurant in Jerusalem. To the man he was now absolutely sure was Rudolf Lobel, the Hunter of Mauthausen.

NINETEEN

"My son-in-law thinks it's impossible, and my friend Vince in New York thinks I've flipped out," Daley said. "I don't know what to think."

"A Nazi here in Israel," Rose said softly. "I don't know either."

The shock had left her face. Now she merely looked thoughtful.

"I could play devil's advocate, if you like."

"At least you're not telling me I've lost my marbles." He laughed shakily, still unhinged by the dream.

"At first I thought maybe it was part of your nightmare spilling over," she admitted, "but now that you've explained it . . . It must have been a horrible experience, liberating that camp."

"It's something you never forget. Not that you think about it consciously, but it's always there. Sometimes I think it's why I became a cop. My father wanted me to join the force. I wanted to be a coach. But after the war . . ." He paused, remembering the confusion of those years.

Coming home had been a bigger adjustment than he'd imagined. He'd felt out of sync, aimless. He'd gone to school, then dropped out. After what he'd been through, his life seemed frivolous. He'd worked in construction, losing himself in the sheer physical labor, and when that also paled, he enrolled again in school. And then it all seemed to pull together. At Mauthausen he'd felt powerless to help the victims. But he realized there were other victims, and those he could help. Police work had been the natural choice, and he'd never regretted it.

"Anyway, I think if it hadn't been for the war, I'd have been coaching in some high school. It's complicated."

"I understand." Rose reached for his hand, stroking it as a mother would a child's. "But, John, it's been so many years. And you admit you didn't know Lobel, you just saw him at the trial. You never spoke to him. People change in forty years."

"I know that. And if it were just his face, than I'd agree with you. But the first time I saw him something clicked in my mind. I didn't know what it was then, but later I realized, it wasn't his face. In fact, his face has changed. It's his walk. A person can change almost anything about his appearance, but the one thing he can't change is the way he walks. Lobel had this bouncing kind of walk and I noticed it every time he walked into the courtroom. And another thing. Lobel had a deformed ear. They'd cut his hair short for the trial and it was obvious from where I was standing. See, his profile was toward me all the weeks of his trial and I was bored half the time, and fascinated half the time, and I kept staring at his ear."

"But this man's ears are normal," Rose said.

"Think about it. Do you remember seeing them?"

Rose was silent for a moment.

"You didn't," Daley said, "because his hair covers them. But I saw them. Outside the hotel the first day. The wind blew his hair back and I saw it."

"What did Ilan say when you told him?"

"That it was improbable a Nazi would be here."

"It would seem so," Rose said, "simply because there are so

110

many people here who might recognize him. He'd be taking a tremendous chance, and for what?"

"Attending a medical conference doesn't seem enough of a reason," Daley admitted. "But I can't get rid of the feeling it is Lobel. He's a doctor, a hunter, the right age, and I tell you, when I look at him some instinct tells me it's him."

"I know it's not very scientific, but I believe in instinct. But tell me this, John, let's suppose you're right and you've seen Rudolf Lobel. Where do you go from here? What do you do about it, if anything?"

"Two options. Do nothing or go to the authorities here. I'm tempted, the more I think about it, to forget about it. If I'm wrong, and there's a pretty good chance I am wrong, then I could ruin the life of some innocent man. I'm not sure enough to take that chance. Anyway, I keep asking myself, is it my problem? I'm not an Israeli, I'm not a Jew. What's Lobel to me?"

"But you're not satisfied with those conclusions, are you?"

Daley pulled her to him. "You must be one hell of a teacher, Rose Malloy! Do you read your students' minds too?"

It was as if the fates were conspiring against him, Daley thought as he walked down the tree-lined path to the Yad V'Shem Museum, dedicated to victims of the Holocaust. No way he could forget about Rudolf Lobel here.

Inside, the black walls and ceilings mirrored the grim mood of the tourists who somberly shuffled by. Daley paused by a map of the camps in central Europe where red lights showed extermination camps and yellow the main concentration camps. He found Mauthausen there on the Austrian-German border, near Linz, its yellow light glowing.

The group made its way through the section devoted to the Resistance, past the exhibits of familiar photographs, still powerful enough to shock, to the art museum, where paintings done by victims were displayed. It was in the Hall of Names, with its black stalls of books listing the names of those who had perished, that it began to get to him. The utter simplicity and silence of that room was like a tomb. He stared at the black iron sculpture of hands reaching upward and felt his

111

breath being squeezed out of him. He was queasy, feeling as he did whenever he awoke from that dream. He felt perspiration breaking out on his forehead, and he had that dry, metallic taste in his mouth.

Rose looked up at him with concern.

"Are you all right? You look awfully pale."

He needed to get out. He was feeling almost as if he'd stepped into his nightmare, stepped back into time, when he'd been a young GI marching with Vince into that hellhole.

"I'm going out for some air," he said.

He made his way around a group of French tourists toward the exit, then he suddenly stopped, feeling as though he'd been punched in the gut. He was staring at a blown-up photograph. A pile of naked skin and bones that could barely be called a human being lay on the ground. Three young soldiers, American soldiers, stood looking down at him. Daley sucked in his breath. His eye flew to the caption on the right: "Liberation of Mauthausen, 23rd April, 1945."

He felt Rose's hand on his arm. He was unable to force his eyes off that photograph, even though he thought he might be sick right then and there.

He stumbled away, pushing past a group of schoolchildren, not knowing where he was going, needing desperately to be away.

He heard Rose call his name, but he kept going until he reached a stairway. Tall black pillars, each containing the name of a country in gold in both Hebrew and English, seemed to bar his path. And on each was the number of Jews killed.

Daley turned, his eyes searching for an exit sign. SON OF MAN FORGET NOT DEEDS OF TYRANNY. The words were like a blow.

The last thing Rose had said to him before they'd gone back to sleep was, "What are you going to do?" He'd been unable to answer her.

"John," she said softly.

He turned to see the same question in her tear-filled eyes.

After lunch the group reentered the Old City, this time through the Jewish Quarter, where police checked their purses

112

and packages. At the ancient temple wall, no more than sixty yards in length, Yael explained to them how the men and women were separated according to religious law. On the left, Daley watched the men, wearing either skullcaps or tall hats, swaying and praying as they faced the wall. On the other side, separated by a flimsy fence, women were poking little scraps of paper into the chinks of the wall.

"They're writing prayers and wishes," Rose said. "I'm going to write something too."

She dug in her purse and pulled out a pencil and paper. Daley watched her mingling with the praying women, slipping her paper into a crack in the wall. He turned back to the men then, a few feet away, and he saw the group of doctors, with Dr. Dailey in their midst. A tour guide was gesturing toward the wall and excavations alongside it. At the edge of the group Daley spotted the hunters. Daley again felt his body respond in that old familiar way . . . muscles tense, adrenaline going. The white-haired man seemed to be listening intently.

Daley now knew the answer to Rose's question. And he knew he would have to stalk him as craftily as he would a quail.

"I hope we get to see some of those excavations," Rose said, rejoining him, "especially the Cardo."

"Rose, let me take a picture of you. Stand over there, by the gate."

She turned and saw the doctors. Her face paled.

"It's him, isn't it?"

Without another word, she slipped her camera from around her neck and handed it to him. Casually, she strolled to the fence, positioning herself by the doctors.

Daley put the camera up to his eye and aimed it. He focused it on the white-haired man. And snapped.

TWENTY

Daley sipped his bourbon, picking halfheartedly at the dinner in front of him. He avoided Rose's eyes, painfully aware of the unspoken thoughts that seemed to hang in the air. From the start he'd told himself that Rudolf Lobel was not his business, that he wasn't going to get involved. That was before the Yad V'Shem.

"John?"

He looked up.

"It might help if you talked about what it was like at that camp."

Daley sighed, pushing his plate away. "It's not exactly appropriate dinner conversation."

"So who's eating?"

"Actually, I never talk about it."

Rose's eyebrows lifted in surprise. "I should think you'd have felt almost compelled to share such a powerful experience with someone. Your buddies in the war or your family. Someone."

"I'm kind of a loner. I don't go around blabbing." He realized, with some surprise, that although he thought he'd been close to Mary Helen, to Vince, to Colleen once upon a time, he'd never opened up to them about that experience and what it was like, or about anything else for that matter. And yet here he'd told Rose Malloy, a comparative stranger, not only about the dream, but about the camp. He was getting old and sentimental, for sure, he thought ruefully.

"I tried talking to Vince once in a while, but he wants to forget about it just as much as I do. He sure doesn't want to talk about it. You should have heard him when we started talking about Otto Mueller! Here's Vince, who once said the whole German race should be slaves for a hundred years, telling me they oughta let Mueller go because he's an old man."

"Maybe the whole subject is too painful for him."

"Maybe." But something told him it was more than that. Vince's sudden anger seemed to turn him into somebody else. Not the Vince he'd known for forty years.

"And, Rose, it's not only Mueller. There're war criminals like Artukovic, the 'Himmler' of Yugoslavia, living in the States, and I read where some priest is writing letters saying don't deport him, he's been a good churchgoer! It makes me sick. I'd have thought if anybody'd think the way I do, it'd be Vince. He was there!"

He fell silent, stirred by an old rage.

"People tell me I'm a good listener," Rose said.

The waiter, with a frown at Daley's untouched plate, cleared the dishes. They ordered coffee. Daley lit a cigarette. His throat burned. He knew he was smoking too much.

"When I was a kid in parochial school I remember old Sister Theresa used to say, 'Hell is worse than your worst nightmare.' Well, Mauthausen was a thousand times worse than anything even Sister Theresa could dream up. We heard stories about the concentration camps, and they even showed us a movie, but we all figured it was propaganda so we'd hate the Germans and fight harder. Nobody believed it." Once he began, Daley found himself unable to stop. "We were marching through this country, the most beautiful country I'd ever seen. I grew up in New York, so what did I know about country? This was storybook. Trees, mountains. And I was thinking how Mary Helen—we were engaged then—would love it. We must have been five miles away when we started smelling this stink. I never smelled anything like it. It got worse and worse and some guys started throwing up. I felt like tossing my cookies, too, but I didn't. I didn't know what it was then. The guys who got there first passed the word back to the rest of us coming up in back, saying things like, 'You're not going to believe it.' I remember the first thing I saw was this barbed-wire entanglement and then what I thought were stacks of wood. And by then the stink was overpowering. Sorry, I warned you this is no dinner conversation." He forced a weak smile.

"No, go on, please."

"Then we got closer and I saw that the wood was really bodies. Just skin and bones, like skeletons. We stood there looking at these naked bodies lying stacked up like wood. Nobody could say anything. We were too shocked. All of a sudden Vince was pulling on my arm and shouting, 'Look, it's moving!' and sure enough, about three bodies down, we saw an arm moving. I thought, Holy Mother of God, there're living people in those piles! We all got to work trying to pull out the ones who were alive. See, the Germans knew we were coming and they tried to cover up the dead. But there wasn't time. And that was the smell—those big trenches filled with rotting bodies. The medical units got there pretty quick because everybody was afraid of typhus. We all had to help because it was just too big a job. You'd have to see those who were left to believe it. I saw this pile of dirty rags on the floor so I went to throw it out and it was a man beaten to death. I don't think he had a whole bone left in his body. Then later I was talking to this lady who knew some English. She looked about fifty or sixty and emaciated. She turned out to be a seventeen-year-old Jewish girl, same age as my sister Peg!"

It was all coming back, the horror, the disbelief. Rose reached across the table and covered his hand with hers. Daley felt his throat close up, but he couldn't stop now. Like a poison he had to rid himself of, it came pouring out. The shedlike structures of the camp filled with floor to ceiling bunks, and people more dead than alive packed like sardines, with no washing facilities. The remains of skeletons and bodies at the bottom of the stone quarry, where inmates had been pushed to their death. The electrically charged fence.

"All of the ones left alive looked like those pictures of starving Chinese the nuns were always showing us. Some of them started to tear cans of food open with their bare hands. The docs told us not to give them water because they'd cramp and die and I saw it happen a couple of times. That really got me. Here were these people who'd lived through this hell and then died that way—drinking water! We gave them a little bread and they grabbed it. Later I found some hidden under pillows, like they were afraid we'd take it away. But the weird thing was the reaction of the prisoners. I couldn't understand it then, but now I do. The same thing sometimes happens to guys let out of prison after twenty or thirty years. I thought when we marched in and liberated them, they'd beat it the hell out immediately. But instead they walked around like zombies. They were so beaten down, so used to being slaves and taking orders, they didn't know what to do. Some of them wandered out of the camp, then came back. They didn't know where to go. What to do. It was like they weren't even human anymore."

"And Lobel?" Rose asked. "Did you see him?"

Daley shook his head. "Not there. He'd escaped before we got there, but I heard about him and I saw a couple of his 'patients' and his 'hospital' where he did his experiments. The stench in that room was enough to kill anybody. I swear you could find any single part of the human body behind those glass boxes. An organ would be cut showing half one way, half the other, like in biology books. I couldn't take it. To me that was the worst. Worse even than the bodies because it was so deliberate, so organized. And the chaplain came around and wanted us to talk about it. But nobody wanted to talk much."

"How did you feel about it?"

"It made me sick, ashamed, and amazed that one human being could do this to another human being. I'd been in a war, and seen buddies blown apart and all, but in a war it seems fair. Kind of like hunting. It's you or him. Not like that. I remember thinking if I ever saw this Dr. Lobel, I'd kill him

117

myself." Daley was silent, remembering. It had been the first time he'd known himself capable of cold-blooded murder.

"Anyway, after that Vince got sent to England and I went to Landsberg, and that's where I saw Lobel. He'd been captured and was on trial. I was standing guard." Daley shook his head. "I couldn't believe he was the same person who'd done those experiments. He looked like anybody else, you know?"

"What are you going to do, John?"

"What would you do?"

Rose laughed. "You don't get off that easy."

"Like I said, I think actually Rudolf Lobel was the reason I became a cop, although it took me a few years. I thought as long as the world's got scum like the animals who thought up that hell in Mauthausen and ran it, there'll be victims like the half-dead zombies wandering around there. And I thought somebody's got to be on their side. It really shook me up. It gave me respect for people's lives, and that's really the problem. If this man isn't Lobel, I have to think what I'd be doing to his life. We talked about it before."

"I know," Rose agreed. "But how could you be sure?"

"I have this instinct. It's part of being a cop. And it's almost always right. It tells me now that he is Lobel."

The waiter poured more coffee. Rose leaned back in her chair and sighed. "You asked me before, John, what I would do. I didn't want to influence you, but I will share with you my philosophy. I try to instill in my students a sense of moral courage. Not easy to do today, believe me. This is the great age of noninvolvement."

"Yeah, tell me about it. Doctors won't help an accident victim because they're afraid of getting sued, and I once saw a dozen people stand around watching an old man bleed to death. And you think one of them would even give a name as a witness? Not on your life."

"I believe we have a moral obligation to do the right thing, to be on the side of justice, corny as it sounds," Rose said. "And you must believe it, too, or you wouldn't have been a police officer for thirty years."

Daley laughed. "Thirty years ago I did. Sure, I was idealistic, but that idealism gets lost in all the slime. What about you? Are you still an idealistic teacher?"

Now it was Rose's turn to laugh. "The burn-out rate is probably the same with teachers. And to be honest, no, I'm not the same as I was twenty-five years ago, either, but something is left."

"I'm not so sure anything's left with me."

"I know there is or you wouldn't have those dreams."

He had seen firsthand the work of Rudolf Lobel, had forever in his nostrils the stench of that camp, forever in his brain the sight of the dead and halfdead, forever in his heart the reality of the cruelty of man. He thought again about the Yad V'Shem and about the photo he'd snapped at the Wailing Wall and knew that, by that simple act, he had crossed a line. He had made a commitment. He was involved and there was no going back.

Taking a pen from his pocket, Daley signed his room number and name on the bottom of the check.

"So?" Rose asked as they got up from the table.

"So we get the film developed right away. That's for starters."

"You're not the cynic you pretend to be." She grinned.

"No, I'm nuts. That's what."

Rose slipped her arm through his. "Then the world needs more like you."

"The gift shop won't open until ten," Rose said, catching up with him the next morning as the group started boarding the bus outside the hotel. "I've got about six more shots on this roll. Might as well finish it today in Bethlehem and we can take it in tonight."

Daley tried to shrug off his disappointment. Without a photograph, he had nothing with which to go to the authorities.

Daley felt the group's excitement, but their enthusiasm didn't touch him. He realized suddenly, it was Christmas Eve. He'd totally forgotten about it. As the bus started down the Mount of Olives he thought that Christmas in Bethlehem should be a peak experience. Instead, his thoughts were dominated by Rudolf Lobel, a man he'd never known.

Although Bethlehem was only seven miles south of Jerusalem, once they left the city the landscape changed subtlely, becoming ancient and Arabic-looking. Catching sight of small boys riding on donkeys, and an occasional shepherd and his flock, brought the word *biblical* to Daley's mind. A line of pilgrims trudging along the road made the picture complete.

In Bethlehem, the bus parked at the foot of Manger Street.

"I'm sorry we must park here," Yael apologized as the bus doors opened. "We will have to walk up the street to the church. As you can imagine, this is the most crowded time of the year in Bethlehem. But before we start up, let me just tell you a word or two about this city. Bethlehem literally means House of Bread in Hebrew. And this city is famous for three events. They are, chronologically, the following. The birth of Benjamin took place in Bethlehem, King David came from Bethlehem and was crowned here, and, of course, Jesus Christ was born in Bethlehem. Today, Bethlehem is one of the largest Arab communities in Israel . . . forty percent Muslim, sixty percent Arab Christian. Now, I know you are all anxious to see the church, so let's go. Please stay together, and we'll stop at the square in front of the church."

Manger Street, Christmas lights strung across it, was lined with souvenir shops selling everything from religious crafts to pencils and pens made in the People's Republic of China.

The Church of the Nativity, the oldest in the country and the principal shrine of Bethlehem, was a fortresslike structure facing the paved expanse of Manger Square. A rather unimpressive Christmas tree stood in the square amid parked cars and groups of tourists.

Yael herded the group together in a corner of the church courtyard.

"Before we go inside, one or two words about the church itself," she said. "The church, which belongs to the Greek Orthodox, is sixth century but it is not the original. In the fourth century there was another church here, built by Constantine after his mother, Queen Helena, made a pilgrimage to the Holy Land. The original church was destroyed, probably by an earthquake, and the Emperor Justinian built a new church on the site two hundred years later. You will notice the very low doorway. People like Mr. Daley"—Yael smiled impishly in his direction—"will have to bend down to enter. The

120

legend has it that the doorway was made so small to prevent unbelievers from riding into the church on horseback. Now, let's go inside."

A large group of German pilgrims led by a priest was gathering in the courtyard as Daley's group entered, Daley stooping to get through the doorway. They paused to admire the fourth-century Byzantine mosaic revealed by the trapdoor opening in the floor, then proceeded through the small and very cold, stone basilica.

"It's so small," Maureen Flanagan said.

Daley and Rose exchanged amused glances.

"She's not going to be happy until she sees something like St. Peter's," Daley whispered.

"Armenian, Greek, and Franciscan priests are responsible for the care and preservation of the church," Yael said, leading them to the narrow stone staircase by the altar, which led to the manger. "Unfortunately, every Christmas there are fights between the monks about which denomination cleans which corner."

Simply lit by hanging lights, the grotto, scene of Jesus's birth, was set in the wall of the cave and marked by a silver star. A small flame burned nearby. Several people got down on their knees to say a prayer.

Despite his preoccupation with Rudolf Lobel, Daley felt a stirring of emotion. His thoughts turned to Mary Helen. How she'd have enjoyed being here. They'd never traveled much. They'd always said later. And there were always other things to spend money on. Things that seemed more important at the time. Daley realized suddenly, he was the one who had said later, he who had always been too busy, too involved in work, who'd decided on priorities.

Colleen's accusation came back to him. . . . "You didn't know Mother," she'd said. Had there been things Mary Helen felt and wanted that she'd never shared with him? Had he cheated her? He'd never thought about it before, but now the possibility filled him with guilt.

He felt Rose's hand on his arm. He looked up.

"Everyone's going, John," she said.

They left the church via the courtyards of cloisters and convents, passing bearded Greek priests in long black robes, purple-robed Armenian priests, and Franciscans in simple brown. Daley saw the graceful spire of a mosque in the distance, heard church bells toll from somewhere, and then the haunting music of Gregorian chant. Yael was discussing what seemed to be part of the church they had just left but which was really Santa Catarine, a Catholic church run by the Franciscans.

Daley couldn't concentrate. The past weighed on him. He took a deep breath of the cold air, trying to regain his equilibrium. What was done was done, he told himself.

Next to him, Rose snapped a photograph.

"Last shot," she whispered. "Now we can get the roll developed as soon as we get back to the hotel."

The main square had filled up with tourists. In the middle the Germans began singing "Silent Night." A hush fell over the crowd.

The spirit of Christmas was all around them in the singing of the pilgrims, the biblical landscape, the Arabs in their traditional garb. Try as he might to shrug it off, the past tightened its grip on him.

He was flooded with memories of how Christmas used to be when Colleen was growing up. He and Mary Helen had knocked themselves out for her on Christmas. It had been the highlight of the year. He felt his eyes mist up, remembering how he and Colleen made a tradition of picking out the tree together, how excited she got when they unpacked the familiar ornaments and began decorating it. He could almost smell the pungent fragrance of the cookies and fruitcake Mary Helen baked every year. He remembered the sumptuous Christmas dinner, the family all together around the table, laughing at old reminiscences, the kids racing around the house and nobody minding the noise for once, or the mess. And Colleen, her face flushed, eyes shining, higher than a kite from it all, and Mary Helen always saying, "She's going to work herself right into a sickbed," which she never did. How could Colleen have forgotten all that, he wondered. Or had she. He wished to hell he could, because the memories, representing loss, brought sharp stabs of pain instead of pleasure.

Rose took his arm.

"Oh, John, isn't it wonderful?"

The Germans' voices brought him abruptly back to the present.

"Stille nacht, heilige nacht, alles schlaft, einsam wacht, nur das traute hochheilige paar, holder knabe im lockigem haar . . ."

Even in German the song was beautiful, touched something deep inside. Daley looked over at them, and suddenly his blood froze.

There, across the square, singing along with the pilgrims, was the Hunter.

Daley felt his heart speed up. The camera, he thought, and remembered even as he started to tap Rose that she'd said the film was finished. He moved away from her and began working his way through the crowd, keeping his eye on the doctors and the white-haired man. When he got close enough he would ask one of the physicians who he was.

The Germans finished singing. There was a burst of applause. The pilgrims started to leave the square, momentarily blocking the doctors from view. Daley swore to himself and squeezed past an English-speaking group. Elbowing his way around the fringes of the crowds, Daley managed to creep up behind the doctors, working his way through their midst.

"Inside, we will stop by the mosaic," the guide was saying in English.

He knew he should stop and ask someone to identify the white-haired man, but some impulse compelled him to push through the spectators. It was an urge almost beyond his control, and a move he would regret.

Daley stood directly behind him. Leaning over his shoulder, he said, "Herr Dokter Lobel."

There was no response.

Daley tapped him on the shoulder. He felt the bones through the man's coat. The man turned. They made eye contact. Daley felt a chill.

"Dr. Lobel," he said again.

The man shook his head impatiently. A look of annoyance crossed his face.

"You have made a mistake, sir," he said.

Daley stared into his eyes. Cold, ice-blue eyes. The eyes of a beast, a devil, he thought.

123

Another song began in German as the pilgrims neared the church. The guttural sound of the language intensified the revulsion that filled him.

"No mistake," Daley said.

"A mistake, Mr. Daley."

TWENTY-ONE

"Ruven, is anything wrong?"

Ruven Levi realized by the concern on Gerte's plain face that his agitation showed. He shook his white head.

"I'm fine, Gerte."

She seemed unconvinced. "You don't look well. Perhaps you are not dressed warmly enough."

"No, no, I am quite warm," Levi protested.

"Who was that man that spoke to you?"

"No one. To tell the truth, I am still tired from my trip."

Their guide was leading the doctors and their wives across the square. Up ahead he saw the German pilgrims making their way into the church. Gerte and Josef fell into step with him.

"Isn't that the way?" She laughed. "I am always exhausted before I get on the airplane, having spent weeks getting ready to travel, and then it takes weeks after I come home to recover!"

"Is it worth it?" Josef teased.

"To see places like this, yes."

"Ruven, perhaps you should not join us on the rest of the touring," Josef suggested. "After all, you have surely seen all the sights, and we will still see you at the conference sessions and the reception this evening."

Abandoning the afternoon tour of Hebron was tempting in view of the strange encounter with the American. Josef and Gerte were giving him the perfect out. Something told him he should seize it, but stubborn pride made him rebel against the idea of allowing Mr. John Daley to intimidate him.

"You're wrong, Josef," Levi replied. "I haven't seen everything. In Israel there are always new sights. The Cardo, for instance. I had not seen the latest excavations and, believe it or not, I had not taken the walk on the ramparts of the Old City before."

"It was wonderful," Josef said.

Levi agreed. He'd been to the Old City hundreds of times, of course, but the relatively recently established walk upon the rooftops was quite special. It had given him an entirely different feeling for the Old City. It was the stillness that first captivated him, and then the spectacular view of both the still-expanding new city of Jerusalem and the teeming alleys and narrow streets of the Old City below.

He'd stopped at one point, enchanted by the toll of church bells overlaid by the muezzin's haunting call to prayer. The hammering of stone cutters somewhere below gave him a sense of timelessness. And as if that had not been enough to stir him, there was the recently excavated Cardo, the main street of Jerusalem during the Crusader time. He'd trod the ancient stones below street level in the Jewish Quarter, admiring the Roman columns where modern Israeli artists now sold their pottery and paintings. He'd imagined how busy, beautiful, and full of life the city had been even then, in Roman times. And if not for the opportunity the conference tour afforded, who knew when he'd have taken a day off simply to wander the Old City?

"Still," Gerte said, as they reboarded their bus, "if you are not yet recovered from your trip, perhaps you should rest."

"I promised to show you my country," he said, "and I am a man of my word."

The guide counted heads. Levi took his seat. From the window he caught a glimpse of John Daley's head above the rest of his group as the Americans climbed aboard their bus. He felt his heart lurch and he turned quickly away.

Dr. Lobel. Daley had called him Dr. Lobel. A name he had never expected to hear again. Indeed, had hoped never to hear again. More years than he cared to admit had passed since he had heard that name spoken aloud, yet in the flash of an instant, decades had been wiped away like dust. He could not suppress a shudder.

Just outside the city limits the bus stopped to pick up a hitchhiking young soldier. Levi stared at the landscape. In the summer it would bloom with orchards and the lush vineyards that produced the famous, very sweet Hebron grapes. Now the land was dry and brown.

The mountains of Hebron came into view. He heard Josef and Gerte remarking with delight on the sight of grazing sheep on the hillside, small Arab boys trotting on donkeys along the road, timeless Arab villages with their solid stone houses, the doors and windowsills painted green to drive away spirits, the men sitting in front talking or playing sheshbesh.

It was a landscape he ordinarily loved, but his stomach was churning sourly. He was unable to concentrate on the guide's words or on the scenery. He knew he would have to regain control, to not allow the confrontation with the American to get the better of him.

He leaned across his seat to talk to Josef and Gerte. He forced a smile.

"Do you see the terraced hills?" he asked. "The olive trees, the vineyards . . . the same agriculture is practiced now as three thousand years ago. It's quite amazing."

He pointed to where an old man was sowing a field by hand.

"Ruven, what a feeling it must be living in such an ancient land." Gerte sighed. "We in Europe think our monuments are old and they go back only eight hundred years or so!"

"And we Americans think anything over one hundred years is ancient," a physician from Minnesota chimed in. "This country puts things in perspective."

A sense of perspective was what Levi normally possessed.

Now his inner turmoil told him John Daley had changed all that.

What, he wondered, was the connection between Daley and Rudolf Lobel? And what was it that caused Daley to call him Lobel? He pondered the possible similarities. Lobel and he would be the same age. There were similarities of build, of coloring, although Lobel's nose and chin had been more prominent, longer than his own. Surely not enough for anyone to confuse him with Rudolf Lobel. Except, perhaps, for the ear. Even if Daley had seen his ear, and he could not be certain he had, surely his ear was in itself not enough for him to be taken for Rudolf Lobel. Or was it?

Levi lifted his hand to his thinning white hair, smoothing it down over his left ear. Countless times in his professional career he'd come across that same rather common congenital deformity. A "cup ear," it was called, a condition which today, unlike in his youth, was fixable. Before antibiotics the risk of infection was high, and as he was one of those unfortunate individuals prone to forming keloids, surgery had not been an option for him. And as Levi felt the ear beneath his long hair he was again struck by the ironic fact that while he'd reconstructed thousands of faces and bodies, he was unable to correct his own.

Ruven Levi was a master of the art of rationalization. He told himself now, as he did so often, that if not for his ear, he might never have specialized in reconstructive plastic surgery. And he took pride in knowing he was one of the pioneers in the relatively new field. He liked to tell himself that his own deformity was what made him sensitive to the emotional pain suffered by his patients.

The bus wound its way slowly through the streets of Hebron, past glass and pottery factories and the heavily guarded military station, toward the Cave of Machpelah, the Tomb of the Patriarchs. Levi could feel the hostility in the expressionless stares of the Arabs, and he took note of the number of men wearing the red kaffiyehs, the symbol of PLO supporters, and the long brown coats of the women, a style adopted by fanatic followers of the Ayatollah in Iran and spread throughout the Middle East via television. The sense of danger in this fanatic West Bank city mirrored his own inner tension.

"One is surrounded by history here, Ruven," Gerte said, "which goes to show that even in so modern a country, one never escapes the past."

Levi felt a jolt, suddenly reminded of a recent discussion at his sister-in-law Rivka's apartment. It was his birthday, and Rivka had gathered a few friends together for a celebration.

"Ruven, you never change," Tsvi, one of his oldest friends, had remarked enviously as Rivka served the cake she had baked.

"We all change," he'd replied offhandedly.

"No one changes. I'm the same person now that I was at sixteen," Rivka had protested. "Only the outside has changed. I am fatter, I have gray hair and lines in my face. But inside I am the same."

"I agree with Ruven," another woman responded. "I'm certainly a different person than I was at sixteen or even at thirty! If I were to meet myself as I was twenty years ago, I would not recognize myself. Rivka, you had a terrible temper when you were young. I remember, even in school! And now you never get upset. We only delude ourselves, thinking we don't change."

"Then you don't believe in the redemption of criminals?" Rivka's neighbor, a teacher, challenged. "Or in the power of psychiatry to help change people? The modern world is based on the idea that people can and do change."

"The Bible says, 'The Negro will not change his skin, nor the tiger his stripes,'" Rivka argued. "Nahon? Right, Ruven?"

"I think a person goes through stages in life, dictated by circumstance. A human being is amazingly adaptable." He'd looked around at the group. He didn't have to see the tattooed numbers on their arms to be aware of their common background. "We saw that in the camps."

"You are talking in generalities," Rivka said. "My Ronit was a temperamental, demanding baby and to this day she is emotional and, I admit, a little spoiled. But my Ezra was sweet and docile the moment he was born, and show me a gentler man. How have you changed, Ruven, since you were a young man?"

"I say," another friend interjected, before Levi could respond, "we are simply an accumulation of our past experiences and we never escape our past. Never. I am sorry to disagree with Ruven, but that's my belief."

If anyone had managed to erase the past, he had, he told himself, thinking of John Daley. And was that not proof that a man was composed of many men? Like the other refugees, he had come to Israel and created a new life for himself. He was not who he had been, he told himself. Rudolf Lobel and Mauthausen were behind and had nothing to do with Ruven Levi. Nothing.

Yet, John Daley, for whatever reason, believed him to be Rudolf Lobel, the Hunter of Mauthausen. Levi thought of the man some years back who had been innocently riding a city bus when a woman, most likely deranged, started screaming, accusing him of being a Nazi. A crowd quickly gathered, the man was forced off the bus and nearly torn limb from limb. His accuser had been mistaken, but Levi had followed subsequent reports of the case with particular interest. The man's life had been ruined. He'd been forced to leave his job; his wife had left him; he died not long after, shunned by neighbors and friends. Daley was a retired detective. If Daley really believed him to be Rudolf Lobel, who knew what he might do about it?

He remembered suddenly the photograph Daley's woman companion had snapped at the airport. He was almost certain he was not in it. Still, he felt a chill. There was no doubt that Daley was dangerous.

The bus neared the Tombs.

He heard Zev behind him entertaining the others with one of his amusing medical stories.

". . . and my obstetrician friend had a reputation for infallibility. When a patient came to him and asked, 'Doctor, will I have a boy or a girl?' he would think and say, 'A boy, Mrs. Cohen.' Then he would take out a black notebook and write, 'Mrs. Cohen, girl.' If he said a girl, he would write in his book, 'boy' and the date. So when the woman delivered, if she had a boy and he had told her she would have a boy, she told everyone he had predicted correctly. If he said boy and she had a girl, she would go to him and say, 'Doctor, you told me a boy and see, I have a girl.' My friend would shake his head and say, 'No, Mrs. Cohen, I remember I told you a girl. See, I even wrote it in my book,' and he would take out the book and show her where he had written 'Mrs. Cohen, girl.' "

Levi forced a laugh, although he had heard the story before. He got off the bus and started up the wide stone steps leading to the Tombs, past crippled beggars and children pestering the tourists to buy chocolate. He was feeling dizzy, almost light-headed. The stress was not good for a man his age. He longed to be home, alone in his hunting room with his music, his books.

He took a deep breath in an attempt to regain his inner composure. Out of the corner of his eye he saw another tour bus pulling up on the street below. His heart pounded pain-fully as he recognized the sign on the front and saw John Daley staring out of the window.

Levi turned away, startled by the violence of his response. For a moment he was swept back in time to the days he'd lived in constant fear of discovery. He'd hated the feeling of vulnerability, which no amount of reassurance on the part of his friends had allayed. He shuddered at the memory. It had taken years and a steely determination to regain his confidence and control.

Levi again thought back to the discussion at Rivka's house. He'd insisted he was a different man now than he had been years before. He knew, were a survey to be taken among his friends and associates, the consensus would be that Ruven Levi was a gentle, patient, giving person. A man who gave of his time and skill to charity. A man who was active in the community. A devoted husband. And he had lived so many years in that role that he, too, had come to believe it to be a true assessment of his nature.

Yet, those who'd known him as a young man would have described him as cunning. Cold, calculating, ruthless. In con-trol. A man who did not allow sentiment to get in the way of reason. If the Ruven Levi of today was a fiction, then who and what was he?

The other bus had pulled to a stop. The tall figure of the American detective climbed down the steps.

Levi felt as though he'd been abruptly wakened from a dream, forced into harsh reality. He had told his friends that a man was composed of many men, that one could change with time. But the fear that John Daley had instilled in him and his own reaction to that fear told him more clearly than any argument that the person he believed he had become was no more than a mask he had created for himself.

As his mind sprang into action Levi was surprised to discover himself experiencing an excitement, a thrill he had not felt in a long, long time. A lifetime ago he had outwitted those bent on his destruction. And he'd taken his success as proof of his superiority, for he had always recognized himself to be superior to most people. Certainly to John Daley. Now, once more, he was about to be put to the test. He was not a coward, had never run from a challenge. I am a survivor, he told himself. And when it came right down to it, all that really mattered was survival at any cost. He thought about the partridge and quail he hunted and the various ways in which they protected themselves. He, too, would find ways to protect himself as he always had.

It came to him that Rivka, in quoting the Bible, had been right after all. "The Negro will not change his skin, nor the tiger his stripes." Ruven Levi knew that he was who and what he had always been.

TWENTY-TWO

It was raining outside CIA Headquarters in Langley, Virginia, as the four men took their seats around the table. The slim, graying man who had called the meeting glanced out the window. The traffic would be snarled if the rain continued. But then he told himself he was being an optimist thinking they could come to some resolution by rush hour. He, himself, despite his talk with Vince, had not reached a definite conclusion about how best to handle John Daley.

"Shall we get started?" he said, opening the top-secret folder in front of him.

An hour later they were only slightly closer to agreement.

"We should leave things to his friend for now," the youngest, a clean-cut athletic type, said earnestly. "Give him a chance to work on Daley. He might persuade him to forget the whole thing."

"We can't wait too much longer," a red-faced, fleshy man warned with a shake of his head. "I say we need to be aggressive in this situation. There's too much at stake."

"I agree with Bob," a tall look-alike for textbook pictures of

133

Abe Lincoln remarked, nodding in the direction of the young man. "We can afford to sit tight for a little bit, but I think we have to contact the Israelis."

"I think it's asking for trouble," the square-jawed young man said stubbornly. "It could backfire."

The three older men exchanged the briefest of glances, silently acknowledging the gap of age and experience.

"I hear what you're saying, Bob," the graying man replied, adjusting the glasses on his aquiline nose. "Still, we have a problem. You have to admit that, and we haven't come up with any alternate solution."

The younger man frowned. "I realize that, but—"

"It's getting late," the heavy man protested, "and we're just going over old ground here. Let's sum things up and make a decision. I don't know about you fellows, buy my stomach's playing a Sousa march!"

"Okay." The man in charge picked up a pencil, twisting it in his hands. "Here are our options. One, we do nothing. This could lead to complications, embarrassments, if you will, if it gets out of hand."

"But there's not much probability of that," the younger man said. "We agreed."

"True," the fourth man murmured. "Still, every possibility must be taken into account. There is the chance it could get out of hand. Especially dealing with an unknown factor like Daley. And then—"

"And then the proverbial shit hits the fan," the fat man burst out, jowls quivering. "And I don't want to be around when it does!"

"The second option," the leader continued smoothly, "is to actively involve our newest player, which we've also agreed is less than satisfactory. From what his friend says, we're dealing here with a less than cooperative character in John Daley. An independent, feisty, if you will, spirit."

"Why not hold off action until Vince has a chance to work on him, if he hasn't already? We can follow it closely," the young man said.

"It seems clear to me," the Lincoln look-alike said. "We contact the Israelis with our proposal. Nothing else we can do. We can't rely entirely on his friend."

The younger man looked worried. "I still don't like it. You're concerned about embarrassment, think how much worse that would look. And, anyway, the Israelis aren't going to like it."

"They may not like it," the fat man said, "but they don't really have much choice. Look, Israel's in the process of upgrading her air force. She needs U.S. help, and the way things have been going lately, it doesn't look so good. We're in a real good bargaining position. Israel gets the help she needs with the planes. And we keep the fan shit-free!" He laughed and closed his folder. "At least for now!"

The gray-haired man put the pencil down and fiddled with his glasses once more. He looked around at the other three.

"We're agreed then? One, we keep a close watch on Daley. Two, we contact the Israelis. If Daley goes to them, at least they can stonewall. Make any identification difficult."

Lincoln nodded. The younger man raised an eyebrow, then shrugged his broad shoulders. The fat man glanced pointedly at his watch.

"It's getting late and we're all tired, but we have other ground to cover before we adjourn," the leader said. He turned to another folder. "What about the Hunter?"

The steady patter of rain against the window was the only sound in the room as the men exchanged glances. This was an uncomfortable subject, yet one that could not be avoided.

"An agreement was made," the Lincolnesque man said, breaking the uneasy silence. "There's no getting around that fact."

The young man's features darkened with distaste. "And for what?" he said bitterly.

"What is he now, anyway, seventy? Seventy-five?" Glancing at the darkening sky, the heavy man scowled. "Jesus, look at that rain!" His fingers drummed impatiently on the table. "I say we owe him nothing. He's an old man. What can he do?"

"That's just the point," the Lincolnesque man commented dryly. "If he has what he says he has, then he can do quite a lot."

They fell silent once more. The gray-haired man knew they were waiting for him, hoping he would make a decision they

135

could live with. He removed his glasses and slowly wiped them with a handkerchief while he gathered his thoughts.

"It would all seem to hinge on what Daley does," he said thoughtfully. "If Daley is persuaded to forget about him, then we need not do anything. I propose we watch that entire situation and talk to Jerusalem."

The fat man sighed heavily, pushing his chair back from the table. "Nobody's answered the question about what to do if Daley starts making waves."

The gray-haired man closed the folder in front of him. "Why, then we'll be compelled to explore other options."

No one needed to ask what those options might be.

Vince couldn't sleep. Not even a glass of warm milk with honey helped. He sat at the kitchen table munching on a salami sandwich. Thinking. He reviewed the meeting in his mind over and over. Wondered what he could have done or said differently. Wondered if he'd been wrong to have made that first phone call. Maybe he should have ignored the whole thing. Maybe he'd made too much of Daley's call saying he'd seen Rudolf Lobel.

He finished the sandwich and rummaged through the well-stocked refrigerator for something else to calm and comfort him in his distress. He took out some cold ravioli. He didn't bother removing it from the Tupperware but took a fork and dug in.

There was nothing else he could have done, he told himself, knowing Daley as he did. Daley wouldn't have called if he hadn't been steamed up. He thought back to the man's question. "What might be our chances of getting Mr. Daley to cooperate?" Maybe that was where he could have lied, said, "Excellent." Daley had only a week or so in Israel. What could he do in that time, anyway? The more he thought about the meeting, the more miserable he felt.

He'd answered honestly. He'd felt at the time he had no choice, but now he was plagued by the possible consequences.

The overhead light snapped on as Angie, in her robe and slippers, padded into the room.

"Are you sick?" she asked anxiously.

"Nope, just can't sleep."

She lowered herself into a chair next to him.

"Do you want some warm milk?"

"No, thanks. Had some."

"You were so quiet tonight at Cathy's. Is anything wrong at the restaurant? Is there a problem with the new bartender?"

Vince leaned across the table and patted his wife's hand affectionately.

"He's okay. Everything's fine. Didn't you ever have nights when you couldn't sleep? You know, you lie awake thinking about all kinds of crazy things, like who's going to win the pennant next year, or should I change the lunch special, or should I plant roses or tulips."

Angie looked relieved. "Well, if you're sure you're okay. Maybe you should get a checkup."

She yawned sleepily and got up.

"Good idea," he said. "Don't wait up for me. Maybe I'll take the dog for a walk."

She leaned down and kissed his forehead. Vince had the urge to confide in her, to share with her his feelings of conflicting loyalties, but he didn't dare. Wistfully, he watched her go out of the kitchen.

He remembered the conversation with Daley about Otto Mueller. Daley cared. That was the thing about Daley. Whatever he might pretend, however he might seem, he cared, and cared deeply, about things. He remembered the day they'd marched into that camp. He'd been as shocked as everybody else. Some of the guys threw up and others broke down. Vince remembered crying like a baby. But Daley hadn't done either. He'd just stood there taking it all in. Only Vince knew that for almost forty years it had eaten into Daley. Most people never saw that side of him. And Daley was right, if there was such a thing as right. Vince sighed.

He had a loyalty to Daley. Christ, they went back so far. But for all his pragmatism, Vince was intensely patriotic. He still got choked up when they sang "The Star-Spangled Banner" at ball games. And he knew without a doubt that his best friend, John Daley, had in his power the ability to hurt the country he loved. Vince was equally distressed by the knowledge that he held in his hands the power to destroy his friend.

"It's up to you," the other man had said.

Vince glanced up at the clock. It would be six o'clock in the evening in Israel. He told himself Daley was probably out for dinner or having a drink somewhere.

The house was still. Angie had probably fallen back asleep. Vince put on his hat and coat. Although it was cold, he left the car in the garage and walked the three blocks to the imposing stone building. He knew the door would be open as he climbed the well-worn steps.

Inside, it was dimly lit and cold. Empty but for the flickering candles and a couple huddled close together in the front pew. With a heavy heart, Vince plodded down the nave and turned to the confessional.

In a Jerusalem apartment a Hanukkah party was in progress. As the guests in the living room began singing Hanukkah songs, an Arab maid entered from the kitchen and indicated to the host that he was wanted on the telephone.

He excused himself and picked it up in a bedroom, pushing aside a pile of coats to make room for himself on the bed. As he listened his face hardened in anger.

"I don't like it," he said.

He ran his fingers absently over the silky fur of a jacket. A lively melody filled the apartment.

"No," he sighed after a moment. "No, don't tell Goldschmidt."

He laughed shortly with a mirth he didn't feel.

"As my mother used to say, with friends like that, who needs enemies?"

TWENTY-THREE

It was with a feeling of frustration that Daley watched the doctors disappear into the Tomb of the Patriarchs. He longed to leap out of the bus, run up the broad stone steps, and confront Lobel. He imagined himself pulling the white hair back, exposing the ear, and shouting to the crowd that there was a Nazi war criminal among them. But the doors of the bus remained closed, trapping him inside as Yael filled them in on the three-thousand-year history of Hebron.

"Hebron," she was saying, "is one of the four major holy cities, the others being Jerusalem, Tiberias, and Safed. According to tradition, four couples are buried here . . . Abraham and Sarah, Isaac and Rebecca, Jacob and Leah, and, as legend goes, Adam and Eve."

Daley eyed the mosque impatiently. Although he wanted another go at Lobel, he realized that calling him by name in Bethlehem might have scared him off. Now there would be nothing stopping the man from leaving the country and returning to wherever he'd come from.

"Hebron was Jewish until 1919, and then in 1929 there was

a massacre in which over sixty Jews were killed by the Arabs," Yael said. "The British evacuated the remainder to Tel Aviv and Jerusalem and only in 1967 did the children of the old Hebron residents come back. But today, as you may be aware, Hebron is a very tense place. It is for this reason, we must stay together at all times."

"A tourist bus was stoned the other day," Maureen Flanagan said. "I read it in the *Jerusalem Post.*"

"That's nothing," Jack Duffy commented. "I heard they executed an Israeli settler last week."

"You must remember we are on the West Bank now and unfortunately, especially since the new Jewish settlements, these incidents do occur," Yael said, "but we will go together into the Tomb and then stop briefly for a drink. If we remain together, we shall be quite safe."

The doors of the bus opened. Daley stood impatiently at the entrance to the building, which dated from the time of Herod and had been at various times different churches and then, finally, a mosque. If Lobel succeeded in leaving the country, he told himself, the Nazi would have again evaded justice. He would have to be stopped.

They paused to have their bags checked by Israeli soldiers. Then Daley, along with the other men, put on a black paper skullcap. He moved to the front of the group, hoping to get another look at Lobel if the doctors were still there.

Inside the mosque, he saw only two Arab men praying on the oriental rugs in the center of the floor. Disappointment coursed through him. The second room, containing the tombs of Isaac and Rebecca, was empty but for a lone Israeli guard. An elderly religious Jew swayed in prayer in the smallest room, used as a synagogue at certain hours and containing the tombs of Abraham and Sarah.

The outside courtyard was also empty. The doctors had gone.

"You certainly get a different feeling here," Rose remarked as they left the tiny one-room synagogue and the tombs of Jacob and Leah. "I feel like I'm in prison with all the soldiers and guards. And the way the Arabs stared at the bus! I'll be glad to get back to Jerusalem."

"Me, too," Daley agreed, not adding it was for different reasons. He was thinking of the film. And his next move.

At the base of the steps Yael escorted them to a small, squat building identified by a sign as THE JEWISH HEBRON SETTLERS GIFT SHOP. Daley noted the small shops across the narrow street, and the taxis and cars parked in front. Among them was an empty tour bus with the sign RECONSTRUCTIVE PLASTIC SURGEONS on the front.

"And now," Yael said, herding them inside the building, "we have time for a rest and, as we say, coffee in, coffee out! You will find a nice selection of souvenirs here and refreshments. We will stop approximately twenty minutes, and again I must impress upon all of you the need for staying inside. Do not leave the building for any reason. If time permits, later, we will stop at a glass factory."

"Rose, something to drink?" he asked.

She shook her head. "No, thank you, John. I want to look at the embroidered dresses."

She joined several of the women at the rack of long dresses.

Bypassing the jewelry and displays of wooden and religious objects, Daley wandered to the snack bar and ordered a coffee and cake. He took a seat by the window where he could keep an eye on the bus outside. The doctors must have been taken to a glass or pottery factory, he decided, seeing only Arab women in long brown coats and white head scarves on the quiet street

Daley finished his snack and headed to the front of the shop and the display of postcards, remembering he'd promised to send one to Vince. He selected a card of Bethlehem for Vince and one of the Tomb to send to the guys at work. He paid for the cards and turned to the rack of dresses, curious to see what new bargain Rose had found. She was not among the women admiring the dresses. When Maureen Flanagan came out of the ladies' room, he asked her if she had seen Rose inside.

"No," Maureen said. "Last I saw her, she was talking to an Englishman over by the jewelry. I don't see him, either."

Daley was uneasy. He told himself that Rose was sensible. She was intelligent. Surely she would have better sense than to defy the guide and leave the group. But he also knew her

141

weakness was shopping for bargains. He glanced across the road at the line of shops. Leather bags, carpets, the famous Hebron glass and pottery plates and vases were temptingly displayed in doorways.

He looked back over his shoulder. Yael and the driver were drinking coffee and conversing in Hebrew. He quickly strode outside and crossed the street. The Arab proprietor approached him the moment he entered the crowded shop.

"May I help you? Hebron glass. Very good prices."

Daley saw at a glance that Rose was not there.

"Did you see an American woman?" he asked. "This tall with short dark hair. She was wearing a green coat."

The Arab shrugged. "We have many Americans. Very good prices."

He made a quick tour of the next shop. A French couple was examining handmade rugs. Again he asked the owner about Rose. The man thought a moment.

"Yes." He nodded. "There was a lady here a little while ago. She looked at some plates but her husband took her away."

"Husband?"

"A tall man, with light hair."

"Where did they go?"

The man shook his head and turned back to the French couple.

Daley's nervousness grew as he rapidly inspected the rest of the shops on that side of the street. It was over a half hour since they'd all gone into the gift shop. He told himself Rose had probably rejoined the group. Nevertheless, he crossed the street and went into the last shop. He didn't know why he felt so unnerved . . . whether it was the encounter with Lobel or the insistence of the guide that they were in a fanatically hostile territory. He sensed danger everywhere.

"Rugs? Very good quality, all handmade." A young Arab boy held one up for his inspection.

Daley took the rug, his eyes scanning the shop. He saw her in a far corner sipping a tiny cup of Turkish coffee and chatting with a robed Arab.

He dropped the rug, as angry as he was relieved.

"Rose!"

She turned and waved.

"John, wait till you see the marvelous rug I found!"

He strode through the shop. Her smile faded at his expression.

"What's wrong?" she asked.

"Nothing except that I've gone through every damn shop on this street looking for you! Didn't you hear Yael? You were supposed to stay with the group."

"Oh, John, I'm sorry!" She looked stricken. "How thoughtless of me. You're right, of course, but I met an Englishman, lovely man, who told me about the exceptional bargains in this shop. He told me I'd be quite safe with him. According to him, the tour guides tend to exaggerate the danger."

Daley grasped her elbow as she put her coffee cup down, said good-bye to the proprietor, and picked up her package.

"Where's your friend now?" he asked.

Rose turned around. "That's odd. He was here just a few minutes ago. Now I don't see him."

"Didn't your mother ever tell you not to talk to strangers?"

Daley tried to keep his voice light in an effort not to betray his feeling that something was wrong. He didn't know what, but he trusted the instinct that was warning him now of danger.

Rose laughed. "Honestly, John, don't you know I'm a liberated woman?"

They stepped outside into the cold winter light. Across the way Daley saw their group coming out of the gift shop.

"There they are!" Maureen Flanagan called out.

It was the last thing Daley heard.

He felt his legs buckle as a blinding pain seared his brain. He saw the pavement rising up to meet him. He was vaguely aware of blood, of Rose's anxious face bending over him. And then, before it all went black, his stunned mind registered a tour bus, the doctors' tour bus, passing by.

TWENTY-FOUR

"I feel as if it's all my fault," Rose said miserably. "If you hadn't gone looking for me, it never would have happened."

Daley put a comforting arm around her shoulder. "Hey, come on, Rose. No guilt. Didn't you hear what Yael said? These rock-throwing incidents happen all the time. It looked a hell of a lot worse than it was. Superficial scalp cuts bleed a lot."

Rose looked skeptical as they rose from the dining-room table. Christmas Eve celebrations were in full swing as the hotel's Father Christmas roamed the room distributing sweets.

"I still say you should go to bed and rest."

"Not tonight," he said grimly. "It might be my last chance to get another look at Lobel."

Even though the painkiller was wearing off, he wasn't about to give in to the sharp throbbing in his temples.

"I'm coming with you," Rose said. "I'd feel even worse if you had a reaction to the injury or the pills."

"I'll be okay. This is no way for you to spend Christmas

Eve. You should stay, go out with some of the others, watch the Mass on TV."

"And miss out on an adventure?"

She was already slipping on her coat. Daley shrugged, inwardly pleased. Remembering that Dr. Dailey had said the physicians were staying at the King David, he'd called the hotel and found out that a reception for the doctors was scheduled that evening.

"I never imagined in my wildest dreams I'd spend Christmas Eve in Jerusalem hunting down a Nazi! It's bizarre!" Rose sighed as they climbed into a taxi outside the hotel.

"At least you know it's one Christmas you won't forget."

Daley leaned back as the driver took off. Luck had been against him. Because of his accident and the first aid he'd required, they'd returned to the hotel too late to take in the film. Now he'd have to wait until tomorrow. He was afraid tomorrow might already be too late.

The taxi pulled into the circular driveway of the King David Hotel, a stately building from the British days. A hotel doorman opened the door for them. Inside the hotel, Daley immediately went to the reception desk on the right. In response to his question, a clerk told him the reception for the medical group was taking place in a room to the right of the lobby.

"It should be over shortly," the clerk said.

Daley and Rose crossed the lobby, proceeding through the Sabra Coffee Shop to the veranda. Directly beneath them sat the hotel swimming pool, an aqua jewel in the night, and, beyond, the spectacular view of the Old City.

"Without a name or a picture, I don't have anything to go to the police with," Daley said. "We can see the lobby from here. As soon as they come in we'll go back inside and separate. If you see him, ask another doctor immediately who he is, but try not to let him see you."

Rose shivered. "The man frightens me, John. I tell myself he's an old man, but knowing who he is, what he was capable of doing . . ." She gave a nervous little laugh. "In fact, this is really ridiculous, but when I saw you suddenly fall with all that blood streaming from your head, the first thought that went through my mind was that you'd been shot. By him! Of course it was totally irrational, but I'm afraid now that he knows you know who he is, he's dangerous to you."

Daley took her hands in his. They were cold. He saw the anxiety in her face. He didn't bother to deny the truth of what she said.

"Look, Rose, it isn't your affair. You can back out anytime. I don't want to involve you in something you don't want to be involved in, especially if there's a possibility of danger."

She shook her head. "Remember what I said about moral responsibility? What kind of a teacher would I be, to say nothing of a human being, if I backed out? Count me in."

Daley glanced at his watch. It was nine-thirty. The reception had started at seven-thirty. It couldn't last much longer. He was thinking they should go back inside when Rose suddenly grabbed his arm, pointing with her other hand.

"John, there's the Englishman, the man I met in Hebron!"

He looked through the window to the coffee shop. A tall rangy man in a slightly rumpled suit was paying his check at the cash register.

"I should tell him about the rug," she said. "After all, he took me to the shop. He seemed to know a great deal about Bedouin weaving."

As they entered the coffee shop the man was leaving. Daley had no time to waste on him. He saw that the lobby had suddenly filled and most of the men were wearing the by-now familiar medical conference badges.

He caught a glimpse of the Englishman sitting behind a newspaper in one of the comfortable chairs as he pretended to study the coffee-shop menu posted just outside the doors and Rose made her way through the knots of people to the gift-shop area in a hallway adjacent to the lobby. He spotted Dr. Dailey as he scanned the crowd in the elegant room. Several groups were gravitating to the dining room. Others headed for the elevators and the exit. Most of them congregated in the lobby. He saw Rose seemingly absorbed in the display in the gift-shop window. A sudden tenderness filled him. She looked up at that moment and caught his eye. Her shoulders lifted in a barely perceptible shrug.

There was no sign of Lobel. Damn! Daley reached into his

pocket for a cigarette, furious with himself, certain that he had scared him off.

The pain in his head had become an insistent throb. Every bone ached from the fall. He was about to call it a day, believing that by now the man was probably safely out of the country, heading back to Europe or South America or wherever he'd been hiding all these years. He started toward Rose, telling himself wryly that he could now claim the dubious distinction of having allowed the Hunter of Mauthausen to escape justice, when he saw the expression on Rose's face suddenly change.

Three men were calmly strolling toward the door. The one in the middle had a distinctive, bobbing walk.

Daley felt his heart speed up. He forgot the pain in his head, the bruises on his body. He met Rose in the center of the lobby as Lobel and his companions entered the revolving door.

"I didn't have a chance to ask anyone who he was," Rose whispered breathlessly.

"Take my arm," Daley instructed as they swept out the door into the night.

Ignoring the waiting taxis, the three men walked down the circular driveway. Daley and Rose followed at a discreet distance.

"If they turn around, stop and look in a shop window," he told her.

There was little foot traffic on King David Street, although the narrow street was filled with cars. A block or so from the hotel they turned, following the trio up a short hilly residential area that wound around until they found themselves on a quiet street that circled a little park. Daley glanced at the street sign on the corner building, taking note of the name, Nahum Sokolov Street.

Daley watched the men go through a wrought-iron gate to the entrance of a four-story, stone apartment building. The front door shut behind them.

"What do you make of that?" Rose asked.

"He's obviously visiting an Israeli doctor."

Daley studied the building, waiting for a light in one of the dark windows to go on. None did, telling him that the men had either entered a back apartment or one that was already illuminated.

The brass directory listed the tenants in both Hebrew and English. Quickly Daley scanned the names for M.D.s. He found four.

He took out a small notebook and pencil from his jacket pocket and copied the names. Horowitz, Eli. Maron, Yehuda. Levi, Ruven. Davidson, Bracha.

Retracing their steps to the hotel, they took a taxi back to the Intercontinental. He had done all he could for tonight. The day, which now seemed to have begun a year ago, was wearing on him, and Daley needed another pain pill. Nevertheless, his mind was already planning the next moves. Tomorrow he would take the film to be developed. He would revisit the apartment building and try to talk to the physicians and find out from them the name of their friend. And then he would go to the police. He was suddenly very, very weary.

"John, promise me you'll go right to sleep," Rose said as they entered the elevator in their hotel. "And please call me if you start to feel sick."

"I will to both." He forced a smile through his pain and kissed her, touched by her concern. He walked her to her room and headed down the long corridor to the elevator.

He stopped halfway down the hall and, taking the notebook from his pocket, stared at the names. Horowitz, Maron, Levi, Davidson. The name Ruven Levi seemed to leap out at him at the same instant he was jolted by a preposterous thought.

Ruven Levi. R.L. Rudolf Lobel. He had seen the name Ruven Levi on the conference sheet Dr. Dailey had given him. Was it possible that Lobel, the 'Hunter of Mauthausen', was living in Israel as Ruven Levi? The thought was too outrageous to be seriously considered, but he refused to discard the remote possibility. He'd seen stranger things in his career.

He had reached the elevator and pressed the button when he heard Rose call his name. He sensed the panic in her voice before he turned to see her scurrying down the corridor. At close range he saw the wild, fearful look in her eyes, the flush on her face as she cried out!

"My room's been broken into! Oh, John, it's a mess! All my things strewn all over the place. My overnight case is gone, my jewelry, my little radio. And . . ." She paused, a stricken look crossing her face. "My camera!"

For the second time that day Daley had a premonition of danger, only this time it included Rose as well.

TWENTY-FIVE

"I feel very bad about your camera," Yael said for the third time. "It is the first time something like this has happened on one of my tours."

"It's certainly not your fault," Rose said.

"Still, I am sorry. All your wonderful pictures!"

"Yael, is there a place nearby where I can buy a camera?" Daley asked.

"In the city, of course, but no shops will be open this early."

He was impatient to be on his way. A camera was crucial if he was to have a photograph to take to the police. But even as he recognized that need, Daley was forced to admit that his chances of catching sight of Lobel again were no better than Rose's were of retrieving her stolen camera. If Lobel had spent the night in that apartment house, then Daley might, if he was lucky, catch sight of him coming out.

"Do you have a camera I could borrow? Just for today?"

Yael shook her head sadly. Then, a moment later, brightened.

"I have a friend who may have one, and I know he will lend it to me. Come. We'll go for a little walk. The place I'm going to take you is worth seeing anyway, and only five minutes from here."

Yael briskly led them out the hotel entrance and up the steep road to the right. A few minutes later they stopped. The guide nodded toward a small chapel.

"This is the Chapel of the Ascension. I think you will find it interesting, and perhaps you will have a chance to go inside later. But what I wanted to show you was this."

She pointed across the road to a small, unassuming coffee house identified by a sign as THE TENT.

"My friend works here," she said, leading them through a somewhat dilapidated inner courtyard. "This place dates from British times, and I think it is very special. It is not what it once was," she sighed, "but you can imagine what it was like then, in the old days, with British officers and their wives having afternoon tea. All very elegant and proper. I like to come here alone sometimes to relax and have a coffee and look at the view."

They sat at a round metal table perched at the rim of the Mount of Olives. Rose caught her breath at the sight of the Old City spread below them, its ancient walls and buildings golden in the early morning sunlight. Daley's mind was too full of Rudolf Lobel to respond to the view or the atmosphere.

While they drank small Turkish coffees flavored with cardamom, Yael conducted a rapid conversation in Arabic with a young man, and by the time they had finished their coffee, she had handed over to Daley a small Instamatic camera.

"There is even film!" she announced happily.

By nine o'clock Daley was retracing his steps of the night before. He noted in the daylight the architecture of the old stone buildings, some with Arab influence, different and more interesting than the boxy Tel Aviv apartment houses.

Although only minutes from the busy King David Street, the quiet neighborhood had a well-established look about it. He passed an affluent-looking gentleman walking a cocker spaniel and several young matrons pushing strollers. And then he found himself at the park. By American standards it was not much of a park, containing only some benches and a few simple pieces of play equipment. There was no grass to speak of and the rose bushes were barren. A group of small boys in skullcaps were kicking a ball around the park. A young mother was pushing a toddler on a swing while two elderly ladies, oblivious to the shouts of the boys, gossiped on a bench.

Daley lit a cigarette and smoked it, staring at the building the doctors had gone into the night before. The white-haired man, the man he knew to be Rudolf Lobel, either knew someone who lived in that building or, outlandish as it seemed, actually lived there himself. And if so, he had to be one of the four physicians whose names were listed on the directory. The name Ruven Levi kept pushing its way into his consciousness. R.L. For thirty minutes Daley smoked one cigarette after another and waited.

A woman who looked as if she might be a maid went into the building. An elderly man came out and was picked up by a taxi. There was no sign of the white-haired man.

Daley left the little park, crossed the street, and pushed open the wrought-iron gate in front of the building. He studied the directory once more. Underneath Ruven Levi's name were the words "Reconstructive Plastic Surgeon." Logic told him Levi's apartment was the one the three men had entered. Still, he intended to check out all of the physicians.

Bracha Davidson's apartment also served as her office. She was, Daley discovered, by the three pregnant women in the waiting room, a gynecologist. The receptionist informed him that Dr. Davidson was busy with a patient and would not be available until noon.

Eli Horowitz's door was opened by a bearded young man in a Harvard sweatshirt. Daley heard a violin concerto playing in the background.

"Dr. Levi?" Daley asked, ready to go into his prepared story about wanting an appointment with Ruven Levi.

"I'm Dr. Abrams," the man said with an American accent. "This is Dr. Horowitz's apartment, but he's not here now."

"When will he be back?"

The American shrugged. "June or possibly July. He's in the States and I'm renting the apartment. Did you want to leave a message for him?"

"No, thanks." Daley turned as if to go, then stopped as though a thought had just occurred to him.

"Tell me, do you know any of the other physicians in the building?"

"No, can't say I do," Abrams replied. "Actually, I'm not an M.D. I'm a linguist. Harvard." He laughed, looking at his sweatshirt. "Guess it's evident. We arrived only two weeks ago and haven't had time to meet anybody."

The middle-aged woman who opened Yehuda Maron's door stared at Daley as though she'd seen a ghost.

"Mrs. Maron?" he asked.

Her hand flew to her throat in an instinctive gesture. Daley recognized fear in her eyes.

"Something happened!" she wailed as tears rained down her lined cheeks.

"I'm looking for Dr. Levi," he said quickly.

Relief seemed to pour out of her. It took her a moment to recover. She sniffled, then laughed.

"I'm sorry! I thought it was Yehuda! He's been in the hospital." She shook her head, then stepped aside to let him in. "I'm sorry, please come in. My husband had a heart attack two weeks ago, and every time the telephone rings or the doorbell, I become frightened."

Daley mentally checked Yehuda Maron off his list.

"I was looking for Dr. Levi," he repeated.

"Oh, yes, upstairs."

"He was recommended to me," Daley said. "I heard he was very good in his field."

"Dr. Levi has a fine reputation, but he doesn't take many new patients anymore."

"Maybe he'll make an exception."

She shrugged. "Who knows. However, I'm afraid you will not find him home now. I saw him go out early this morning."

"That's too bad. What is he like?" Daley said, adopting a chatty tone.

"We've lived in the same building for almost ten years, but I couldn't tell you that. He is very polite. Quiet. But we don't know him. And since his wife died, he keeps to himself. Some men are like that. He should marry again."

Daley thanked her, filed away the information that Levi

was a widower, and climbed the well-worn steps to Ruven Levi's apartment. If Levi was a widower, the chances were no one was home. He wondered if he dared force the lock and enter, search the apartment for some link to Rudolf Lobel. But as he stood in front of the door he heard the drone of a vacuum cleaner.

He rang the bell. Immediately a dog began barking. He pushed the bell again and waited. When the door opened he found himself looking down at a diminutive, dark-skinned Yemenite woman in a housedress. The fragrant aroma of baking bread filled the apartment. A wire-haired German pointer pushed past the woman, sniffing Daley excitedly between barks. Daley bent to pat the dog.

"Dr. Levi?" Daley asked.

The woman shook her head.

"Is he here?" Daley asked.

"No here."

She started to close the door.

"I have an appointment."

The woman looked at him blankly. Daley realized she barely understood English. He pointed to his watch.

"Appointment." He strode past her through the foyer, into the living room.

"No here. Later. Come back."

Daley was mentally memorizing the large, comfortable room. He noted old Persian rugs on the stone floor, oil paintings of landscapes in heavy gilt frames, dark, ornately carved furniture. An expensive stereo was the only modern touch. Daley scanned the record collection. Operas and classics.

"No here," the woman repeated nervously. "Later."

"I'll wait," he said. "Appointment." Again he pointed to his watch.

The woman eyed him uncertainly. Then evidently giving up, went back to her chores. Daley strode down the hallway, into another, smaller room.

This was evidently Levi's study, although hunting room might have been a more appropriate name. For while bookshelves lined the wall on one side, most of the room was devoted to hunting trophies.

Daley moved to the bookcase and studied the titles. Medical books in English and German. History books in English. What looked like novels with Hebrew titles. What one would expect of a physician.

He turned his attention to the rest of the room. The stuffed head of a wild boar dominated the second wall, and on the others, a collection of hunting trophies . . . antlers, stuffed partridges, an antelope skin, an artful display of porcupine quills. A handsome saddle with handmade Arabian bridles hung over the fireplace.

Daley was drawn to the gun rack by the fireplace. He couldn't help admiring Levi's collection: a semiautomatic FN, an over/under 4 Italian Beretta, an Italian semiautomatic Fabarm, and a German Mauser hunting rifle. He couldn't resist picking up the most valuable, a rare German Kessle double-barrel shotgun. Handmade. He'd have given a hell of a lot for that gun, he thought enviously. He inspected a display of hunting knives that lined the other side of the fireplace.

The drone of the vacuum started up again. The dog padded into the room, sniffed around, and then approached him, nuzzling his leg.

Daley absently patted him as he studied the framed photographs of smiling hunters in varied locales, hoping to catch a glimpse of the white-haired man in one of them. Disappointed, he tried the desk drawer. It was locked.

He glanced into the bedroom on his way out. No photographs except one of a sweet-faced woman dressed in an outdated costume.

Ruven Levi, Daley decided, as he bid good-bye to the Yemenite housekeeper, was a man of means. Of culture and taste. And, like Rudolf Lobel, an avid hunter.

The taxi driver dropped him off at the area known as the Russian Compound, off Jaffa Road. There, by the incongruous Russian Church, a building that with its green-domed cathedral looked as if it had been lifted from the heart of Moscow, he strode to the small guard house in front of the Jerusalem police station. Although Daley recognized the flimsiness of his story minus a photograph, he knew he had no choice but to proceed anyway.

A policeman in navy uniform asked for identification. His

NYPD identification card seemed to impress the guard, who, after making a telephone call, directed him to the police building, a gracious two-story stone structure. The inside of the building smelled of paint. Daley followed a young secretary in civilian clothes up a flight of stairs to a windowless office. It was more like a cubicle, furnished with a cheap wooden desk and, like most Israeli buildings, cold. The walls were decorated with posters, a cheap calendar, and several photographs. A plug-in electric heater provided the only warmth, a fluorescent hanging light the only illumination.

A young officer, in a short navy jacket and light blue shirt, rose from the cluttered desk and offered his hand.

"Mr. Daley," he said, gesturing to a chair, "please sit down. It's not often we get visitors from the New York Police. I'm Tsvi Roth. . . . Coffee?"

"Thanks."

"Turkish or Nes?"

Daley had learned it was near to impossible to get what he termed real coffee. Israelis seemed to drink only instant Nescafe or the thick, black, and very sweet Turkish coffee. Only in the hotels could he order what they called "filter," a cup with a drip filter on top.

"Nes," he said. "Thanks."

"I was in New York," Roth said. He pushed a button on the black phone and spoke Hebrew. *"Shnei nes, b'vakashah."*

"When was that?"

"Two years ago. I studied at the University of Colorado. Then drove across the U.S. It's a great country. So how do you find Israel?"

"Very interesting. In fact, more interesting than I'd bargained for."

The secretary brought a metal tray with two cups of instant coffee and two pieces of cake.

"How's that?"

Daley sat back and lit a cigarette.

"I don't know how else to say this except to just come out with it. There's a Nazi war criminal here in Israel."

Roth's eyebrows lifted slightly. He, too, lit a cigarette from the half-finished pack on his desk.

"At least you're not laughing," Daley said.

156

When he'd finished his story the young policeman was still not laughing, but Daley sensed his skepticism.

"You realize, of course, it is highly unlikely that Rudolf Lobel would be here in Israel," Roth said. "He would be taking too great a chance of being recognized, even for an important medical conference."

"I realize that," Daley said. "But the similarities. The ear, the walk. The age, coloring."

Roth eyed him silently. "I understand, but still it doesn't seem probable. However, I'll get a list of everyone attending the conference. We can make a check." Again he pushed a button. Another policeman came in. There was an exchange in Hebrew.

"Do you know a Dr. Ruven Levi?" Daley asked.

"I know of him. And I think my mother-in-law knew his wife. Levi is very well-respected. He's known for his reconstructive work for the military and for terrorist victims. He always took the cases no other surgeon would touch. He operated on one of our officers very recently. An incredible job! The man's face had been nearly destroyed in an explosion. Levi's semiretired now. Why do you ask about him?"

Daley described following the three men to the apartment house and his morning visit.

"Dr. Levi friends with a Nazi! It would seem out of the question that Levi would associate with a Nazi. Especially"— a flicker of a smile crossed the young policeman's face—"as Levi is a survivor of the camps."

"What camp?" Daley asked.

Roth shrugged. "I don't know. He's German, so it was most likely Dachau or Auschwitz."

"What about the fact that both Lobel and Levi are Germans, besides being plastic surgeons?"

"Israel is full of Germans who immigrated after the war. More than you'd realize, because so many changed their names from German or Polish to Hebrew ones. And plastic surgery is not an uncommon specialty. In any event, there isn't anything much I can do, Mr. Daley. I suggest you go to the National Police Headquarters. It's not far. They have a special unit there that deals with Nazi criminal investigations."

Daley was about to offer his theory that Levi and Lobel were one person, but something in the younger man's attitude told him it wouldn't make any difference. Roth found it hard to believe that Dr. Ruven Levi would even know Rudolf Lobel. He'd never believe that Ruven Levi was Rudolf Lobel. Passing the buck, he realized, knew no national boundaries.

The young man stood and offered his hand.

"Good luck. And have a good stay in Israel."

It was a short taxi ride to the Israeli police building, a huge, modern, white-stone affair set back from the street. Daley asked for the Nazi criminal investigation unit, noting that the officer behind the reception desk who asked for his passport didn't raise an eyebrow. He'd had the feeling Roth had been humoring him, and he didn't know what to expect from the next encounter. After a short wait he was directed to the second floor and the Special Investigation Division.

This time it was Malka Rubenstein, a motherly woman in civilian clothes who listened to him.

"Mr. Daley, it was good of you to come to us," she said when he'd finished his story. "However, all the files concerning Nazi war criminals are in Jaffa. If at all possible, you should make an appointment with the Division of Nazi Crimes there."

Daley felt his frustration returning.

"How long will you be in Jerusalem?" she asked.

"Our group goes back to Tel Aviv today."

"Good. Jaffa is really a part of Tel Aviv. So it should not be inconvenient for you."

"You mean there's nothing you're going to do here?"

"As you told me, Lieutenant Roth is checking the list of the physicians attending the conference. We will be in touch with Mr. Goldschmidt in Jaffa after you have seen him. This is really his area. But you may be sure that your information will be carefully followed up."

She tore a slip of paper off a pad and wrote in English.

"Here you are. This is the phone number in Jaffa and the address."

She stood and offered her hand. Daley was about to mention his theory that Lobel might be an Israeli, but she was clearly ending the interview.

"One last thing," he said as he got to his feet. "Do you know Dr. Ruven Levi?"

She brightened. "Why, yes, as a matter of fact. My brother-in-law is an anesthesiologist at Hadassah Hospital. He's often worked with Dr. Levi. He says he's one of the best. Or was. He's getting on now." She shook her head sadly. "A word of advice, Mr. Daley. If you are trying to connect Rudolf Lobel to Dr. Levi, you are, as the Americans say, barking up the wrong tree. Ruven Levi is absolutely above suspicion."

"You're probably right," Daley conceded, inwardly adding to himself that no one was.

On the main floor he asked for, and was directed to, a public telephone. He took several asimonim from his pocket and the slip of paper she had given him and dialed the area code for Jaffa.

Malka Rubenstein's motherly appearance underwent a change as the door closed behind John Daley. She looked like what she was—a twenty-year veteran of the Israeli police who had seen everything. The wrinkles in her forehead deepened as she frowned, and she absently ran her stubby fingers through her short gray hair. She sighed heavily and turned her chair from the desk toward the wall where her young granddaughter's latest artwork hung. The smiling rabbit and the huge yellow sun failed to cheer her as they usually did. She had hoped John Daley would not come. And she felt doubly bad as she swung around in her chair and picked up the telephone, because she liked him. She made snap judgments of people and prided herself on their accuracy. Daley was not only not a kook, as might be expected with such a story, but was intelligent. Decent. Her frown deepened and she reached with her free hand for a cigarette.

She almost hoped the switchboard would be busy, but her call went right through. She wasted no time on preliminaries.

"John Daley just left," she said.

As she replaced the receiver Malka Rubenstein knew this to be one of those infrequent times when she hated her job.

TWENTY-SIX

Yossi Aroni was on a routine patrol in the Golan Heights when the Jeep in front of him hit a mine. The explosion shattered the windshield of the Jeep Yossi was driving. The driver of the lead Jeep, a twenty-four-year-old soldier from Haifa, was burned to death. Yossi, in the days immediately following, considered him lucky. He had survived, but with a noseless face so lacerated by shards of glass that the features were nearly unrecognizable.

Yossi Aroni was, as Tsvi Roth had told John Daley, the sort of case Ruven Levi took on. The sort of case where the chances of failure were great, the sort most surgeons shied away from.

Levi had operated on the young soldier before leaving on his European vacation. Now, nearly three weeks later, it was time to view the results of the initial surgery. Levi carefully snipped away the last bandage. Seeing the anxiety in Aroni's eyes, the doctor squeezed the young man's hand reassuringly.

Anyone else would have been repulsed by the sight of the shiny raw-looking flesh. Levi, with his usual scientific detachment, was pleased. He noted with satisfaction the fine sutures where he had taken the skin of the forehead, made it into a flap, turning it down to rebuild the nose. Additional surgery would be required, of course, but Levi had no doubt that in time he would rebuild for Yossi Aroni a face as nearly normal as humanly possible. Despite his years and his semiretirement, he knew he was still among the best.

"Tov me'od," he said to the young soldier. "Very good."

He was rewarded with a noticeable relaxation of tension, a glimmer of gratitude in the dark eyes.

Levi thought about the young soldier as he left the Hadassah Hospital and made his way home for lunch. He hummed to himself, his pleasure in the soldier's progress causing him to put aside the thoughts of John Daley that continued to plague him.

"I'm Dr. Ruven Levi," he told himself as he stopped in at a tobacco shop for a newspaper, "and I have nothing to fear from John Daley."

He was feeling so good that he made a sudden decision to attend the afternoon session of the medical conference, after all. Not wanting to run the risk of running into the American again, he'd told Josef he was coming down with a cold and thought he might stay home and rest. But there were two interesting papers scheduled, and he could be in Tel Aviv in an hour.

His usual confidence returned as he anticipated the awe and gratitude of the soldier's family over the miracle he had performed. There was no reason to allow John Daley to intimidate him. He would forgo his normally substantial lunch, have Mazal fix him a sandwich, and he would go to Tel Aviv.

As he climbed the stairs to his apartment he smelled the *mlawakh,* the freshly baked Yemenite pitas with margarine inside that Mazal made for him.

His spirits lifted as he let himself into the apartment. Buzz pranced up to him, sniffing excitedly. Levi put his paper down and patted the dog affectionately.

"Good Buzz. Good boy."

The animal followed him to the kitchen.

"Shalom, Mazal." Levi helped himself to one of the fragrant, still-warm breads from the basket on the table and bit into it. Mazal smiled happily at his appreciative sigh.

Levi was about to instruct the maid to fix him a sandwich when she spoke up.

"Someone came today for an appointment."

Levi frowned. He had private office hours only one afternoon a week. He couldn't recall having made any appointment.

"Did he leave a name?"

Mazal shook her head. "I told him you were not here, but maybe he didn't understand. He spoke in English."

Instantly Levi was on guard.

"What did he look like?"

"Very tall and big. He had dark hair but some silver in it, and blue eyes, I think. He is not so young, but not old."

The description fit John Daley. The thought of John Daley tracking him to his home totally banished Levi's buoyant mood. He felt as if a noose were tightening around his neck.

"He wouldn't go away," the maid continued. "Then he must have decided he was wrong because he went away."

"He waited? You let him in?" Levi asked sharply.

"He would not go away," she repeated. "I'm sorry. Did I do wrong? He said he had an appointment."

"What did he do here?"

Mazal shrugged. "I don't know. I was working. He waited."

Levi saw the woman was near tears. He softened his tone.

"It's all right, Mazal. In the future, do not let anyone inside when I am gone. Do you understand?"

With the dog padding close behind, he left the kitchen and went to his study, closing the door behind him. He took a key from his pocket and unlocked his desk drawer. The blue leather book was lying under a pile of receipts. He opened it, picked up the telephone, and dialed.

Long distance was unpredictable. Today, he thought ironically, he wasn't entirely unlucky. His call went through immediately. Yet to Levi it seemed an eternity before he heard a voice on the other end. Wasting no time on preliminaries, Levi came right to the point.

162

"There is someone who says he knows me. Someone who believes me to be Rudolf Lobel."

There was a slight pause on the other end before the other party replied smoothly, "We are aware of the situation, Doctor."

Levi could not keep the surprise from his voice. "And how do you know?"

"We have our sources."

The receiver felt slippery in his hand. He realized he was perspiring despite the cold apartment.

"I want to know more about John Daley. Who is he? What is he doing here? What does he want with me?"

"He's an American tourist, a retired police detective. He has a daughter and grandson in Tel Aviv."

"But why—" Levi began.

"You have nothing to worry about, Doctor," the other man broke in comfortingly. "You should not react. You are perfectly safe."

"Perhaps I should go away for a few days," Levi suggested, "to the Galilee, or the Negev."

"I shouldn't. It is best to go about your usual routine. We will take care of the situation. Of Mr. Daley and of you. Haven't we always?"

Levi stared at the head of the wild boar for several moments after he had hung up. Despite the reassurances he had been given, he was uneasy. His hand absently patted the sleek gray and black head of the dog. He had forgotten the young soldier, the euphoric feeling of accomplishment his elegant surgery had given him. Also forgotten was his plan to drive to Tel Aviv for the afternoon session of the conference.

He knew he must trust the man he had just spoken to. But his own experience and philosophy convinced him that a man could trust only himself.

When Ruven Levi was tense or nervous only one activity relaxed him. After relocking the desk drawer he went into the bedroom and changed into worn overalls, a plaid shirt, and sleeveless hunting vest. He put a red cap on his head, and then after putting bread, fruit, and a thermos in his backpack, loaded the old double-barreled Spanish shotgun and Buzz into the Willy Jeep he'd used for hunting for thirty years.

Fifteen minutes later he was outside the city of Jerusalem. He drove south in the direction of Beersheva until he came to the stretch of land he was looking for. It was a good place for partridge. He turned off the highway. The Jeep bounced down a dirt road belonging to a moshav. He parked and, with Buzz prancing happily by his side, set out across the field.

The beauty of hunting for Levi lay in the total absorption required first to spot the brown-gray birds, which blended in with the surrounding countryside, and then shoot them at just the right time in midair. Today, however, he found himself unable to achieve that desired concentration.

He was painfully aware that his life now rested in the hands of others. "We will take care of the situation," he had been told. He had no choice but to trust. Only Buzz could be trusted to be his friend, Levi thought. Human beings—even the most well-meaning—were unreliable. Self-serving. All but Frieda.

He sighed as memories of his wife and the steps that had led him to his present precarious situation came back to him. He was remembering the refugee camp after the war and Frieda as she looked the first time he had seen her. A painfully thin woman with cropped dark hair and incredible hazel eyes that stared out of a haunted face.

The faintest rustle caught his ear. Levi pursed his lips to simulate the sound of the partridge taking off. A moment later he saw a bird skimming parallel to the ground. Levi quickly raised his gun in position and, waiting until the partridge soared up, fired. The bird fell to earth.

Levi patted Buzz. "Go, go get it!"

The dog raced forward in the direction of the partridge.

Frieda's face came back to him. She had been lovely, even in her emaciated, sickly state. He'd been immediately drawn to her. So drawn that he'd thrown his usual caution to the winds and, acting impulsively for the first time in his life, followed her to Israel. He loved her. Knew she had to be a part of his life no matter what the risks.

Buzz bounded back with the bird in his mouth. Levi clipped it on to a hook on the side of his belt, then bent to pat the dog.

The satisfaction he normally took in a difficult shot evaded him today. His mind was too filled with fears of the future and memories of the past. And he kept reverting to the theme of trust.

Had he not trusted Frieda, he would have been a citizen of Buenos Aires or Rio de Janeiro. Life in Israel in the days after the war had been incredibly difficult—not that he'd ever planned to stay. He'd planned to marry Frieda and then leave. Many of the immigrants left Israel to join families in the States, in Canada, in South America. But Frieda was an ardent Zionist. Levi recalled her tears, her pleas when he told her he wanted to leave Israel to try his life elsewhere.

He found it impossible to deny her anything, and so for the first and only time in his life, he had trusted another's judgment instead of his own. His "friends" had not been pleased.

A soft "tut-tut" sound caught his attention. He whirled around in time to see another partridge running across the rocky field, nearly indistinguishable from the thorny plants. When it was flying overhead Levi aimed and fired. An easy shot. This time he missed.

It was a shot he should have had, he thought with annoyance, but told himself he was distracted. It reminded him of his first year in Israel after the war when he'd been so jumpy, so nervous that he hadn't been able to shoot anything. Everything, it seemed, was reminding him of the past.

He took the water canteen from his backpack and poured some in a plastic cup for the dog. He noticed holes in the ground indicating the presence of porcupine and thought he would come back at night to hunt them. Maybe he would have better luck. He took a slice of bread and cheese from the pack. Sitting on a rock, he munched, washing the food down with gulps of tea from his thermos. Buzz had finished lapping his water and was eagerly sniffing the ground.

"Good Buzz, find the birds," Levi said. "Find the partridge."

Frieda, he sighed, I should not have listened to you. But he knew he couldn't blame Frieda for his mistake. She had loved him enough that, had he insisted, she'd have followed him anywhere.

While he'd been a general surgeon before the war in Germany, his interest had always lain in plastic surgery. People had been doing a variation of plastic surgery for a hundred years or so, but the organized form of the field started only around 1940, the great need stemming from the terrible injuries inflicted by the war.

Israel, with its thousands of war-maimed, presented a unique professional challenge, and he had always been a man to respond to challenge. The irony of knowing that he was saving former victims intensified the joy of his pioneering work. When, in those early years, he had the gnawing feeling that he had committed a fatal mistake by becoming an Israeli, he was able to repress it successfully. Gradually, with time, his confidence had returned. He had built a life. He had a career, a wife he loved, friends, hunting. Now, nearly forty years later, a stranger, John Daley, was threatening to resurrect the insecurity and fear of the past.

Levi finished his bread and cheese. He put the cup back on the thermos and replaced it in the backpack. Getting to his feet, he, with Buzz alongside, turned back in the direction of the Jeep.

"We will take care of the situation. Of Mr. Daley and of you," he had been told. Could he trust the man? And if not, then what?

Buzz stiffened. Levi's hunter's eye spotted a partridge, barely visible in a clump of thorny bushes. He heard the soft flutter of wings as it suddenly took off. This time he was ready. He waited until it was a brownish speck overhead and fired. An instinctive surge of satisfaction in the perfect shot warmed him as he sent Buzz after it.

Ruven Levi stood in the field watching the dog bounding toward the fallen partridge. John Daley was no match for him, he thought, with no attempt at modesty. And anyway, if he understood the implication of "We will take care of the situation" correctly, then the American detective's days were numbered. He did not have anything to worry about. He watched Buzz pick up the bird and start back. When the animal reached him Levi praised and patted him, took the dead bird from his mouth, and clipped it alongside the first. He felt the buoyancy of his morning mood returning.

He had lost neither surgical nor hunting skills, he thought proudly. Equally intact were the survival instincts that had kept him alive all these years. If anyone should fear, he told himself, it should be John Daley.

TWENTY-SEVEN

"The thing I keep coming back to is this—why would a Nazi come to Israel, where he'd run the greatest risk of being discovered? That's the one element that doesn't make any sense."

Daley finished his bourbon and signaled to the bartender for another. He and Rose were sitting in the intimate Peacock Bar, adjacent to the hotel dining room.

Rose sipped her brandy, pensively staring at the blue tiled floor.

"Maybe that's the key," she said thoughtfully. "It reminds me of the Edgar Allan Poe short story 'The Purloined Letter.'"

"Oh?"

"The story is wonderfully ironic. An investigator is searching for a stolen letter. He knows who the thief is and he takes the man's apartment apart looking for secret drawers, hollow bedposts, and the like in a frantic search for all the conceivable hiding places. But instead of being cleverly concealed, the letter turns out to have been in plain sight all along. He never thought to look in the most obvious place."

"Which is what Lobel might have counted on," Daley said. "Reminds me of something that happened to me. I used to have lunch every day at a deli around the corner from the station. One Sunday, Mary Helen and I drove out to the country and stopped at a fruit stand. I saw a man in shorts buying peaches. We looked at each other and we both knew we recognized each other but it was obvious we didn't know from where. It drove me crazy all day, trying to think where I knew him from, and then finally I told myself I didn't know him. He just looked like somebody I knew. Turns out he was the waiter from the deli, but the reason I didn't place him was because we were both out of context."

"John, I just thought of something else. Wait here!"

Rose hurried out of the bar. When she came back a few minutes later her face was flushed with excitement. She thrust a small plastic medicine bottle at him.

"Look at this!"

Daley took the bottle, noted the white tablets inside.

"It's the aspirin I bought the night we arrived. Remember, he helped me? Look, the labels are all in Hebrew! He knew Hebrew! What are the chances that a visiting European doctor here for a conference would know Hebrew?"

Daley knew what was coming next was a confirmation of his own growing suspicion.

Rose clutched his arm. "John, is it possible that Lobel isn't just visiting Israel? Is it possible that he's actually living here, masquerading as an Israeli?"

"Dr. Ruven Levi," he said softly. "Jerusalem."

The police headquarters in Jaffa was a plain, brown-cement building in the midst of a run-down industrial area lined with auto parts shops and tiny coffee houses. Even less impressive than the building was the third-floor office belonging to the Unit of Nazi War Crimes Investigation, a division of the National Department of Criminal Investigation. A one-room space containing a desk, two chairs, a file cabinet, and the inevitable plug-in electric heater. Dominating the otherwise bare walls was a huge map of Germany. The caption DEUTSCHLAND UNTER DER HITLER-DIKTATOR 1933–1945 stood out in bold letters.

Eli Goldschmidt was a stoop-shouldered man in his seventies, with the pallor of one who has spent too much time indoors. Sparse gray hair and rimless spectacles perched on a long, arched nose gave him a birdlike look. His slight frame seemed lost in a shapeless gray sweater.

Greeting Daley cordially, he offered him a glass of tea. He listened intently, his blue eyes behind the glasses never leaving Daley's face. When Daley finished Goldschmidt removed his glasses and carefully wiped them on a handkerchief. He pushed up his sweater sleeves and leaned back in his chair. Which was when Daley saw the tattooed numbers on his forearm. The old man saw his glance.

"There are only seven of us working in this division," he said simply. "A small staff for a big task. We are all survivors. Before we go any further, let me tell you a little about our office and the procedures we follow, Mr. Daley. This office began after Eichmann, in 1961, to continue the work of collecting evidence against Nazi war criminals. And that work is far from complete." His lips tightened, making his face appear even more wizened.

"Of the seventy thousand Nazi war criminals who came onto Allied books in 1945, some fifty thousand escaped any retribution. I see the numbers shock you. And they should. We look for witnesses, such as you, in order to bring to justice the criminals still at large, like Rudolf Lobel."

"I remember Lobel's trial. He was sentenced to life. I never remember reading about his release."

"No, there was nothing in the papers. Not like the recent furor over Walter Reder in Italy."

Daley remembered the outcry when the Italians freed the former SS major at the request of the Austrian Government. Outraged villagers demonstrated, claiming that Reder massacred over eighteen hundred of their relatives in reprisal for partisan attacks against German military units. Daley, too, had been outraged at the Austrian Defense Minister's description of Reder's release as a "humanitarian matter."

"No, nothing in the papers," Goldschmidt repeated. "However, the fact of the matter is that Rudolf Lobel served only two months of his sentence. We have been searching for him for years. How he escaped was never determined, but it was

170

obvious he had help. We assumed from Odessa, but in recent years we have come to suspect another source."

"And what was that?" Daley asked.

"I mentioned earlier that about fifty thousand war criminals escaped retribution. The majority found a haven in Latin America. That fact has been well-publicized, but that is only a part of the story. In the postwar scramble to acquire sources of information against the Russians, any concern with the evil past of intelligence agents recruited by the Allies was dismissed."

"You mean all those Nazis became agents for the Allies?" Daley demanded.

"Not all. We do know for a fact that the United States State Department and Army Intelligence did recruit hundreds of former Nazis wanted by Soviet Bloc countries for war crimes."

"I knew some were, but hundreds?"

Goldschmidt nodded. "The U.S. worked with Britain to prevent the extradition of the former Nazis to both Eastern and Western European countries. It is suspected that Mengele was arrested by the U.S. and then let go. Was this a bureaucratic foul-up? Did they indeed not know who he was? Or was Mengele freed in exchange for information? Was he part of Safehaven?"

"Safehaven?"

"An elaborate policy network was set up to keep them in the American and British zones of Germany. They allowed a number of unnamed collaborators to emigrate undercover from Leghorn, Italy, to South America under a legitimate refugee operation code-named Safehaven."

"Safehaven," Daley said softly. He was remembering the trials, the pathetic parade of witnesses, the evidence, the final sentencing. Had it all been a hoax, an elaborate sham? His anger was growing at the idea.

"And Lobel, was he an agent?"

"That I don't know. His escape has always intrigued me. Certainly it is possible. After all, Klaus Barbie, 'the Butcher of Lyon,' was hired by the U.S. Army Counterintelligence Corps as an informant and then helped to escape to Bolivia through the escape route known as 'the Rat Line.' "

171

"I fought in that war," Daley said bitterly. "I saw buddies killed. I saw things I never hope to see again, but all the time I told myself it was for a reason, a good cause. We believed in the United States . . ." He couldn't go on, felt strangled by rage.

"Your government was in good company," Goldschmidt remarked wryly. "The Rat Line was helped by a Croatian priest, a Father Dragonovic, who was attached to a Croatian seminary in Rome. So there was even a Vatican connection. The war was over, and the Allies turned their attention to other concerns—the Cold War and competing with the Soviet Union for German scientific and engineering talent. Have you heard of Project Paperclip?"

Daley shook his head.

"Over a hundred German rocket experts were slipped into the U.S. by government agents at the close of the war. Many were kept in your country illegally for years and then secretly escorted to Mexico and guided back across the border at El Paso to give them legal but inconspicuous points of entry. Arthur Rudolph was one of them. That was Project Paperclip. I suspect, Mr. Daley, that Rudolf Lobel's escape, like Otto Mueller's, was engineered by U.S. Intelligence as part of Operation Safehaven."

"Mueller, too."

Daley felt as if he were being hurled back in time to the camp. He saw the skeletal faces of the prisoners, smelled the stench, relived the gruesome experience that had haunted his dreams for nearly forty years. And, finally, he saw the face of Rudolf Lobel staring expressionlessly ahead as witness after witness testified to his barbarism. He saw himself, a young MP, trying to make some sort of sense of it. And he suddenly realized that it was only with Lobel's sentencing that he began to feel some relief from the pain. Lobel's life sentence had seemed a moral victory, and Daley had rejoiced, believing justice had been served. Now, listening to Eli Goldschmidt, he understood with a growing sense of betrayal that the scope of Allied-Nazi postwar collaboration was far wider than he'd suspected.

"You must remember the time," Goldschmidt said, kindly. "There was tremendous fear on the part of the West over the

172

Russians. The U.S. and British believed they needed the information the Nazis could provide. It was worth it to them. But back to Lobel." Goldschmidt became all business once more. "What comes next?"

"The next step is to collect any and all evidence from survivors of Mauthausen. When we have a reliable picture of evidence then legal steps can be taken—in the case of Rudolf Lobel, extradition to Germany for trial. However, in this case we do not have the luxury of time. If Lobel is here for the medical conference, then he will be leaving very shortly."

One of his strong points, Daley believed, was his ability to quickly and accurately size up people. Some instinct had prompted him to keep to himself his theory about Ruven Levi when talking to the Jerusalem police. Goldschmidt, he believed, was intelligent, thorough, single-minded. A cop's cop, if there was any such being. And Daley trusted him.

"Do you think it's possible that Lobel could be living in Israel? That maybe he's been here all along?"

He had known that Goldschmidt wouldn't laugh. The other man studied him from behind his glasses for a long moment before speaking.

"I think we both know, Mr. Daley, that anything is possible. I doubt it very much, but I can imagine several scenarios that fit your theory. After the war, there was a huge influx of immigrants. It would have been relatively easy for an imposter to enter the country, as most people had no documents. Certainly, had Lobel wanted to come to Israel at that time, he could have, either legally, by getting a certificate of permission from the British or from a Jewish agency, or he might have applied for a tourist visa and then remained illegally. That's a bit farfetched, but it is possible the British authorities would have given a tourist visa to a physician. But the most common way would have been through illegal immigration. You know there were over two hundred thousand Jewish DPs and it was a mess. No papers, no documents." Goldschmidt nodded. "Oh, yes, I would say it was possible, but not likely. Our sources have reported Lobel in South America as recently as five years ago."

"Isn't it possible that this Dr. Levi I told you about is actually Lobel?"

Daley could only guess at the thoughts going through the old man's mind. Goldschmidt was silent as he stared at the oversized map of wartime Germany. He seemed to have retreated to a far-off, private place. After a moment he seemed to snap back to the present.

"You can be certain that that possibility will be thoroughly checked out. First, however, there is the matter of the evidence."

"How do you get this evidence, and what sort of evidence could you expect after all these years?"

"To answer your first question, the evidence and testimony from the survivors is obtained by means of advertising in the newspapers. We generally place an advertisement which requests that survivors of such and such a camp please contact us. Besides the advertisements, there are in Israel associations or congregations of what we call 'Landsmen,' people who come from the same European communities. Congregations of Jews from Warsaw, for example. There are even congregations of survivors of certain concentration camps. As to evidence, this I admit is more difficult to obtain. But documents are sources of information. The Nazi Rausch, for instance, claimed to be fighting on the Russian front at the time witnesses testified that he was a guard at Dachau. We found a witness who had a document signed by Rausch. This document proved that Rausch was lying. And, of course, photographs are extremely important for identification."

"You have photographs of Lobel then," Daley said. "I know I'd remember that face."

Goldschmidt picked up the phone, punched a button, and spoke in Hebrew.

Five minutes later an old man shuffled in carrying a large gray booklet. He placed it on the desk.

"Todah." Goldschmidt dismissed him.

"These are the photo spreads," Goldschmidt said, opening the album. "We are very cautious about pictorial identification. We use different photo spreads to avoid transference from one witness to another. You will note each photograph is numbered, and different numbered photographs are in each booklet. As I recall, there are no individual photographs of

Rudolf Lobel. However, I remember seeing an excellent group shot of the Mauthausen staff."

Daley leaned forward, catching an occasional glimpse of men in SS uniforms as Goldschmidt turned page after page of old black and white photographs.

"It should be here on the next—" Goldschmidt stopped. A look of confusion crossed his face. He shook his head slightly, mumbling something in Hebrew.

"What is it?" Daley asked.

Goldschmidt's face seemed to have turned even more pallid as he turned the album over so that the page was in front of Daley. There was, as the old man had said, a formally posed group portrait of the Mauthausen Concentration Camp staff, all in Nazi uniform. For an old photograph, it was remarkably well-preserved. The faces clear and focused. Only one thing marred it. In the second row, atop the shoulders of the third man on the left, where there should have been a head, there was instead a neatly razored-out hole.

Eli Goldschmidt's gnarled finger pointed at the hole.

"Rudolf Lobel."

Daley looked up and met the eyes of the other man. He knew there was no point in asking questions. It was obvious that Eli Goldschmidt was as stunned as he.

TWENTY-EIGHT

They don't make movies like they used to, Vince thought, settling back in his chair before the television. On screen, a tall and manly Gary Cooper strode down a dusty Western street. Vince reached for his beer. He had seen the film a half dozen times, but it hadn't lost its appeal. Nowadays all they made were "T and A" pictures that were more raunchy than funny or talky movies with no point, guaranteed to put you to sleep. No class, not like *High Noon*. His son-in-law made fun of the old films, saying they were too black and white, all good guys and bad guys. Vince didn't know what was wrong with that.

A Honda commercial burst on the screen at the same time the phone rang. Vince pushed himself out of the chair and waddled to the kitchen. His heart did a quick flip when he heard Daley's voice on the other end.

"Got your message," Daley said. "Anything wrong?"

"Everything's great here. How's things over there?"

He'd been relieved when he called Daley's hotel and found out he wasn't there. He told himself Daley might well have

176

forgotten about the Hunter or have come to the conclusion he'd made a mistake.

"Depends what things," Daley said. "I'm getting a crash course in history. This is an amazing country. You and Angie should take a trip."

"Yeah? Maybe we will for our fortieth."

Vince hoped maybe the whole thing had blown over, but his hopes were dashed a moment later.

"Vince, I'm sure it's Lobel."

"Come on, Daley, don't start in on that again. How could it be? If Lobel's been in South America all these years, it wouldn't make sense for him to leave."

"Who says he's in South America?"

"I don't know. Aren't most of them?"

"Maybe not."

"Why would he take the chance of going to Israel?" Vince pursued the same argument. "Somebody'd recognize him for sure."

"Vince, I think he's been here for years, passing himself off as an Israeli."

Vince forced a laugh, although his insides were churning.

"You better not tell anybody that or they'll lock you up."

"I already have."

"What do you mean?"

"I went to the police."

Vince groaned. "Jesus, Daley, what the hell did you do that for? They must've laughed you out of there."

He should have called Daley right away, should have immediately used all his power of persuasion to convince Daley he was wrong. Instead, he'd stalled, hoping desperately that his interference wouldn't be necessary. He'd gambled and lost, and now he feared Daley had gone too far. By his action, Daley had taken matters a crucial step forward.

"I got another kind of history lesson today," Daley was saying, "only not the kind the kids read in history books. All about how hundreds of those Nazi bastards were recruited as agents by the U.S. and the British after the war. We actually knew who they were and what they'd done, and we hired them, then helped them hide."

"Yeah, I heard those rumors too," Vince said as casually as

177

he could, "so maybe we helped a few scientists. You ask me, most of what you read's a lot of Commie propaganda."

"I'm not talking one or two, I'm talking hundreds of war criminals. Vince, you know anything about Safehaven?"

This time Vince felt his heart jump into his throat.

"What's that?"

"When you were in England were you involved in intelligence work?"

"Me?" Vince snorted. "Do I look like James Bond? All I know about spies is what I see on TV. I told you before, all I did was typing and filing in an office. The most boring thing I ever did in my life. What's all this about anyway? What's it got to do with Lobel?"

"Safehaven was the operation that helped the Nazis after the war. I want to find out if there's a connection between it and Lobel."

Maybe, Vince thought desperately, there was still a chance that he might lessen the damage.

"Hey, Daley, I'm telling you I don't know anything about any of that, but I tell you what. You did the right thing. You went to the police, you told them, and now it's their baby. So now you can relax and leave it to them. You have a good time. See the sights. You earned it. Hey, how's Colleen? You seen her or Yoni? Angie keeps asking me."

Daley refused to be deflected. "Vince, if I find out Lobel escaped and has been hiding out all these years because of American help, I swear I'm going public with it. I'm going to make a stink like you never smelled in your life."

Vince's shirt was sticking damply to his back. He shifted uneasily from one foot to the other.

"That'd be a big mistake."

There was the slightest pause. When Daley replied his voice had a hard edge.

"What do you mean?"

"Take my word, it would be a mistake."

"Goddamnit, Vince, if you have something to say, say it plain. Don't bullshit me! We've known each other too long for that crap."

Vince felt his own temper rising. "All I have to say is, don't be a horse's ass! You think you're going to change the world?

178

Didn't thirty years on the force teach you anything? And if it is Lobel, and I don't believe for a minute it is, but let's say it is, and he knows you recognize him, what's going to stop him from going after you?"

"So what else is new."

"So is it worth your life? It's history." Vince made a conscious effort to control his anger, his fear. He took a deep breath, and when he went on his voice was calm and measured.

"Daley, I'm talking to you like your friend. Your oldest friend. Leave it alone. For all our sakes."

Vince was afraid he might have said too much. For a moment he wished he had the courage to tell Daley all, but things had gone too far. Daley said he'd make a stink. Vince knew him well enough to realize it was no idle threat.

"I'll do what I have to," Daley said before hanging up.

Vince was glad Angie was at a church bingo game. She'd have known immediately something was wrong, and confiding in Angie would be harder than confiding in Daley. He stood by the telephone, trying to pull his confused thoughts together.

"It's up to you," he'd been told. He tried to console himself with the thought that he'd done all he could to stop Daley. Yet he'd known all along it would be futile. Daley was always his own man. Stubborn as an ox.

Vince felt suddenly chilled. He was not a drinking man, but he went to the liquor cabinet in the den and poured himself a cognac. He should have called Daley right away, before he'd had a chance to go to the police. Daley had set the ball in motion with that action and Vince felt inextricably a part of it. He downed the cognac in two swallows. It didn't help. The chill that seemed to originate somewhere inside him was taking hold of the rest of his body. He'd experienced that feeling only a couple of times in his life—once or twice during the war when he'd thought for sure he was going to die, and when an armed robber had broken into the restaurant one Saturday night when he was closing up. The feeling was naked fear.

The familiar theme of *High Noon* poured from the television set. His son-in-law was right. The film was simplistic, he thought. Today it was hard to distinguish the good guys from the bad. More and more the gray areas seemed to dominate. Maybe it had always been that way and he and Daley had just never recognized it.

A young, patrician Grace Kelly stared adoringly at the strong, silent Cooper. For the first time they seemed to Vince to be cardboard caricatures, their actions foolish posturing. For an instant he felt a wave of nostalgia for a more innocent time, when he knew what was right. Or thought he did. Then, with the pragmatism that was so integral a part of his nature, he snapped back to the present and the reality of his situation. He turned off the set.

As he picked up the telephone in the kitchen, Vince prayed to himself that things hadn't gone too far. Prayed that he was not condemning his best friend. As he dialed he realized that he didn't know, might never know, what effect his action would have. The only thing he knew for certain, he thought grimly, listening to the ring, was that he had no choice. For him some areas were still black and white.

It took Vince less than two minutes to say what he had to say.

"We've already taken steps to stop him," the man on the other end said when he had finished.

Which was, Vince knew as he hung up, what he had feared all along.

"Daley," he sighed aloud. "Daley, you goddamned stubborn mick. I warned you."

It didn't make him feel any better.

TWENTY-NINE

Something told Daley Vince was lying. His reaction to Operation Safehaven was too quick and pat. And Daley realized he never did find out why Vince had called the hotel and left a message. He thought back to the discussion they'd had about Mueller. Vince's attitude hadn't made sense. Then. But if Mueller had been helped by Safehaven, and Vince had known about it, his cavalier attitude became comprehensible.

Daley stood on the hotel balcony, staring out at the sea. It was a glorious winter day. Unusually balmy for December, Israelis said. The promenade was a winding ribbon, made colorful by pedestrians. Out on the beach a group of husky teenage boys kicked a soccer ball. A young couple by the water's edge was involved in a game of *matkas,* the paddle game similar to Ping-Pong that had originated on the Tel Aviv beaches. Young mothers gossiped, keeping watchful eyes on small children. "Banana Beach," Ilan had laughingly called it, so nicknamed he claimed because in his youth that section of the beach, sheltered from the surf by a rocky reef, was the preferred spot for mothers, whose main occupation seemed to be peeling bananas and force-feeding their children.

The carefree scene belonged, he thought, on a travel poster entitled "Come to Israel." Only the ever-present soldiers patrolling the boardwalk reminded him of the grim reality underscoring everyday Israeli life. But then, he thought, thinking of his conversation with Vince, he'd learned long ago, things were seldom what they seemed. Daley considered himself as cynical as any cop. He was no longer surprised to discover the trusted, faithful bookkeeper absconding with millions or the choirboy murdering his family. His career had been filled with such seeming paradoxes. And so why not the U.S., which on one hand sought, tried, and sentenced war criminals and employed and aided them on the other? He knew he shouldn't be shocked but he was. And he couldn't help the anger.

It was, he told himself, somehow not so bad when you discovered your neighbor was a crook, but quite a different story when it was your brother. Americans, he thought, were tolerant of the scandals of other governments—almost as if they expected other governments to be corrupt or decadent. But when it turned out to be Nixon who lied and cheated, they were outraged. And Daley felt as if he'd been betrayed by his family.

If Vince had been involved in intelligence and knew about the U.S. recruitment of Nazis, it would explain his never talking about that period of his wartime activity. Maybe Vince was still involved. Daley'd meant it when he told Vince that if he found out Lobel had escaped with help from the U.S., he'd go public. "A mistake for all of us," Vince had responded. The "for all of us" could only mean that Vince was venturing more than simply an objective opinion. If Vince meant to frighten him off, he thought grimly, he'd achieved just the opposite.

Daley felt the need to talk. His first thought was Rose, but the group had a free morning and she had gone to the Tel Aviv Museum. It surprised him that she would have immediately come to mind. He couldn't get used to the idea that in such a short space of time he had come to feel not only a physical attraction but something deeper. Admiration for her plucky spirit and confidence in her judgment and, although he found it hard to admit, a growing sense of closeness. There hadn't been a repeat of their night in Jerusalem, but he knew it was inevitable. He didn't know how far the budding relationship would go, or even how far he wanted it to go, and he was almost grateful for the mental diversion Lobel provided.

Sadly, he realized he could no longer trust Vince. Rose was away. That left only one person.

The thirty-four-story Shalom Tower, Tel Aviv's tallest building, was situated in the heart of old Tel Aviv—a stone's throw from Allenby Street, with its furniture stores, bakeries, bookstores, kiosks, jammed sidewalks, and screeching buses. From the Shalom Tower it was a short walk to the busy intersection of Allenby and King George Street, where the colorful Shouk ha Carmel sat practically in the middle of the Yemenite Quarter. On the twisting streets of the Kerem Ha Teimanim one could practically smell the sea, along with the pungent aromas of grilled meat and fish wafting from the oriental restaurants.

The Migdal Shalom contained offices, a department store, a supermarket, several restaurants, a wax museum, and Mayerland, an amusement area for children. It was also where Ilan had his law office.

Daley nodded to the two girl soldiers at the foot of the escalator and rode to the third level. Ilan was sitting at a small round table in the back of the Ali Baba Restaurant.

"You caught me just in time," Ilan greeted him. "Another hour and I'd have been gone. Our plane leaves this afternoon."

Daley sat down. The portly waiter shuffled over, and Ilan ordered coffee and *borekas.* Daley accepted a cigarette from the pack of English cigarettes Ilan offered.

"Right after you called I tried to get Colleen on the phone but she was out. Probably shopping for some last-minute things."

"Just as well. I really wanted to talk to you."

"Now you've got my curiosity aroused."

"Remember what I told you about seeing a Nazi?"

"I remember."

"I'm sure it's him."

Daley caught him up on what had happened in Jerusalem . . . how he had heard Lobel talking in the restaurant with the hunters . . . how he'd followed him to the apartment house . . . his sessions with the police in Jerusalem and in Jaffa. The photograph of the Mauthausen staff with the missing head of Lobel. Even Rose's stolen camera. When he'd finished Ilan regarded him thoughtfully.

"I'll tell you, John, when you first mentioned it I was skeptical. After all, on the face of it, it's pretty unlikely Rudolf Lobel would come to Israel for a medical conference for all the obvious reasons. And even if he had, it's just as unlikely that you'd recognize him after all these years. And I'll tell you something else. If anyone but you came to me with this story, I'd forget it. But you're not anybody."

As the two men silently acknowledged a mutual respect, Daley was reminded of his initial response to Ilan when they'd first met in New York. He'd been immediately impressed by Ilan's confident professionalism and charmed by his quick, sometimes biting wit. He'd recognized then that the young Israeli was not only clever but had the ability to cut through the bullshit to get to the heart of whatever was under discussion. If not for Colleen, he thought, they'd have been good friends. It was funny, though, that his anger at Colleen was stronger than any resentment he felt toward the man facing him.

"What about those names I gave you?" Daley asked.

"I called a friend who promised to look into it, but I haven't heard back from him." Ilan smiled ruefully. "This is Israel. Things take time. I'll call him again."

"Tell me what you think about this," Daley said. "I don't think Lobel came here for a conference. I think Lobel's been here all along. For years. Posing as an Israeli."

This time the normally expressionless face of his son-in-law registered surprise. Ilan slowly let out his breath.

"Cities of refuge for the stranger among them," he said softly.

"What's that?"

"The Bible," Ilan said. "Numbers, either Thirty-four or Thirty-five. The Lord told Moses that when the Israelites passed over Jordan into the land of Canaan, Moses should

184

choose six cities of refuge. I don't know if I can quote it exactly, but it goes something like this. 'For the children of Israel, and for the stranger and for the settler among them, shall these six cities be for refuge, that every one that killeth any person through error may flee thither.' "

"Lobel's crimes were hardly in error."

"Wait. The Bible also takes care of that," Ilan said. "As I recall, the passage goes on to say that if the manslayer kills with a stone in the hand, or a weapon of wood in the hand, and a man dies, then he is a murderer and shall surely be put to death. This passage always intrigued me, being a lawyer. The Bible stipulates that if the manslayer at any time goes beyond the border of his city of refuge, the avenger of blood shall himself put the murderer to death with impunity. This idea of refuge or safehavens, you see, goes way back to ancient times."

"Safehaven," Daley said bitterly. "Maybe that's where they got the name."

He went on to tell Ilan what he'd learned from Goldschmidt.

"It's one of those skeletons in the closet," Ilan said, with a look of distaste, "and people in the intelligence community have known about it for years. People started to get wind of it only when the dirt about the 'Belarus Brigade' was made public. Are you familiar with that?"

Daley shook his head.

"The Belarus Brigade was a unit of White Russians who volunteered for service with the SS during the war. They did a lot of cute things like dropping children down wells and tossing grenades on them. Anyway, many of them emigrated to the U.S. There's a community of them today living in a New Jersey town called South River. So how did they get there? They'd been granted U.S. citizenship as a reward for cooperation with American intelligence in Europe after the war. It wasn't only Israel that had safe havens. You've got your own so-called cities of refuge. But Lobel here in Israel." Ilan's face became somber. "It's intolerable."

"If he gets away, again, I'll feel it's on my head," Daley said. "I'm afraid I might have scared him off, and by the time the police get their so-called evidence, he'll be gone. You've got contacts. Can you do anything?"

Ilan was thoughtful. "If Lobel has been living here as an Israeli, I doubt if any of our people knew it. I'll make some calls."

"Thanks," Daley said.

"I'm doing it as much for myself as for you." He paused. "My mother's family were all killed at Auschwitz."

The waiter brought the bill on a slip of paper. Daley reached for his wallet, but Ilan waved him off.

"On me. Listen, John, we're leaving in a few hours, but when we get back I'd like us to get together. All of us."

Daley immediately felt his defenses go up.

"It won't work."

"Colleen's been upset since you two saw each other. Believe me, she wants to make it up to you. It's time."

"I don't think it's possible."

Ilan grinned, reminding Daley suddenly of his younger, brasher self. "We both know anything's possible."

Back on the main level, Daley paused by the escalator to admire the huge mosaic on the wall. Talking to Ilan had relieved some of his tension. He could trust Ilan to follow up, make the promised calls, and hopefully get the wheels moving. He would have been less relieved had he known that by involving his son-in-law, he had widened the circle. And widening the circle meant increasing the danger to himself.

He turned from the mosaic and started toward the exit. He passed a falafel stand. Several people stood in line while a swarthy young man adroitly prepared the snacks, stuffing the pitas with chopped vegetables, tahini, and round falafels. A man in a business suit standing at the counter caught Daley's attention. Daley stopped. It was the Englishman.

As the man reached in his pocket for change, the events of the past two days ran through Daley's brain like a film. What were the chances of encountering him three times—in Hebron, the King David Hotel in Jerusalem, the Shalom Tower in Tel Aviv? Slight, unless they were not chance encounters after all.

The Englishman was eating his falafel standing up. Daley

quickly turned. Retracing his steps, he passed the escalator and ducked into the supermarket. Wending his way through the narrow aisles, he left the building through the market door.

And if the Englishman was following him, Daley thought, walking swiftly to the corner, it was possible he'd been set up in Hebron. Lured out of the restaurant in search of Rose so that he'd become a target. But on whose orders? Instinctively, he reached up to touch his forehead, where his wound was still tender.

He hailed a cab on Allenby and told the driver to take him to the Sheraton. The Englishman was nowhere to be seen. The driver turned off Ben Yehuda to the narrow Ha-Yarqon Street, which ran parallel to the sea and the beachfront hotels. Traffic was congested, and the taxi was forced to inch along.

A line of police vans and fire trucks ringed the front of the hotel. Paying the driver, Daley climbed out of the cab and pushed his way through the excited crowd that had gathered. A soldier stopped him at the cordoned-off entrance.

"I'm a guest," Daley said.

The soldier insisted on seeing identification.

Daley reached for his passport. "What happened?"

Before the soldier could respond, Daley saw Rose through the glass door hurrying to him, her arms outstretched in an almost childlike gesture. Even from a distance, Daley saw her distress. She pushed through the revolving door. At the sight of her pale, stunned face, Daley felt his heart speed up. She stumbled into his arms.

"Oh, John! It's horrible! That poor man!"

A sob rose in her throat. She clung to him, her body shaking.

Daley pulled back and lifted her face. It was filled with anguish.

"Who? What's going on?"

"Dr. Dailey, the man you were talking to in the restaurant in Jerusalem! He's dead!" She started to cry. "It's so senseless, such a tragedy."

Daley tightened his arms around her. And it was only then that he looked up to see firemen hosing the ugly, gaping blackened space on the seventh floor of the hotel.

The soldier handed him back his passport.

"Terrorists," the young man said, stepping aside to let them into the hotel.

Daley pocketed his passport and, with one arm around Rose, went through the door. Where Vince's veiled warning failed in frightening him, the sudden death of the doctor from Ohio succeeded. Their common name had resulted in the luggage mix-up. Now Daley wondered if the bomb that had killed Dr. Dailey had been intended for him.

THIRTY

"Jane wants you, Jim, and she doesn't look happy."

Jim Banning looked up to see his wife, elegant in a black cocktail dress, signaling him from under the mistletoe in the living-room doorway.

"Some exciting spy crisis?" the woman teased.

"More likely a kitchen crisis," he replied.

"Do you people ever have ho-hum days like we realtors?"

Banning smiled, "More than I'd care to count. Excuse me."

The slim gray-haired man made his way through the guests and uniformed waitresses passing hors d'oeuvres to where his wife was standing. She didn't look happy.

"Telephone," she said darkly. "It's Carl, and if you leave before dinner, I swear I'll never forgive you."

He patted her rump affectionately. She trailed him through the foyer into his study and stood with her hands on her hips.

"I mean it, Jim. This would make the third year in a row that you ducked out because of some problem or other. Honestly, isn't there anyone else there who can handle things? You might as well be an obstetrician with a beeper!"

"Don't get all steamed up," he said smoothly. "It's probably nothing."

But they both knew his aide never called him at home unless the matter was pressing.

James Banning was a stickler for efficiency. If there was one thing he despised, it was sloppiness. After listening to what his young assistant had to say, he hung up the phone and swore aloud. Something he rarely did. Somebody, he thought, as he picked up the receiver again and dialed, had screwed up but good. He wondered if people were becoming more incompetent or if he was becoming less tolerant.

"Margaret," he said smoothly when he heard the woman's voice on the other end, "sorry to disturb you, but I'd like to talk to Jay."

There was bound to be a flap over this. His small group had been responsible for keeping the lid on things, and Banning was all too aware of the consequences if things were mishandled. The Lobel affair, he thought, as he waited impatiently, was the sort of item the press would gleefully seize on. And Banning was also aware of the repercussions. It wouldn't end with a news story. The Rudolf Lobel business was like the first pebble in an avalanche. Seemingly insignificant, but potentially disastrous. They'd barely weathered revelations concerning Nazi scientists and agents—distasteful perhaps, but understandable given the peculiar temper of the times. But Lobel was another matter entirely. They might not be able to ride out the storm his story would create.

His wife had left to rejoin their guests. He was already wondering how quickly he could round everyone up for a special meeting. Bob, he knew, had planned to take a few days off over Christmas to visit his family in Massachusetts, and Andy had the flu. Maybe it could wait a few more days.

"Things have been bungled in Israel," he said simply when his party got on the phone. "What the hell's going on, anyway? It's like sending an elephant to kill an ant!" He fumed as he relayed the disturbing news his aide had told him.

His annoyed expression changed to one of bewilderment as he listened. Then he let his breath out in a long sigh.

His wife appeared in the doorway as he hung up.

"So?"

He barely heard her. He was planning ahead to the meeting he knew could not be postponed or delayed if they were somehow to repair the damage John Daley had caused.

As he'd expected, no one was happy about the unscheduled session. Andy, out of a sickbed, sniffled and wheezed, his jowly red face even puffier than usual from medication. Bob was clearly put out at having to delay his trip. George's craggy, Lincolnesque features had taken on a distinctly melancholy cast as he toyed with his pipe. And half a dozen cups of strong coffee hadn't done much to make up for Banning's own lack of sleep.

"The situation was under control as long as John Daley and his lady friend . . . what's her name?" Andy asked.

"Rose Malloy," the young man promptly replied.

"Malloy. As long as they were the only ones involved," the fat man continued, pausing to blow his nose. "But he couldn't stop with the police. Now he's involved his son-in-law, and the son-in-law's started asking questions of the wrong people."

The four men stared bleakly at each other. The gray-haired man shared their unspoken feelings of depression. It was one of those situations where there clearly could be no winner. A situation they all wished would simply disappear. Further frustrating them was the knowledge that it was a situation they had not invented but had inherited. "Cleaning up somebody else's shit pile," Andy had termed it. An apt description, Banning thought. And even less just was the fact that if things blew up, as they now threatened to do, the blame would be laid squarely on them. Each man knew the peril, not only to the Agency and the prestige of the nation, but to his own individual career.

"The son-in-law is a definite problem." George tapped his pipe on the side of his chair.

"More of a hurdle to be overcome, I would say," Banning replied. "Judging from his professional background, I believe he can be approached. Reached on some level."

The youngest man shook his head doubtfully. "But we're dealing here with an Israeli, Jim. A Jew. That might make a

191

real difference. He's bound to look at it slightly differently. More emotionally."

"True, but his training's on our side. He'll be able to separate emotion from necessity. And"—Banning paused—"he's also a family man. He has priorities and I think we can reach him."

"So, given that the son-in-law becomes cooperative, the question still left is John Daley," Andy said, "He's widened the circle, and Christ only knows what else he's going to do if he's not stopped. I tell you, he should've been stopped right away!"

"Let's take another look at this bombing incident," Banning said, shifting topics. "A bomb blasts a hotel room in Tel Aviv and kills an innocent American tourist. Oddly enough, the tourist has the same name as John Daley of New York, and his room is exactly one floor below the other Daley. What are the choices? Was it a random terrorist attack? Bungling on the part of our friends? We know now it wasn't any of our people. It's definitely not our friends' style. At least not on their home ground."

He paused, took a sip of the coffee that had grown lukewarm, and looked around the table.

"And a random attack is too coincidental," Bob offered.

"Which leaves another possibility. Lobel," Andy said. "He knows Daley's onto him. He must be running scared."

"That's a little farfetched, wouldn't you say? A guy in his seventies?"

"Yes and no," George said. "He has people in his debt. And some of them are pretty unsavory. I'd imagine he could call in those debts when necessary. And if Lobel's taking matters into his own hands," he continued, "then perhaps the real issue becomes not John Daley but the Hunter."

Banning had reached that conclusion himself over the long, restless night, but for different reasons. He personally believed that a terrorist attack was as likely the cause of the blast as Lobel, although in studying the files on Lobel he was aware of the fact that he had the range of contacts to pull such a thing off. Still, the fact that something appeared too coincidental was no reason to assume it was. It was Banning's gut-level feeling that if things were to be blown, it would be Lobel rather than John Daley who would ultimately blow them. In concentrating on Daley, he'd decided, they ran the danger of ignoring the more real threat of Lobel. It all came down to the question of which man had more at stake. In his opinion, the one in the greatest peril presented the greatest danger.

He'd thought of all this and more as he lay in bed watching the night give way to a pearly dawn. Lobel, he decided as he'd finally given up on any hope of sleep and gone to shower, had to be stopped. Although he'd come to that decision, it was his style to allow others to reach his conclusions independently. It took longer, was at times frustrating, but James Banning had found over the past twenty years that it made for better, more harmonious working relationships. And, as he often told himself, in what was often a dirty business, one needed some veneer of civility.

"I think you've put your finger on it, Bob," he said in the tone of a pleased schoolteacher, "and I think now is the time we need to focus all our attention on Rudolf Lobel."

THIRTY-ONE

The stylishly dressed crowd spilled out of the concert hall into the spacious modern lobby of Tel Aviv's Mann Auditorium. A line quickly formed at the coffee bar. Cigarettes were lit. Conversation filled the air as friends greeted each other. The Israeli Philharmonic Orchestra, founded fifty years earlier, had a fiercely loyal following. Most of the people were season ticket holders of years standing—a goodly fraction having inherited their tickets from parents who were counted among that first generation of subscribers. As a result, attending the symphony was as much a social event as cultural, and at intermission the entire lobby reverberated with the camaraderie of a kibbutz.

Dr. Ruven Levi was neither a season ticket holder nor a resident of Tel Aviv. But he loved the symphony. And when he'd returned home from his afternoon of hunting, he'd been unable to resist Yacov's invitation.

"I've even wrangled tickets for Josef and Gerte," his friend bragged, with typical Israeli pride in his use of *protexia,* or influence. "Weissenberg is playing Brahms Concerto Number One. It's been sold out for weeks."

Rather than tiring him, the hunting expedition had revived Levi. Attending the concert appealed to him.

"What about the evening session?" Levi had asked his friend.

And that was how he'd heard the news. Out of respect for the Ohio physician, the evening session was canceled. Yacov had gone on to describe the tragic event, and when Levi had hung up, after agreeing to meet at the auditorium at eight o'clock, his spirits were practically soaring.

The talk during intermission centered on the hotel bombing.

"Did you know John Dailey, Ruven?" Gerte asked.

Levi shook his head. "No."

"We met him in Toronto last year," she went on, "with his wife. A really nice couple. They have two young sons, one in medical school. What a tragedy! At least no one else was killed. Only a maid slightly injured."

"Some of the people are leaving early because of it," Josef said. "Americans mostly."

"If not for such incidents, Israel would be a tourists' paradise," Yacov commented. "I don't mean to downplay what happened today, but such things always get magnified and blown up out of all proportion in the press. There's more terrorist activity going on in France and Italy than here in Israel and less security."

"But how, with all the security, could it have happened?" Gerte asked. "It makes me feel so unsafe." She shuddered.

The discussion swirled around him. Levi excused himself and went to get a coffee. There was no doubt in his mind that the death of the Ohio surgeon was a mistake, that the real target had been John Daley. Proof, he told himself, as he paid for the coffee and stirred sugar into the small cup, that the promise made to him would be honored.

Levi sipped the thick black Turkish coffee. A mistake had been made, but he knew that was not the end of it. There was no way Daley could protect himself, he thought, as he slowly made his way through the knots of people to where his friends were standing.

* * *

After the concert Yacov suggested they go to the Apropos, a popular restaurant in the auditorium complex, for dessert. There was a line waiting to be seated, but they decided to wait rather than begin searching elsewhere.

"The Habima will be just as crowded," Yacov said, "and by the time we get the car and go to Dizengoff, and try to find parking, it will be the same as waiting here. Anyway, I like the atmosphere."

The Apropos was one of those sleeky modern white-and-chrome-and-glass restaurants possessing a flashy look that the younger people seemed to like, Levi thought. He personally found such places sterile and too trendy. Still, the atmosphere, which was alive, sophisticated, and very Tel Aviv, appealed to him.

"I don't mind waiting," Gerte said. "I don't look forward to going back to the hotel. Just thinking about it makes me shiver."

"It's too bad they can't get those terrorists as easily as they can get people like Otto Mueller," Yacov commented acidly.

Levi looked up. "Otto Mueller? What's the connection? Mueller was an old man in his eighties. He died of a heart attack."

Yacov shook his head knowingly. "It wasn't a heart attack. There were people who didn't want him to come to trial."

"Why is that, Yacov?" Josef asked.

"Ah, our table," Yacov said. "Come. I can taste that chocolate cake already!"

They followed the good-looking young hostess to a table by the window on the enclosed patio area and sat down.

"Now what was that about Otto Mueller?" Levi asked.

Yacov put the menu down. "Only this. I heard that if Mueller came to trial, there were some things that would have come out that would have been an embarrassment to people in high places. Like with Klaus Barbie. You know all those so-called French Resistance fighters who were really collaborators are shitting—excuse me, Gerte—in their pants. They know damn well that Barbie can hurt them."

"Oh, Barbie!" Gerte exclaimed excitedly. "I read recently

196

he was taken to the prison infirmary with food poisoning and he claimed it was intentional!"

Yacov nodded with a smug smile.

"But how do you know this, Yacov?" Josef asked. "And what things would have come out at Mueller's trial?"

Yacov leaned forward and lowered his voice dramatically. "I can't say what things, but I have a nephew in the 'shoo-shoo' business."

"Now I am confused. What is shoo-shoo business?" Gerte asked.

"Just an Israeli joke," Levi interjected, trying to keep his voice light and not betray his inner turmoil.

"Exactly," Yacov said. "Here in Israel that's what we call intelligence work because when friends and relatives ask an agent what it is he does, he always puts his fingers to his lips and goes, 'Shhh-shhh.' " He laughed heartily. "Like the old story of the American CIA agent who comes to Israel looking for a particular Israeli spy and finally, after much investigation, goes to the apartment where the spy reportedly lives. It is all very hush-hush. Top secret. He stops on the first floor and knocks on the door and a woman answers. 'I'm looking for Mr. Cohen,' he says. The woman eyes him up and down and says, 'You want Cohen the tailor or Cohen the spy?' "

Levi laughed with them at the old joke, although his insides were churning.

"So," Yacov went on, picking up the menu as the waitress came to take their order, "my nephew told my sister and my sister told me that it wasn't a heart attack that did that old bastard in. I'll have the chocolate cake and a café au lait."

Levi ordered the first item he saw. For the second time that day his sense of well-being had been abruptly shattered. The story of Otto Mueller reminded him all too clearly that he, too, was expendable. Which meant he was in double jeopardy —from John Daley and from those who had promised to protect him.

A wave of panic swept through him at the thought of his vulnerability. Then he told himself that he must take control of himself and of the situation. With a supreme effort, he stilled his fear.

The topic had switched from Otto Mueller and the bombing

to the latest financial crisis in Israel. Salaries were being frozen and there was a threatened strike by the city garbage workers.

"We are a country always living beyond our means," Yacov lamented as the waitress brought them their desserts.

Levi picked at his torte. A smoldering resentment, fanned by his fear, began to build against the man who had set out to ruin his life. John Daley. He could not rely any longer on others to get Daley. Levi did not feel entirely comfortable relying on others. He never had. It was always safer to take care of things oneself. And Levi knew it was that extra measure of security he needed. A part of him began to respond with excitement to the challenge facing him. There was no way he would allow himself to be hunted and slaughtered like that fool Mueller. He would outsmart them all.

A plan was beginning to take shape in his head. A plan that delighted Levi's love of the ironic. John Daley would have to be eliminated. But not before Levi used him for his own protection. The man determined to destroy him would be the one to save him. And in the elimination of the New York detective, which he personally resolved to undertake, Levi would take his revenge.

So daring a scheme would take planning and cunning. And it would involve the help of others. Levi thought of the shattered faces and bodies he had repaired over the years, individuals who swore they owed their lives to him. It was time, he told himself as he finished his dessert, to cash in on some of those old debts.

THIRTY-TWO

Ilan decided not to mention his meeting with Daley to Colleen. For the first time since her father's arrival in Israel, she seemed her old exuberant self. It had been far too long since they'd had a vacation by themselves. The prospect of Egypt had brought the color back to her face and the lilt to her voice. Even the mention of Daley, he knew, would put a cloud over things. Get her to brooding over their inability to reconcile the differences that kept them estranged.

He thought about that as the taxi headed out the Haifa Road to the airport. A waste. Two people who cared about each other as much as Colleen and her father. But they were too much alike. Stubborn, proud people. Ilan knew she'd been waiting for him to call or come by or make some conciliatory gesture. And, if he knew his father-in-law, Daley was waiting for Colleen to do the same.

After the trip, Ilan told himself, he'd try to arrange a meeting. He sensed that if Daley were to leave Israel with bad feelings between them, Colleen would suffer as much as in the early days of their marriage when she'd longed for word from him. And that was a period he'd rather not relive.

But for now, with a vacation ahead of them, he was not about to bring up the subject of Daley. He didn't have to. The news bulletin on the car radio did it for him.

Colleen uttered a high-pitched cry at the mention of the name John Dailey. She was staring ahead, her face drained of color. Ilan instinctively put an arm around her as he told the driver to turn the volume up.

When he heard the description, "American physician from Ohio," she let her breath out. Tears spilled out of her eyes and Ilan felt her body trembling.

"Oh, God!" She sighed. "I was sure it was Dad. You don't think it really was, do you? That they made a mistake?"

"No. There was a doctor with the same name. Remember, he told us about that suitcase mix-up at the hotel?"

Colleen reached into her purse for a tissue as the airport came into sight. She blew her nose and wiped her eyes.

"I don't think I could stand it if he died like that. With our not speaking."

"You can change that. Somebody has to make the first move."

Colleen snapped the clasp shut on her purse. Her lips tightened. "If I felt it would work, I would. I know him. It's no use."

Ilan knew that the report of the hotel bombing had upset her. It upset him as well, but for a slightly different reason. Midday was a strange time for a terrorist to plant a bomb in a tourist hotel. The chances of injuring tourists was slight. However, if a bomb was meant as a warning, then midday was ideal. He thought back to what Daley had told him about Safehaven and he was worried.

As Ilan checked in Colleen went to find a phone.

"I'm going to call the hotel just to make sure," she said.

By the time Ilan finished checking in, Colleen had returned. The dead man was, indeed, Dr. Dailey from Ohio. They headed to the waiting area by their gate. Ilan was relieved that Colleen seemed to have put the bombing out of her mind. She settled into a seat and was soon engrossed in an English paperback. Ilan opened his newspaper, but before he had a chance to do more than skim the headlines, he heard his name paged over the loudspeaker.

"It's probably Ben," he sighed.

Colleen laughed. "Don't let him talk too long. I'm getting on that plane, with or without you!"

He grinned, thinking of his talkative partner. Ben thought nothing of calling him at odd hours and places and talking for hours. Only the fact that he was one of the best in his specialty of taxes and a good-hearted soul kept Ilan from losing patience.

But when Ilan reached the information desk an airline official led him not to the courtesy telephone but to a small office behind the counter area. There he faced a stranger.

"Mr. Bar-Lev?"

Ilan nodded.

The man indicated the only other chair in the tiny office.

"Please take a seat. This won't take long."

The man who emerged, twenty minutes later, looked totally different from the man who had entered. Ilan was practically shaking with rage and frustration. They had not yet called his flight and so he felt he had a moment to collect his thoughts before returning to Colleen. He ducked into the men's room and leaned over the sink next to a bedraggled American kid who was trying to wash off what looked like a week's grime. Ilan lathered his hands as if cleansing away the unpleasantness of the conversation.

A man should not have to make such choices, he thought bitterly. And for a brief moment he considered defying the order, and although it had been couched in politeness, it was indeed an order that had been given him.

"Do nothing."

Ilan splashed water over his face. Then he took his pocket comb and ran it through his thick dark hair. Two bearded Hasidim came into the room, conversing in Yiddish. Their eyes swept over him as though he were invisible. They looked at the American as if he were another species of animal.

Ilan heard the first announcement of Flight Number 243 to Cairo. He looked at his face in the mirror, wondering if Colleen would detect his distress.

201

He strode out of the men's room into the busy terminal. He'd done as his father-in-law had asked. He'd called Ezra. His friend had responded as he'd known he would. Positively and immediately. Of course he'd see what he could find out.

"Did Ezra call you?" Ilan had demanded of the stranger.

"He didn't have to," was the response.

And so Ilan knew that his father-in-law's actions were being watched. And, thinking of the bomb that had killed the Ohio doctor, he feared Daley was being more than watched. Stalked. The stranger's perfunctory denial did little to dispel his worry. And so he had placed a condition of his own.

Do nothing! Ilan had always had a quick temper. He'd learned, through steely self-discipline, to control it. He'd learned to mask his feelings with an air of indifference, with humor. Such devices were effective but they took a toll. He was an erratic sleeper, and his doctor had diagnosed the beginnings of an ulcer. But now that temper was flaring as he mentally replayed the brief meeting in the airline office.

"Do nothing."

Ilan was suddenly reminded of an early childhood memory. He'd run into the house from the street where he'd been playing with friends and had found his mother weeping over a photo album. The sight had shocked him. It was the only time he'd ever seen his mother cry, and he approached her timidly, fearfully.

"Ima, why are you crying? Are you sick?" he had asked.

She'd gathered him to her and shook her head. Then she pointed to where a family picture was pasted in the album. Unfamiliar faces smiled at him.

"That's all that's left," she had said. "Just a picture."

And the seven-year-old boy had grieved with her, not understanding, but feeling her grief. Years later he had understood. And now he felt as though he were mocking that old sorrow, as if he were desecrating the unmarked graves of his family by the bargain he had struck.

I'll be damned if I will, he thought furiously as he caught sight of Colleen's red head in the lounge. She was craning her neck, looking for him. From a distance she looked to him suddenly vulnerable. A rush of tenderness swept through him for her and for Yoni. And Ilan knew that no matter how deep his rage against Rudolf Lobel might go, how deep his commitment to his country, his number one priority was his family. Colleen and Yoni. If Colleen were to lose her father now, he knew she would never forgive herself for their rift. And there was another compelling consideration. In a few years, frighteningly few, Yoni would be in the Army.

"Think about that," the stranger had said conversationally.

Ilan didn't have to think hard. It was something every parent lived with from the moment a child was born. And each time a soldier died, the entire country mourned. Hopelessly outnumbered by her enemies, Israel depended on the best equipment and weapons for her protection. Without the new fighter planes, Israel was at a disadvantage. As the stranger had bluntly put it, Israel's safety meant Yoni's safety. There was nothing he would knowingly do that might further jeopardize Yoni's life.

"Ilan!"

Colleen's worried look disappeared as she caught sight of him. "Hurry!"

He joined her. They crossed the lounge to the gate and took their places in line.

"What was it?"

For a moment Ilan was tempted to confide in her despite the instructions he'd been given. After all, it was her father who was involved. In a sense he felt he owed it to her. If positions had been reversed, he thought, wouldn't he want to know? Wouldn't he expect her to tell him?

"Ilan?"

Colleen was studying his face.

"Are you all right? Is everything all right? Who called you?"

Ilan smoothed her hair back from her face. He suddenly wasn't sure what he owed to whom. He needed time to think.

"Who called you?" she repeated.

"Ben," he said, forcing a laugh. "He couldn't find some papers he needed, and you know him. Once he gets talking, it takes an act of God to stop him."

Colleen linked her arm through his and smiled indulgently.

"He's a dear, but sometimes I wonder how you can stand it."

They handed their boarding passes to the steward at the gate and walked outside toward the waiting plane.

THIRTY-THREE

"Are you sure you won't change your mind and come to Tiberias with us?" Rose asked.

Daley shook his head. "I've got some things to take care of."

Rose glanced hesitantly at the group boarding the bus, and then back at Daley. A worried frown wrinkled her brow.

"Are you all right, John? Your head?"

"I'm fine. Go on, have a good time. I'll expect a full report."

Rose hesitated. She reached up. Her lips lightly grazed his cheek.

"Be careful, John. Please."

Daley stood for a minute watching the bus as it pulled away from the hotel and disappeared. It had been a long time since anyone had worried about him. So long, he had nearly forgotten what it was like. He didn't want to think about resuming his life at home, a life where his only personal contacts were Vince and his sister Peg. A life, he had to admit, in which hardly anyone gave a damn if he lived or died. It was a life he hadn't minded because he'd grown so used to it. Rose Malloy had changed all that. A "shipboard romance," she'd called it. Well, better that than nothing, he thought. But Daley knew he could not go back to his old ways.

With a sigh, he forced his thoughts from Rose to the present . . . and Rudolf Lobel. Time was running out, he thought grimly. Lobel was probably preparing to leave the country . . . if he had not already done so.

A maid was making the bed when Daley entered his room. Without waiting for her to finish, he picked up the telephone and gave the operator Eli Goldschmidt's number. The person who answered didn't understand his English. Daley was turned over to someone else, who asked him to hold. After several minutes a third individual informed him that Goldschmidt was unavailable. Leaving his name and number, Daley hung up.

He found Tsvi Roth's phone number in the little notebook he carried on him. The call to Jerusalem went through immediately. This time Daley was transferred three times before being asked to wait. Finally he was informed that Roth was in a meeting. He left a message. He was almost surprised when he reached Malka Rubenstein on the first try.

"How did it go with Mr. Goldschmidt?" she asked pleasantly.

"The procedures are time-consuming," Daley said. "I'm afraid Lobel will get away while they're hunting witnesses and evidence."

The woman clucked sympathetically.

"We cannot be too cautious in such cases. I'm sure you realize that, Mr. Daley. You can rely on Eli Goldschmidt to follow through. And rest assured, if it is Rudolf Lobel you saw, he will be apprehended. I appreciate your concern, but I suggest you leave things to Mr. Goldschmidt and enjoy the rest of your trip."

Daley started to tell her about the missing camera, the bombing in the hotel, the razored-out head of Lobel, but she cut the conversation short.

"I'm sorry, Mr. Daley, but I must go now. Thank you for calling."

For the next half hour Daley tried calling both Roth and

Goldschmidt. Each time he was told they were unavailable. After trying Goldschmidt's office for the fourth time and being told that the man was out of the office, he slammed the phone down, swearing under his breath.

He almost expected to be told that Goldschmidt had left for the day, but when he gave his name to the officer at the entrance, the man picked up a phone, spoke in Hebrew, and moments later asked Daley to follow him.

Eli Goldschmidt was talking on the telephone when Daley entered his little office. He looked up and motioned to the chair. Daley sat down and waited impatiently until the man had finished his conversation.

"Decided not to wait for you to call me back," Daley said.

"Did you call me?" The old man looked surprised.

"Only about six times."

Goldschmidt frowned. Then shrugged his bony shoulders. "We have a new operator. I'm afraid I haven't been getting all my messages. But never mind. I was going to call you today."

"You've had a response to the advertisements?"

"Nothing yet. But these things take time. However"— Goldschmidt's seamed face came the closest Daley had seen to a pleased look—"we have located a woman who remembers Rudolf Lobel."

Daley's heart gave a little jump. "So the photograph won't be crucial."

"Perhaps not. She lives in Haifa, on a kibbutz that is composed mostly of camp survivors. I've sent a car for her. Hopefully, she'll be able to identify him—if he attends the final session of the medical congress this evening." He glanced at his watch. "In fact, she should be here any moment."

"Have you found out anything about Dr. Levi?"

Goldschmidt went to the metal filing cabinet and pulled open the top drawer. He removed a manila folder, then, sitting back down, opened it on the desk. "It is much as I thought. Ruven Levi is well-known. As you would say in America, his life is like an open book. At least his life since he has been in Israel. Dr. Levi was a part of the illegal immigration that took place after the war. According to this, he was in a DP camp, then came to Israel in 1947. Married a German refugee that same year."

"Any children?"

Goldschmidt looked up from the file. "His wife was a survivor of Dachau. She was sterilized there."

"Where was Levi during the war?"

"Bergen-Belsen."

"What about family?"

Goldschmidt shook his head. "His family all died in the war."

"There must be people who knew him from before," Daley said, "schoolmates, neighbors, friends. And there must be records from medical school."

"You were in the war, Mr. Daley," Goldschmidt said. "Remember the chaos? Hundreds of thousands of refugees from all over Europe crowded into the DP camps. No papers, nothing from the past. I, myself, had nothing left of my old life but one photograph of my parents, which I somehow saved. My birth certificate, my school diplomas . . . everything else was lost. It was evidently the same with Ruven Levi. Not at all unusual. To make matters worse, he was originally from Königsberg, which is now a part of Russia and called Kaliningrad. You can appreciate how difficult, if not impossible, trying to get any documents from there would be today. When he came to Israel all Levi needed to do was take an oath that he had earned a medical degree. This he did, like many physicians. And from all reports he has led an exemplary life since. He is, as I've said, highly respected."

"So you don't believe he could be Lobel."

Goldschmidt paused for the slightest beat.

"I didn't say that."

"Do you have any photographs of Dr. Levi?"

"I am working on that. The passport office has not been able to locate his photograph. I have a call in to the branch of the police where they keep records of drivers' licenses and identity cards. They have not yet called me back. There is a great deal of what you would call red tape here in Israel. Not like in your country. Here everything, unfortunately, takes time."

"So no picture of Ruven Levi. And the photo I took of Lobel in Jerusalem was in the stolen camera. It all seems a little too convenient."

"Perhaps." Goldschmidt closed the folder. "And yet, we have had an increase in crime. The camera was, after all, part of a general burglary of Miss Malloy's room. Tourists are always prime targets."

"Like Dr. Dailey," Daley said grimly. "If he was the target."

Goldschmidt's pale eyes met his, and this time the old man did not reply. Goldschmidt's assistant peeked into the room. The two men exchanged a few words in Hebrew. Then Goldschmidt stood and beckoned to Daley.

"The car is here from Haifa. Come."

"Her name is Ida Karpinsky," Goldschmidt told him as they rode down in the elevator. "She has been in Israel since '48. We were lucky to find her, and she is eager to cooperate. Seems her sister died in Lobel's hospital."

The elevator doors opened. Daley saw a tiny, fragile woman perched on a wooden bench at the end of the hallway. She ignored the activity around her, the coming and going of officers and visitors, staring straight ahead like a passenger waiting patiently for a train.

"Geveret Karpinsky?" Goldschmidt said when they were within earshot of the woman.

"Ken." She turned.

Daley looked down at the woman's upturned face. Her thin lips curled slightly in what might have been a smile. But Daley was unaware of that. Shock, then disappointment as bitter as any he had ever felt shot through him as he stared down at her expressionless eyes and the red-tipped white cane in her gnarled fingers. Ida Karpinsky was totally blind.

THIRTY-FOUR

Daley slipped into the conference room through the rear door and took a seat in the last row. The hall was shrouded in darkness except for the screen on which a series of slides was being shown. As his eyes adjusted to the lack of light, he spotted Goldschmidt sitting to the right, near the lectern. The old man appeared to be intently studying the slide of a burn victim as the speaker, a young man with a French accent, described the grafting techniques used on the patient in the picture. But Daley knew Goldschmidt's concentration was a pose. Eli Goldschmidt, like himself, was thinking only of Rudolf Lobel. And both men were aware that this might be their final chance of identifying the Hunter of Mauthausen.

As the last slide flashed off the screen and the lights went on, Daley surveyed the audience. The group seemed smaller to him. Many of them had probably gone home early, some prompted no doubt by the death of Dr. Dailey. And thinking of the jovial, mild-mannered doctor, he felt a twinge of guilt. If not for him, it was possible the Ohio physician would have been among those asking questions of the speaker.

His eyes lingered briefly on each white head, although he was certain, as he had confided to Goldschmidt, that Lobel would not show up. He wondered if it might have made more sense for them to have gone to Jerusalem to watch the apartment house of Ruven Levi.

Daley was trying to catch Goldschmidt's eye when a man sitting in the aisle seat of the third row turned to speak to a colleague behind him. In the fraction of a second it took for Lobel's face to register in Daley's stunned brain, the Nazi spotted him.

Daley had no time to signal to Goldschmidt. He moved swiftly toward the exit by the aisle where Lobel was seated. Lobel, however, had had a head start.

There were only two obvious ways out of the hotel. One was the doorway leading to the beachfront. The other, the stairway to the main lobby upstairs and the front entrance. Opting for the closest, Daley sprinted across the lower lobby and pushed past a startled tourist at the door. He stood for a moment on the sidewalk to catch his breath. Cars and taxis zoomed by. A group of teenagers jostled each other good-naturedly. There was no sign of the old man.

Ruven Levi was unusually agile for his age. He had been a physical fitness advocate long before exercise became fashionable. And so the moment he spotted John Daley in the last row of the conference room, Levi was able to quickly excuse himself and reach the lower lobby before the American.

Within seconds he was out the door. There was no time for him to retrieve his car from the parking lot. Walking rapidly, he kept an eye out for taxis. It was only a short walk to the Dan Hotel, where there were bound to be cabs. He would take one to Dizengoff, sit inconspicuously in a crowded cafe, and decide on his next move. But he would have to be quick, for he had no doubt Daley was after him. He allowed himself a swift backward glance. Any moment, Daley would burst through the door. Levi jogged nearly to the corner and turned. It would be safer to stick to the quiet, dark side streets. Impulsively, he abandoned the idea of the Hotel Dan, deciding instead to walk to Ben Yehuda and catch a cab there.

By attending the last session, Levi knew he ran the risk of

running into Daley, a fact he had considered as he had driven to Tel Aviv from Jerusalem. And while he knew it would have been more prudent to stay away, some perverse streak in his nature egged him on. It was the same perverseness that kept him from leaving home, even though he knew Daley had tracked him there. The challenge of the hunt, he thought. It never failed to get his juices flowing, making him feel like a young man. Yet, Levi was forced to acknowledge to himself that the risk was not as great as it appeared. For he had taken steps to ensure that John Daley would be taken care of.

Still, he felt like a hunted animal. Somewhere out there in the night, John Daley was stalking him. He told himself he would simply have to be more clever, more alert. He glanced back over his shoulder. The street was empty. In another moment he would be at Ben Yehuda.

It seemed at first that the large, silent shape springing suddenly out of the darkness was an animal. A Doberman or German shepherd. Startled, he backed away, nearly stumbling to the pavement. It took a moment to realize that the creature looming over him was not an animal but a young man.

A cry of surprise strangled in his throat as his attacker threw him to the ground. He caught a glimpse of a young, swarthy face in the moonlight. Curly black hair. A black shirt. Gold chains around his neck. And something else—the silver gleam of metal. In a movement so quick that for a horrified instant Levi wondered if he'd imagined it, the man's arm swung up in an arc, then down toward his heart. Levi threw up his hands.

Pain sliced through his side. Some instinct told him, "Play dead. Don't move." Shutting his eyes, Levi forced himself to lie motionless while he felt his heart about to burst out of his chest. A fleeting thought cut through his pain. After all he had been through in his life, he was about to die on a city street, the victim of a common thug. He felt his arm jerked as his watch was roughly pulled off his wrist. He felt himself being turned over on his face as strange hands probed through his pockets, removing his wallet. He was aware of the harsh breathing of his assailant. He lay perfectly still, waiting for the knife to pierce again his body, this time hitting a vital organ, draining away his life. But all he felt was a vicious kick in his ribs, and then he heard the sound of running feet.

He counted slowly to ten, then rolled over on his back. The pain was sharper now as it spread through his body. He touched his side. When he took his hand away it was slick with blood.

Levi recognized his faintness to be from shock rather than from any fatal wound or excessive loss of blood. He struggled to his feet. Dizziness made him stagger back toward the wall of the building from which his attacker had lunged. Again the irony of the situation hit him. He had been escaping from John Daley only to fall victim to an ordinary street hoodlum.

Levi started toward the corner, each step a supreme effort. He held his arm stiffly against his side. He bit down on his lip, until he tasted blood. Tried to concentrate only on putting one foot ahead of the other.

He stopped, numbed by a chilling thought. Yacov had talked about Otto Mueller's being a potential embarrassment. He knew his own story was a far greater menace to those who had promised to help him. Not a heart attack, Yacov had said. Levi was suddenly certain that his attacker had not been an ordinary hoodlum. Or had he? Though he'd missed the money in Levi's secret pocket, he'd taken his watch and wallet, Levi reassured himself. But he was wracked with doubt.

"We will take care of the situation," he had been promised. A bitter taste filled his mouth. Barbie and Mueller had also been promised. What were promises, anyway? He recalled the promises he had blithely made . . . promises to spare lives. Promises he had broken without a second thought. Promises were meaningless.

Levi was sweating. Another wave of dizziness crashed over him. He didn't know how much blood he had lost. Didn't know how much farther he could go.

It was a sudden surge of hate, of pride, a combination of all the characteristics that made up the complex personality of Ruven Levi that kept him from fainting, that pushed him to the corner, where he flagged a taxi. He climbed in and told the driver to take him to Jerusalem. Hate for John Daley, a stupid American detective who threatened to destroy his carefully constructed life. Hate for those who had promised to protect him but had reneged. Pride in his own superior intelligence, which would not allow him to fall prey to those he knew to be inferior beings.

The driver sped on the Gehah Road leading to the Jerusalem freeway, spurred by the promise of a fat fee. Levi leaned back. The cold air blew in through the window, reviving him. He willed himself not to pass out. For the first time in many years, he allowed himself to think back to another life when he had been a different person. He recalled how it had felt to hold lives in his hand. To do as he wished with impunity. To play God. To be, in a sense, God.

The exhilaration of that power, as though he walked astride the world of ordinary mortals, came back in a rush. The closest he'd ever come to recapturing that thrill was in the operating room, but the satisfaction of rebuilding a shattered face was second best to the joy of holding absolute power over others. Levi sighed. It had been a different life, but he had not been a different person. He was the same man, grown older. Grown even bolder out of desperation. He smiled to himself, forgetting momentarily the pain, which had become a dull, steady throb, thinking of how, once again, he was about to play God. This time with John Daley and his grandson.

THIRTY-FIVE

"At least we know he's still here," Daley said, finishing off his bourbon.

"And doesn't the fact that he ran when he saw you mean he really is Lobel?" Rose asked. She looked from Daley to Goldschmidt.

Goldschmidt sipped his club soda.

"Not necessarily. Suppose he is not Rudolf Lobel but someone who vaguely resembles him. And suppose he fears that because of the resemblance, Mr. Daley will cause him difficulty. Embarrassment. That could be a reason for panic. However, we will have the airports and borders watched very carefully."

It didn't make Daley feel any better. To have been so close and to have the man get away was a bitter pill. Seeming to read his thoughts, Rose placed her hand on his.

"There was nothing you could have done differently, John."

Goldschmidt nodded. "Miss Malloy is right."

"And if he is Ruven Levi?"

"I am not discarding that possibility, Mr. Daley. I will be in touch with you."

Goldschmidt got to his feet. The old man, in his shapeless sweater, looked shabby and out of place in the hotel bar surrounded by well-dressed tourists. He bowed slightly to Rose.

"I suggest you try to salvage what is left of your evening."

"What do you say? Shall we salvage the evening?" Rose asked with forced brightness when Goldschmidt had gone. "How about Dizengoff Street?"

Daley shook his head. "I'm not in the mood. I don't suppose you'd be interested in visiting my grandson with me."

"I'll just run upstairs and get my coat."

"Sabba!"

Yoni threw open the door, a wide grin on his face.

Daley tousled the boy's hair, then introduced Rose to Yoni and Esther.

Rose's years of teaching certainly showed, Daley thought. She seemed to know just the right things to say to the boy. Watching the two of them poring over Yoni's stamp collection, Daley was filled with a warm sense of family. It seemed so natural and right . . . he and Rose and the boy. He had to force himself to remember that they weren't family, that the comforting sense of closeness was an illusion. He and Yoni would not likely see each other again. And once the tour ended he and Rose would go their separate ways. The intrusion of reality left a bitter taste in his mouth.

"Sabba, will you come back soon?" Yoni asked when at ten o'clock Daley announced it was time to go.

He paused. "I hope so."

"You must," Esther said. "Colleen and Ilan will be home soon. And I want you to have Shabbat lunch with me. I will make a cholent. And you must bring Rose too."

"I don't know," Daley said, thinking of Colleen. "Our tour has only a few more days and we're going to Masada and Eilat and—"

"And we'd love it," Rose interjected, placing a firm hand on his arm. "We'll check our schedule and call you, but I'm sure we can work it out. And thank you."

Impulsively, she embraced first Esther and then Yoni.

216

Daley shook hands with Esther. He wanted to hug the child as Rose so easily had, but he felt awkward and ill at ease. He started to extend his hand to Yoni when the boy turned his face up to Daley for a kiss.

"Shalom, Sabba. *L'hitraot.* See you."

It might have been Colleen's pert, childish face that he kissed, so suddenly and unexpectedly was he hurled back in time. Equally unexpected were the tears he felt gathering behind his eyelids.

"He's a delightful child," Rose said as they settled back in the taxi. "So bright and open."

"You really think so?" Daley could not hide his pleasure.

"I've seen a lot of children in my time. He's special. I hope you're not peeved with me about accepting Esther's invitation, but I feel so strongly that you and Colleen must see each other again. And I have to admit, I'm looking forward to meeting her."

Daley's euphoria vanished. "I wouldn't count on it."

For a moment the only sound in the car was Rose's sigh.

"John . . ." she began.

"Look, Rose, I know you mean well," he said, "but I don't see any way Colleen and I are going to make peace. It's just one of those things. Period."

He turned away from her, unwilling to continue the subject. The taxi had stopped at a red light on busy Ibn Gevirol Street. Daley stared out the window at the Kikar Malkhe Yisrael, the town hall square. People strolled to and from the cafes and ice-cream parlors that lined the adjacent street.

The light changed. The cab drove on, crossing first Dizengoff and then Ben Yehuda toward the sea.

Tel Aviv, like New York, was a night city, Daley decided. Despite the incredible inflation and the Israelis' complaints of the high cost of living, people seemed to live well. The cafes and restaurants were filled. The shops and art gallerys looked to be thriving. A throng poured out of a movie theater where the latest American film was playing, and another crowd waited to get in for the next show. In the midst of the vitality and sophistication of Tel Aviv, it was hard to keep in mind that this was a land that, according to the papers at home, was constantly under siege.

"Excuse me." The taxi slowed, and the driver, a burly man with a Russian accent, turned around. "Maybe you get out here. It's too much traffic."

He nodded toward the intersection, where traffic was snarled.

"An accident?" Daley asked.

"A wedding in one of the hotels," the driver said, pulling over to the curb. "The hotel is not far. Only two blocks."

Out on the sidewalk, Rose slipped her arm through his. They started walking toward Ha Yarqon Street. The Hilton, the Ramada, the Sheraton were silhouetted against the moon-lit sky. A fresh breeze blew inland from the sea. Daley felt himself beginning to unwind from the tension of the evening. Goldschmidt was a good man. He could leave things in his hands. The time spent with Yoni had served to push Lobel to the back of his mind.

There were other things as important, he thought. Rose, for instance. He turned to her, about to suggest she spend the night with him, when her fingers dug into his arm.

"John! Watch out!" Her alarmed cry pierced the air.

A dark sedan was bearing down on them at full speed. Daley pushed Rose into the doorway of an old stone building. The car jumped the curb, missing them by a hair before careening off and disappearing around the corner.

"Goddamn drunk!" he swore, wishing he had gotten the license number. "Are you okay?"

In the moonlight, Rose's face was ghostlike.

"It's all right," he said, putting an arm around her. "Just a drunk."

She was staring in the direction of the car, her eyes wide with shock.

"Rose? What is it?"

"It was the Englishman. I saw him. The man from Hebron!"

THIRTY-SIX

Returning to his home was taking another chance, for Levi knew Daley might be waiting for him there. It was a chance he needed to take.

He asked the cab driver to let him out a block from his house. Levi forced himself to be extra-alert as he made his way slowly, every step an agony. He noticed nothing unusual. As far as he could tell, he had not been followed, nor was he being watched. Still, he knew it was only a matter of time.

An hour later, his wound tended to, Ruven Levi sat in his kitchen with a cup of tea, a map of Israel spread out on the table in front of him. It never failed to strike him how vulnerable the country seemed when looking at a map. Surrounded by enemies—Lebanon to the north, Jordan to the east, Egypt to the south. Now he knew that, for him, the enemies were within the borders as well. He had to get out.

Buzz padded to him, nuzzling his nose affectionately against his leg. Absently, Levi stroked the animal's sleek head and took a sip of tea. Like Otto Mueller, he was marked for death. He imagined the article that would appear in the newspaper and wondered if it would say heart attack or stroke as cause of death. His thin lips curled in a sardonic smile. He could almost hear his friends remarking, "But he was always in such excellent health!" "Ruven took such good care of himself." Would anyone ever discover the truth? He doubted it.

Levi sighed and directed his attention back to the map. He had to assume several things. One, former protectors had turned against him. The sudden, vicious attack in the night was proof enough for him. It seemed to him he had always known it would end like this. That one day he would be completely alone again, forced to rely solely on his wits for his protection. At times, over the years, Levi wondered why they continued to protect him. Inertia, perhaps, or, more likely, fear—fear he'd instilled. Should anything happen to me, he'd warned them long ago, certain revealing documents in the hands of friends would be made public. That threat had probably kept him alive.

He nearly laughed aloud. If Mueller would have proved an embarrassment to the Americans, he could imagine the sensation the press would make of his story. His capture would prove to be a far greater scandal to the Agency, which hated to admit to a rotten apple in their barrel. For while some of his former colleagues acquired protection in exchange for information, his own arrangement had been based purely on greed.

Secondly, Levi told himself he must assume that John Daley had gone to the police with his story. Naturally they would find it hard to believe, but nevertheless they would feel compelled to follow it up. He let his eyes roam over the map. Assuming the police were now looking for him, the airports would be watched. As he stared at the map it came to him that there was a way out. Risky, but then his entire life had been filled with risk.

He folded the map carefully and finished his tea. Rising stiffly from his chair, he went to the sink and rinsed out his cup. It would be interesting to see Ernst again after so many years. And he imagined the surprise his sudden appearance in Amman would create. Ernst might not be entirely delighted, but then Ernst owed him a favor. It was he who had given Ernst a new face. Ernst could be relied upon to get him to

Syria, where a friendly government helped so many of his former associates.

Levi dried the cup and replaced it in the kitchen cupboard. Thank God he had had the foresight to squirrel away funds in Switzerland. He might yet enjoy a comfortable old age.

As he began to pack a small bag Levi felt himself in the curious transitional state of shedding one life, not yet immersed in another. He felt a stirring of excitement. He had nearly forgotten how it had felt after the war to live on the edge, aware always of the possibility of discovery, despite the cosmetic alteration of his nose and chin. It had been a relief to finally settle into a more normal existence, if one could call it normal to find refuge among his former victims. He had almost forgotten the thrill of being on the run. Almost, but not entirely.

Levi shut the small suitcase and lifted it from the bed. In his study he wrote a brief note for Mazal. A good woman, Mazal. Impulsively, he enclosed some extra money. It would tide her over until she found other work.

He unlocked the desk drawer and took out his well-worn telephone book. Fifteen minutes and two telephone calls later, he was ready.

Gripped by a sudden nostalgia, he allowed himself a final tour of his apartment. Each object seemed to call out to him. He was surrounded for the last time by a lifetime of possessions, a lifetime of memories of his life with Frieda. He paused before his favorite photograph of her. He reached out, thinking to take it with him, then restrained himself. Frieda belonged to this life, which was now dead.

He went to the telephone, picked up the receiver, and started to dial Rivka's number. Then, halfway through, he hung up. There was no point. Yet his heart ached with the knowledge of how he would miss her, and his niece, Ronit.

He returned to his hunting room, and felt tears scalding his eyes. For an instant he doubted he had the energy or heart to begin all over in a strange environment surrounded by strangers. Maybe it would be better to end it all here. The thought of John Daley pushed into his head and the moment passed as quickly as it had come.

He cautiously drew back the curtain and looked out the

window at the dark street. It was empty. He propped the note for Mazal on the kitchen table, where she would be sure to see it in the morning.

He heard the bleat of a taxi horn outside. He bent down and ran his hand over the dog's head.

"Shalom, Buzz. Good boy."

His throat was tight with unshed tears as he pressed the wall button for the hall light and made his way down the stairs, trying not to think that this was the last time he would go this way. It was only his hate for John Daley that kept him from weeping. Hate, and the secret enjoyment of knowing that Daley, the man bent on his destruction, would be the one to save him.

Rudolf Lobel closed the door behind him and stepped into the darkness.

THIRTY-SEVEN

"What was it you called it, a 'shipboard romance'?"

Rose smiled up at him.

"Sounds familiar. Why?"

"I don't know. Just wondering."

Rose propped herself up on one elbow. Looking into her eyes, Daley had the uncomfortable feeling that she was able to read his thoughts.

"John, I think there's a reason behind everything you do and say. Is there something you want to talk about?"

"Not really."

He reached out for her. She let herself be drawn into the circle of his arms, and they lay quietly, comfortably together. Daley felt the strong, steady beat of her heart against his chest. His throat ached with unsaid words. While the need to say them was nearly overwhelming, his feelings seemed too complicated to express easily. He wasn't even sure exactly what it was he wanted to say. Sometime during the last hour since they had made love, he realized he had crossed an invisible boundary. He felt a tie to Rose Malloy . . . something he hadn't expected or wanted to feel. He didn't want to think about the end of the trip and the inevitable parting. For Rose their affair was a diversion. A shipboard romance, she had called it. He mentally reviewed all the reasons she would not want to see him back in New York. Daley was torn between the desire to ask her and the fear of being rejected.

"John, I think I know what's on your mind," she said at last. "You're afraid our sleeping together has obligated you to something you're not ready for. I want you to know I understand and don't blame you, or expect anything more than this. This is the eighties. We're both grown-up people. Some might even say 'over the hill.' "

Daley sank back, resting his head on his arms. Rose was letting him down easy, telling him tactfully that as far as she was concerned this was it. At least, he thought, through his disappointment, he hadn't made a fool of himself, proposing they see each other at home.

"Not that it's going to be easy," she went on. "It's amazing how close you can feel to someone in a matter of days. I know I'll miss you. More than I ever thought I would."

Daley tensed. Now was the time, if ever, to say something. He had a sudden image of the future as a fragile spider web, intricate, beautiful, but enormously fragile. He wanted her, but a part of him was backing off in terror. He knew that if he allowed that part to gain control, he would have crushed that silken web in his hands.

He sensed her waiting. All the reasons he knew it wouldn't work out flashed through his mind before he impulsively, uncharacteristically, plunged ahead.

"You're right, but only partially. I feel a commitment, but you're dead wrong when you say I'm afraid of it. Well"—he grinned—"maybe just a little afraid. But you know something? I've been lying here afraid that maybe you didn't want any kind of . . . of continuation. After the trip, I mean." Suddenly he was panicky, fearful that he had misunderstood her.

"Do you?"

For answer, she reached out for him. Daley couldn't remember ever feeling such utter joy.

Later, in the darkness, Rose asked him, "You weren't going to say anything, were you?"

He felt her fingers lace through his.

"It's taking a risk," she said.

"I never thought about it that way, but I suppose it is. It's funny. I put my life on the line every day for years. It never scared me."

"I imagine. But risking a relationship with another person is another matter. There's potential for a deadlier hurt."

Daley thought of Colleen and he sensed that without saying a word, Rose somehow knew what he was feeling. He squeezed her hand, thinking if he could hold on to that hand every night the rest of his life, he would never ask for anything more.

"First you almost missed Tiberias, now Masada," Daley joked as the taxi entered the city limits of Jerusalem. "You've hardly seen Israel."

"If you think I'm letting you out of my sight now, you're crazy." She laughed. "Masada's been there for centuries. It'll be there tomorrow."

"Unlike Rudolf Lobel."

"If you really feel it's futile, why are we going?"

Daley shrugged. "I've got to try to find out if Lobel and Levi are the same person."

"And if they are, you said yourself he wouldn't sit around at home waiting for you or the police."

"I know. Still . . ." Daley let the rest of the sentence hang in midair.

"I'm going in alone," he said after the taxi had driven off. "You wait here in the park. If I'm not out in twenty minutes, go to the King David Hotel."

He reached into his pocket and took out the slip of paper Malka Rubenstein had given him.

"Call this number and ask for Goldschmidt. Tell him what happened."

Rose shivered. "I don't mind telling you, I'm afraid. Lobel's not just an old man. He's a monster."

"Yeah, tell me about it. But yours truly wasn't working

225

among saints the past thirty years." He kissed her cheek. "There's a nice bench in the sun."

"What if he is there? Then what?"

"I don't know, Rose, but I do know I'll be damned if I'm going to have it on my conscience that I let the bastard get away."

Daley stood outside Ruven Levi's door for a moment before pushing the doorbell. The dog barked, footsteps sounded against the tile floor. Daley braced himself for the improbable confrontation with the white-haired man. The door was opened by Levi's housekeeper.

"Is Dr. Levi home?"

The dog sniffed at him eagerly.

The woman shook her head. "No here."

Daley took a step halfway into the apartment, preventing her from closing the door.

"What time will he be back?" He pointed to his watch. "What time?"

She shrugged. Then lifted an imaginary object to her shoulder and said something in Hebrew.

He looked at her blankly.

"Bang bang," she said, and squeezed an imaginary trigger.

"Hunting?" he asked.

She smiled and nodded her head. *"Ken,* yes. Hunting."

"Hunting," he said. "Thank you."

He walked down the uncarpeted stairway, his footsteps echoing on the stone. He hadn't expected Levi to be there, but he was disappointed just the same. Levi's absence, he told himself, wasn't proof of anything, however. The man was an avid hunter. It was certainly conceivable he had gone hunting. But the dog was there. Would he go hunting without his dog? Not likely. Yet, there could be reasons for that too. From somewhere back in time a conversation suddenly came back to him. He and a few of the guys had been sitting around the lunchroom talking about sports. He remembered one of the men asking Moe Greenstein, "Hey, Moe, how come Jews don't hunt?" Daley remarked he'd never thought about it, but in all his experience he'd never run across a Jewish hunter.

"How come?" he'd asked Moe. "Something in the religion?"

Moe had shrugged. "Not that I know of, but I'm no rabbi. Just not part of the culture, I guess."

But Ruven Levi was a hunter, Daley thought, stepping out of the building into the bright sunlight. A hunter passionate enough to have that trophy room. Unusual for a Jew, unless Ruven Levi was not really a Jew.

He waved to Rose. She got up from the park bench and hurried across the street to him. He was about to suggest they wander over to the Old City but the sight of her face, pale and frightened, stopped him.

"What's wrong?"

"There's somebody watching us, John, in the park. The man reading a newspaper."

A stocky young blond man sat on a bench. Daley watched him put down his newspaper and start to toss bread crumbs to the pigeons. He didn't glance their way, but Daley's instinct told him Rose was right.

Daley suggested they take a Sherut taxi, an oversized sedan shared by other passengers. Sensing Rose's nervousness and trying to divert her, Daley struck up a lively conversation with one of the other three passengers. But she remained tense and quiet all the way to Tel Aviv.

It was a short walk from the taxi drop-off point to the beach area and the hotel. Daley suggested they stop for lunch first, but Rose shook her head.

"I want to get back to the hotel. I feel so vulnerable here."

"With all this?" Ben Gurion Street buzzed with activity.

"I keep thinking about that car last night," she said. "And the man in the park."

"What made you think he was following us?"

Rose's hand tightened on his arm. "I don't know, John. It's just a feeling I can't shake."

"I'm going to go up and take an aspirin," Rose said as they stopped by the reception desk to check on messages, "then if you like, we can have lunch."

"Sounds good to me. I may even try some of that, what was that stuff we ate in Jerusalem?"

They walked toward the elevator. Rose, Daley was glad to see, seemed more her old self now that she was back on familiar ground.

"Hummus. It was good, wasn't it? I wonder if it's something I could make at home. Maybe one night I'll attempt an Israeli dinner, although cooking is not my forte. Would you be game to try it?"

He pressed the UP button. He pictured the two of them sitting over dinner in New York and a wave of happiness came over him.

The elevator doors opened and a young couple with a small child stepped out. Daley and Rose got in. The elevator stopped at the second floor. Rose gasped as the blond man from the park slipped inside, quickly pressing the CLOSE DOOR button. Daley lunged forward toward the control buttons.

"Stay where you are!" the young man ordered, and pushed the EMERGENCY STOP.

"What the hell is this?" Daley demanded. "Who are you?"

Reaching into his jacket, the man pulled a gun.

Rose uttered a sharp cry.

"I'm not going to hurt you," he said to Rose. "Or you, Mr. Daley. I'm with the Mossad. My job is to make certain you don't get hurt."

"Thank God! What a scare you gave me!" Rose exclaimed.

"Let me see some ID," Daley demanded.

The other man smiled. Daley realized he was younger than he appeared. He couldn't be over thirty. Blue-eyed and fair-skinned, he looked almost Scandinavian.

"Would an organization that keeps its headquarters secret allow its agents to carry ID?" he asked almost playfully.

"And if I don't buy it?" Daley asked.

The man shrugged. "It is your choice, Mr. Daley, to believe whatever you wish, but I will tell you this. If you do not believe me, and if you choose to disregard the advice I am going to give you, you do so at your own risk. And"—he nodded significantly toward Rose—"and the risk of Miss Malloy."

The man paused for his words to sink in.

"Stay out of this matter, Mr. Daley," he said, not unkindly. "You only complicate things. You should not have involved your son-in-law in the matter of Rudolf Lobel."

"What's that supposed to mean?"

"You've done your part," the man said, ignoring Daley's question. "Now, please leave the rest to us. Have I made myself clear?"

He looked from Daley to Rose. Then, without waiting for a reply, he replaced the weapon in the holster under his arm, concealing it beneath his jacket, and pressed the UP button. The elevator began its slow ascent.

At the third floor the doors opened. The man stepped out. The doors closed.

Later, when he had time to piece it together, Daley concluded that the phone calls Ilan had promised to make had alerted the Mossad, resulting in the unexpected encounter with the agent. Relieved that he had set things in motion, Daley told himself that if any organization in the world could capture Rudolf Lobel, it was the Israeli Mossad.

THIRTY-EIGHT

Like a decaying tooth, Vince's anxiety about Daley was a persistent, nagging discomfort that refused to go away.

"Grandpa, come on! Mom's going to cut the cake!"

Joey pranced into the den, where Vince had been sitting alone. The little boy was bursting with impatience.

"You're going to miss everything!" he cried. "Come on!"

"I'm coming."

Vince hoisted himself out of his chair with a grunt and followed the boy to the dining room, where the rest of the family was gathered. Normally, there was nothing he enjoyed more than family get-togethers like this one for his grandson's birthday. Tonight, weighed down by feelings of responsibility, he had to force himself to enter into the fun.

Daley, he thought miserably, I know you too well. He couldn't trust Daley to leave the Lobel business alone. Not Daley. He'd push and prod and poke his nose into it until he was satisfied he'd caught the son of a bitch. That was Daley, and Vince knew he'd screwed it up. He shouldn't have come off so strong. He should have known, with Daley, that that approach was bound to backfire. Now the CIA was involved, and Daley would be caught in the middle.

A burst of applause cut into his thoughts. His daughter carried in a large chocolate cake with blazing candles. Vince joined in the singing, his mind still thousands of miles away in Israel with Daley. If only he could replay their conversation. He would talk to Daley differently, use some psychology. Shit, Vince thought, disgusted with himself, he'd used psychology successfully for years handling his help and wooing customers. He knew how to get along with people. Why the hell had he blown it with Daley?

"Grandpa, you want a rose?"

Vince's fourteen-year-old granddaughter was standing in front of him with two paper plates in her hands.

"Huh?"

"A rose, on your cake. You want a rose?"

"Whatever. Sure. A rose would be great."

Vince sat down next to his son-in-law, Frank. His daughter served them coffee.

"You're quiet tonight, Dad," she remarked.

"Too busy eating." He grinned. "No bakery bakes like this." He forced a joviality he didn't feel and dug into the cake. But for once even the rich chocolate failed to comfort him.

Joey was tearing open the paper on one of his gifts. Vince's mind wandered back to Daley.

He knew why he'd blown it with Daley. Daley got under his skin with the Lobel business. Daley made him look at something he didn't want to look at. Like the garbage, he thought suddenly, remembering a visit from Angie's cousin, Louise, a few years back.

Louise had come to New York from the Midwest, and they had taken her around showing her the sights. Vince recalled stopping in one of the specialty gourmet shops that sold exquisite and exotic meats, cheeses, pastries, salads, coffees, wines. The aroma from the street was enough to put ten pounds on you. He was sure there was nothing like it in her hometown, but instead of looking impressed, Louise appeared puzzled.

"Look at that," she'd said, pointing to the sidewalk.

Vince looked but didn't notice anything unusual.

"The garbage!" she cried. "Wouldn't you think the owner of such a beautiful, tasteful shop would care enough to have a boy sweep up the garbage just outside the entrance?"

And that was when Vince had seen it. Mounds of uncollected, foul-smelling garbage spilling out of plastic bags and cans onto the sidewalk and gutter. And he knew why the owner hadn't bothered to clean it up. Like him, he'd gotten so used to it, he didn't even see it. Well, he thought, that was what the Lobel affair was. Just as he'd been defensive when Angie's cousin noticed the garbage, Daley made him defensive about Lobel.

Vince told himself Rudolf Lobel wasn't his fault any more than the garbage on the street was. But Daley had made that claim ring false to him, which was part of the reason he felt so crummy. Okay, Vince told himself, knowing why he'd blown it with Daley didn't help the situation. Daley was still there in Israel. As long as he persisted in hunting Lobel, he was endangering himself. He wondered if maybe it would have been better to level with Daley. To tell him everything and then enlist his cooperation. After all, Daley was a reasonable man. Vince quickly abandoned that idea. Daley was reasonable, but not about Nazis.

"Hey, Grandpa, thanks!" Joey shouted across the table, holding up a computer game. "This is neat!"

"You gotta show me how it works," Vince said.

He glanced at his watch. It was morning in Tel Aviv. There was a chance Daley was in the hotel, and maybe, just maybe, he could undo some of the damage. Or, he thought, at least make himself feel better.

Angie and the girls were in the kitchen gossiping and cleaning up the dishes. His son-in-law had moved to the living room. Vince went to the den and shut the door.

"Happy New Year!" Vince said when he heard Daley's voice.

"Are we going steady or what?" Daley cracked.

"Listen, Daley, just wanted to apologize about the other day."

"Apologize for what?"

"You know."

232

Suddenly Vince was uncomfortable. Wondered again if maybe he should come right out with the whole story.

"I don't. Suppose you tell me."

"I came on a little strong, about that Nazi stuff, but you know us paisanos. We get all steamed up fast. Anyway, how's it going?"

"Great. At least in some respects. I met a woman."

"No kidding! Who is she? An Israeli?"

"Bostonian. You'll meet her."

"Hey, now that sounds serious."

Daley laughed, "I wouldn't post any banns, but she's quite some lady."

"That's great. Listen, Daley, I been thinking a lot and I'm sure you must've made a mistake about Lobel, you know? It could happen to anybody."

Vince sensed Daley holding back. He waited a moment. Daley was conceding nothing.

"Daley, you hear what I said?"

"Yeah, I heard. I didn't make a mistake, but if it'll make you feel better, I'm not involved. The Israelis are taking care of it."

A score of questions leapt immediately into Vince's mind. But they were questions he didn't dare ask. He tried to fathom the implications. The Israelis taking care of it. It could mean nothing. It could mean Daley had really stepped aside. Or Daley could be putting him on, pacifying him. Or . . . Vince didn't want to think of what the other alternatives might be.

"Glad to hear it," he said at last. "What the hell, it's their problem, not yours. You concentrate on your lady friend, okay?"

"Yeah, okay."

"So, Happy New Year."

"Same to you, buddy. And say hello to Angie."

The flea market in Old Jaffa was a shopper's dream, Rose insisted.

"A junk collector's dream, you mean," Daley joked, stopping to pick up a battered copper pot.

"A little of each, I suspect. Now this piece, cleaned up, could be an interesting planter."

233

"Want me to use my famous bargaining skills?" Daley asked as the Arab proprietor scurried toward them.

"Not on this. Save it for something I really want."

The group had been let off the bus by the Clock Tower, and after a quick look around the renovated artist quarter, they were given an hour of free shopping. Rose and Daley had wandered off by themselves, strolling the winding stone streets where fish grilled on open coals and Arab pastries, oozing with sugar and honey, lay out in open trays. Daley bought a round ring of fresh Arab bread and they shared it companionably, breaking off hunks with their fingers. Yael had promised a more complete tour of the art studios and galleries after lunch.

"The artists have made Old Jaffa quite fashionable," she'd told them, "and in the evenings it is the place to come. There are many fine restaurants and cafes."

The bohemian artist quarter, Daley noted, contrasted with the distinctly oriental flavor of the bustling stalls of the Shuk Hapishpeshim, the Flea Market. It seemed as if there was nothing that couldn't be found in its arcades of dark little shops and stalls . . . tapestries, jewelry, ceramics, furniture, pots, shoes, and clothing.

"Like the Village," Daley remarked. "Used to be the pits. Now it's the in place. You know what those condos go for down there? If anybody'd told me twenty years ago what that property would be worth . . ." He shook his head. "Even Vince's place—it was a real hole in the wall when he bought it. Now he's sitting on a small fortune. When we get back I'll take you down there for the best Italian meal you ever had."

"I'd like that. I'm looking forward to meeting Vince."

Daley sobered, remembering Vince's unexpected phone call. Vince had pumped him for information, and he'd held back purposely. He was sure Vince knew a hell of a lot more about the Lobel business than he admitted to. He'd neglected telling Vince about his trips to Jerusalem, or the Englishman. Instead, he'd told Vince the Israelis were taking charge, knowing that would get Vince off his back. What it came down to, he thought sadly, was that he could no longer completely trust his oldest, his only, friend.

"John, look at this!" Rose held up a small ivory perfume bottle with a silver top. "Isn't this exquisite!"

"From Persia," the owner said, materializing suddenly from the dark depths of the shop. "Very old."

As Daley joined in the bargaining over the perfume bottle, the disturbing thought flitted into his mind that maybe it wasn't all as it appeared. He'd been assured the Israelis were actively handling the situation and he'd been reassured by the encounter with the Mossad agent in the elevator.

Yet, he was bothered. Goldschmidt had discovered Ida Karpinsky in the kibbutz in Haifa. There had to be other survivors of Mauthausen in Israel, besides the blind woman, who remembered Lobel. But so far none had responded to the advertisement for witnesses that Goldschmidt said he had placed. Daley remembered his frustration at trying to reach Roth at the Jerusalem police. Malka Rubenstein's polite brush-off. It crossed his mind they were stonewalling. And if that was the case, he was damned if he'd stand by and let them get away with it.

"John, I thought you were finally going to relax," Rose chided, the perfume bottle tucked safely in her purse. "You have that look on your face."

"What look is that?"

"I don't know what to call it but I know what it means. It means your mind isn't here and you're upset."

He patted her arm. "Not upset. Just thinking."

She eyed him skeptically.

"Rose, I think I'll go see Goldschmidt, find out what's going on with the witnesses."

"Do you want me to come along?"

He shook his head. "Thanks, but you've got more bargains to strike." He kissed her. "Tell Yael I went back, okay?"

It was a short walk to the old police building. When Daley asked for Goldschmidt he was told the old man was out. Daley considered waiting, then abandoned the idea. He left the building, feeling at loose ends. Something was wrong but he didn't know what. He only knew his feelings were related in some way to Vince's call, to the Mossad agent who'd followed them from Jerusalem. To the Englishman from Hebron. A vague anxiety was beginning to worm its way into his gut.

He flagged down a taxi at the corner. He started to give the driver the hotel name, but impulsively changed his mind, directing him instead to Colleen's street, overcome by a sudden desire to see his grandson.

He lit a cigarette and tried to analyze his disquiet. The formless apprehension reminded him of the Manzone case. They thought they'd had it solved with a suspect, a confession, circumstantial evidence. But Daley had a feeling, despite appearances to the contrary, something was wrong. He'd kept digging. His hunch paid off. The confession was a phony and his persistence ended in a stunning apprehension of the kidnapper. When reporters asked him what made him suspicious and Daley said he didn't know, they thought he was being modest. He knew he was being honest.

The taxi wound through the run-down streets of Petah Tiqwa to the Haifa Road, and up Jabotinsky. It circled around the fashionable Kikar HaMedina. Daley recognized Colleen's street.

"I'll get out here," he said.

He paid the driver and got out. He started walking to the apartment, then turned and crossed the street in the direction of a cluster of small shops . . . a cafe, flower shop, travel agency, and a little grocery. This time, Daley thought, he wouldn't go empty-handed.

He bought fresh flowers for Esther and was about to go into the grocery for chocolate for Yoni when he spotted the boy across the street, sauntering home from school, backpack slung over his shoulders. Daley called out to him, but his voice was drowned by the roar of a city bus pulling up to the curb, blocking the other side of the street from his view. The doors of the bus wheezed open. A woman got out. The bus moved on. Daley stepped off the curb, then stopped.

For an instant, he was confused. Then, in quick succession, puzzled and, finally, panicky. No more than fifteen seconds had passed. But Yoni had vanished.

THIRTY-NINE

In thirty years as a cop, Daley had been witness to more tragedy than he cared to remember. Had interviewed bloodied and battered victims of muggings, rape, and assault. Even tougher had been the painful task of informing families of the deaths of close relatives. There was nothing more devastating than having to tell a parent his child was dead.

Although for thirty years Daley had identified with the victims, inwardly raging against the perpetrators of human misery, nothing in those thirty years adequately prepared him for the role of victim.

He'd gone through a spectrum of emotions in the hours since Yoni had disappeared. Bewilderment, fear, fury, until now he felt only helplessness, something he hadn't experienced since the war, when he'd come face-to-face with those half-dead skeletons. He'd felt helpless then and felt helpless now. Yoni was gone and there was nothing he could do.

He poured himself another whiskey. He'd lost count of how many he'd had over the long afternoon. He felt no effect. People had come and gone . . . neighbors, relatives, police.

The incomprehensible, guttural sound of Hebrew had become a meaningless drone, like background music in a dentist's office.

Most of the police who'd swarmed through the apartment had gone, but tension and confusion remained. Colleen and Ilan huddled together talking with Rappaport, the officer in charge, and his assistant. They seemed to have aged years. The sight of Colleen's ravaged face was a knife twisting his heart and he turned away, toward Esther, who sat alone on the couch, a small, forlorn figure. We should be pulling together, Daley thought, but if anything, the gulf between us has widened. He felt shut out.

Eli Goldschmidt came up behind him.

"Cigarette?"

"Thanks." Daley took one from the pack the old man offered.

"It must be especially hard, not understanding what's being said," he commented.

"Isn't it possible he just went off by himself with a friend?" Daley asked.

"He wouldn't do that," Esther said suddenly from her place on the couch. "Not my Yonaleh. He always let me know first. Always." She burst into tears. "It had to be the kidnapper."

Although it was the logical assumption, Daley couldn't get rid of the growing fear that somehow Rudolf Lobel was involved in some way.

"And if it is the kidnapper?" Colleen looked from Ilan to the policemen. "What do we do?"

"We are working on the assumption that these kidnappings are politically motivated acts of terrorism."

Colleen paled. "Do we pay a ransom then? Make some statement? What do we do?"

Rappaport faced her squarely.

"We do not bargain with terrorists. Ever."

"But a child's life!" Colleen cried. "Ilan! Tell them we must —we'll do anything!"

Ilan looked as though he'd been struck.

"I can't."

Tears spilled down Colleen's face. Daley felt his own eyes

misting. He wanted to cradle her in his arms, but could not make a move toward her.

"You have to," she shouted shrilly. "My God, Ilan, it's Yoni!"

"Don't you think I know that!" he roared. "Goddamnit, I know it! But all my life I believed we don't give in to terrorists. We don't strike bargains with them. We fight them."

"Even when it's your child?" she challenged.

"Even then."

"It could be Lobel. Maybe his way of warning me," Daley said in the silence that followed.

At the anguished look on Ilan's face, Daley felt a rush of sympathy for his son-in-law. If Lobel had taken Yoni, Ilan had played a part by making those calls Daley had asked him to make.

Colleen's head jerked up.

"Who's Lobel?"

She listened in disbelief as Daley quickly told her about Lobel, and then turned to Ilan.

"Why didn't you tell me?" she demanded.

He shrugged. "It didn't seem important."

"Didn't seem important!" she cried. "My father gets involved with a Nazi criminal who may have kidnapped our son and you tell me it wasn't important!"

"I don't believe Lobel had anything to do with this," Ilan said.

Rappaport lit a cigarette.

"I agree with your husband," he said to Colleen. "If we dismiss the possibility that your boy ran away, or is with friends, the alternative is that he was abducted. And the pattern seems to be that of the kidnapper. This Lobel business . . ." He exhaled a cloud of smoke and sighed. "The whole thing is too improbable."

"A hell of a lot of improbable things have been happening," Daley said. "A man with my name in my hotel is killed. I almost get brained by a rock in Hebron, and nearly run over by an Englishman who keeps showing up every place I am. And when I take a picture of Lobel the camera's stolen before the film can be developed."

"Okay, so these things happened," Rappaport said, "but by

themselves they are not so unusual. In your country, too, Mr. Daley, hotel rooms are burglarized, people are assaulted on the street, and you have, I understand, a problem with drunk drivers. Am I right? And you are not even certain the man you saw is Rudolf Lobel."

"I am certain. It's him."

"But you have no proof. Photographs?" He looked at Goldschmidt.

"No photographs," the old man said grimly. "Not anymore."

"What's happening with the photograph of Levi?" Daley asked. "You were going to get one of him."

"I haven't been able to get it," Goldschmidt admitted. "It's unusual for it to take so long, but sometimes that's how it goes. But now we must get it."

He spoke to Rappaport, who sent his assistant hurrying to the telephone.

"Okay, assuming the man is Lobel, Mr. Daley, how and why would he take your grandson?" Rappaport asked. "Not for money. If anything, he would want to disappear, not draw attention to himself. *Nahon?* Right?"

"You're thinking logically, but that man's mind is twisted. He wouldn't think like you or me. You can't assume what he'd feel or do based on logic."

Goldschmidt nodded in agreement.

"And if Rudolf Lobel kidnapped Yoni," Colleen cried, whirling around to face Daley, "it's your fault! If he took Yoni to get at you . . ." Tears rained down her cheeks. "For once in your life, couldn't you stop being a cop!"

Daley stepped back, almost expecting her to strike him. He felt her anger and grief searching for a tangible target and knew she would lash out at whoever was near, no matter how irrational such an action would be. But instead of attacking him, she sank down on the couch next to Ilan, as though the brief flare-up had drained her of all energy.

"What I want to know is where the hell was the agent watching me?" Daley asked.

"Who is that, Mr. Daley?" Rappaport asked.

"The Mossad agent. He followed me from Jerusalem to Tel

Aviv and told me he was assigned to watch me. He should've been able to see what happened."

Rappaport looked puzzled. "I don't know anything about that, but I'll find out. I'll make a call." He stubbed out his cigarette and headed to the kitchen.

"We will need a good photograph of your son," Rappaport's young assistant said to Colleen.

She nodded, and walked stiffly out of the room. Ilan and his mother remained on the couch. Goldschmidt stood at the window, staring out at the sunset. The young officer was making notes on a lined pad of paper. Daley heard Rappaport talking in the kitchen.

He looked around the living room, remembering the first day he'd come. Yoni's eager welcome. The game of checkers. He felt his throat thicken with emotion. His mind refused to accept the possibility that he had found his grandson only to lose him.

Colleen returned carrying the photo album Yoni had shown him that first day. She sat down and began to turn the pages.

"It is curious," Rappaport said, coming back into the room, "but the man you talked to in the elevator was not a Mossad agent."

"Then who was he?" Colleen looked up from the album in alarm.

"Obviously someone who knew me. Someone who knew I was onto Ruven Levi. Maybe a friend of Levi's. A member of Odessa. I don't know."

The minutes dragged by. Colleen selected a photograph of Yoni, handing it over to the policeman as if it were a precious relic. Rappaport requested, and she gave him, the names of Yoni's friends. Esther, at Ilan's urging, made coffee. They sat around the table, their lonely vigil interrupted only by the telephone as one relative after another called. At last the doorbell rang. Ilan opened the door to a policeman carrying a manila envelope in his hand.

"The photograph of Dr. Levi," Goldschmidt said.

There was no sound in the room as Daley opened the envelope and held the photograph in his hand. A quick glance was enough to tell him that the round, moon face bore absolutely no resemblance to the man he knew as Rudolf Lobel. The ears on either side of his nearly bald head were completely normal.

Daley let the photograph slip out of his fingers.

"This is not the man I saw."

"So much for the theory that Lobel and Levi are one and the same," Rappaport commented.

"So it would appear," Goldschmidt said.

Daley knew he was remembering the razored-out head of Lobel in the group photograph.

Despite the damning evidence of the photograph, Daley was not yet ready to abandon the idea that the two men were the same. If one photograph had been tampered with, why not another?

"Now we must wait," Rappaport said. He began to gather his papers. "This is the most difficult thing to do, I know."

Colleen and Ilan walked with him to the door. Daley went out onto the balcony. Goldschmidt joined him.

"I can't explain that photograph, but I still think Levi is Lobel," Daley said. "You think that's nuts?"

Goldschmidt said softly, "I don't, but, Mr. Daley, you must understand the natural resistance to such an idea. We are a people still bleeding from the wounds of the Holocaust. If you think there was an outcry over your President's trip to the German military cemetery . . ." He sighed. "Well, you can imagine how shocking the idea that we have been harboring a Nazi murderer would be. More than shocking. It is unacceptable. Secondly, the man you believe to be the Nazi is a respected citizen. A man who has done good and valuable work."

"One of the characteristics of a psychopath, which Lobel certainly is, is his inconsistency," Daley argued. "The criminal can be kind and sentimental toward his family one minute and commit an unspeakable crime against another human being the next."

"That's true, of course. Lobel does not have the time to indulge in such a dangerous act for symbolic reasons. Mr. Daley, if he or someone helping him took your grandson, he wants something from you. In which case, he will contact you. I know this will be difficult for you, but I am going to ask that you go on with your tour's agenda. Leave things to the police.

242

There is nothing you can do here, and this time, I promise, we will be watching you. Come, I will take you to your hotel."

"Thanks. I'll get my jacket."

Halfway down the hall, he turned and ducked into the master bedroom. Quickly he strode to the closet and, pushing aside Colleen's dresses, took the shoe box Yoni had shown him that first day. In one swift movement he concealed the gun inside his jacket.

He would leave things to the Israelis, as he had promised Goldschmidt. But not entirely.

FORTY

As he strode down the corridor toward the meeting room, Jim Banning felt like Gregor Samsa, who'd awakened one morning to find himself transformed into a giant cockroach. One minute, things were firmly under control. The next, he was plunged into the midst of a nightmare.

Banning had spent the last twenty-four hours bogged down in the mire of self-doubt and recrimination. They should have taken immediate action against Lobel before the old man had grasped the initiative. But who could have foreseen the boldness of such a move on the part of a man in his seventies? How he had managed to pull it off remained a mystery. Yet, despite the lack of positive proof, Banning was convinced Lobel was behind the disappearance of the Daley grandchild. And by that act Lobel had put them all in the distinctly distasteful position of having to react rather than act.

At the end of the road Banning saw nothing but more trouble for each of them. The idea of a demotion was untenable and a career change was not easy at his stage of life. He'd brooded half the night, reviewing their obligations and lifestyle . . . the house, the private schools for the kids, the ski vacations, the BMW. Not to mention his share of keeping Jane's mother in a nursing home.

As he reached the conference room Banning was filled with a feeling of injustice. He hadn't spent his professional life building his career to have it go down the tubes because of a man he'd never met. Not for the first time, he cursed the corrupt bastard who had struck that unholy bargain with Rudolf Lobel. Christ!

Banning opened the unmarked door. The others were sitting around the table comparing ski resorts. They nodded in greeting as Banning helped himself to coffee.

"Looks like we have a little problem," he said easily, placing his papers on the table.

They reacted to the kidnapping as he knew they would. With disbelief and anger.

"But, Jim, how do we know he did it?" Bob asked.

"We don't, for sure. But, for one thing, Lobel disappeared the same time as the boy. He promised he'd stay put but he's gone."

"He panicked," George mused through a cloud of smoke. "We knew he might."

"He's a suspicious s.o.b.," Banning commented wryly. "As well he should be."

"We should have taken care of him right away," Andy glowered. "We screwed around too long. Now it's too late. He's got the kid."

Bob looked perplexed. "I don't get it. What can the boy do for him? By taking the kid, he's got the whole country looking for him. Why would he do it?"

Banning sighed. "You can be sure we'll find out."

"And Daley?" Andy asked. "He started the whole goddamn mess and then made it worse. Why the hell is he still around? I thought he was being taken care of too."

Banning finished his coffee, then leaned back in his chair. He felt the beginning of a monstrous headache. Andy had put his finger on it. John Daley was an ever-present thorn in his side. It was Banning's belief that they'd made a mistake relying on Vince. Given what they'd been told about Daley's char-

acter, they should have moved swiftly. Decisively. He sighed.
All that was hindsight.

"Daley's off-limits."

Surprise registered clearly on their faces.

"The son-in-law drives a hard bargain," he went on. "His own people had trouble convincing him to cooperate. He agreed only after they promised him Daley would be safe. So that's the way it goes as far as Daley's concerned."

"Which means," George said thoughtfully, drawing on his pipe, "that if Lobel gets away, we still have Daley to contend with."

"That's exactly it, George," Banning said. "Daley told Vince he'd make a stink—and he will—if Lobel gets away."

"We can't afford to let Lobel get away," George said.

"A little late for that," Andy grunted.

"He's already gotten away," Bob seconded.

"Only temporarily," Banning said. "If he's got the boy, and our sources seem to think he does, it's for a damn good reason. He's going to use the boy somehow. And when he resurfaces it will have to be the end of him. Any objections? Discussion?"

"What about those letters or papers Lobel says he has somewhere?" Bob asked.

"I never believed there were any," Andy barked. "It was bullshit on his part."

"But if it's not, then what?" George asked.

They fell silent.

"It may be time to risk that," Banning said at last.

Bob frowned. "What about the boy?"

"We're working with the Israelis on this one," Banning said. "They're not going to let the boy get hurt."

Bob was a new father, and seeing the look of relief on his face, Banning knew the young man was identifying.

What Banning didn't say was that their men were under no such injunction. Getting Lobel was their first priority. In his view, Lobel was a spreading, deadly cancer that needed to be cut away.

"But there's no guarantee, is there?" Bob asked. "I say the old man isn't worth it."

"Bob, I know how you feel," Banning said. "Look, if Lobel

had simply provided information about the Russians in exchange for protection, then we could ride it out. It might not be pretty, but at least it would be understandable, given the temper of those times. People have come to accept that it was actually, from our viewpoint, in our security interests. It's no secret even that Reinhard Gehlen, Germany's most celebrated spy, entered into a pact in '46 with the U.S. Government and established his own intelligence operation with the help of his old Nazi cronies. Even Hoover knew who he was recruiting."

"Jesus," Bob said softly.

"As Allen Dulles put it when asked why he made use of people like Gehlen, 'There are few archbishops in espionage. He's on our side and that's all that matters. Besides, one needn't ask him to one's club,' " George put in.

"But this situation is different," Banning said. "It'd be damn hard to ride this out. Lobel got everything. We've got nothing."

"I say go for it," Andy said.

"I agree," George seconded.

Bob was silent for a moment before nodding.

Banning pretended to study the papers in front of him. It was a dirty business. One of those horrible situations with no winners. The only possible way to approach it was to think in global terms. How did one balance a life, a life of a child, against the prestige of a nation? The question had haunted him all night, caused him to shout at the kids, to argue with Jane, to wake at three in the morning in a cold sweat. Well, you did it by thinking of it as a battlefield situation. And telling yourself that a nation sent an army of kids to fight knowing in advance that many would die. It was a calculated, necessary move for the good of the nation. Dealing in anonymous and large numbers, as opposed to individual and named people, made it acceptable. One talked of "troops," not men. Psychologically, it made a difference. Unfortunate as it might be, the boy would have to be regarded as a military casualty.

"Guess that's it," Banning said, pushing his chair back and getting to his feet. "Unless anyone has anything to add?"

No one answered.

Banning gathered his papers. Then, with an uncomfortable start, it hit him that they were the clichéd "old men" sending young kids out to fight and die. Except, in this case, it was an eleven-year-old boy whose life might be sacrificed. And they couldn't even hide behind the banner of freedom. The bottom line was, they were not protecting home and country and freedom, but a dark and ugly secret.

FORTY-ONE

Rose was waiting for him in the lounge when Daley got back to the hotel. He'd called her from the apartment earlier, and now as he recounted the evening's events she held his hand, nodding sympathetically.

"It's horrible," she said when he finished, "horrible for everyone. For Yoni, and for you." Her eyes misted. "And I can just imagine Ilan and Colleen! Oh, those poor people. How is Colleen?"

Daley didn't want to think about her. Each time he pictured her stunned face, he felt sick.

"She blames me," he said bitterly.

"I don't believe that, John."

"You didn't hear her. And the damn thing is, she's right. If I hadn't gone after him, if I hadn't—"

"John, stop it!" Rose interrupted. "I'm not going to let you blame yourself. First of all, it's not true, and secondly, it's absolutely counterproductive."

"Maybe so, but it doesn't change the fact that she blames me."

"You've been around enough misery to know people don't always act rationally in times of emotional crises. Colleen probably said things she doesn't believe. What did you say to her?"

"What could I say?"

Rose sighed. "Oh, John, it pains me so to sit by and see what's happening between you two. Or rather, what isn't happening. Don't you realize now is when she needs you the most?"

"She doesn't need me."

"She does. Believe me. She needs all the love and support she can get. John, don't you think you can reach out to her? Just a little? After all, you were able to reach out to me."

Looking into Rose's face, Daley saw only compassion and caring. Somehow, it eased the pain in his heart.

"That was different. Rose, I can't talk about it anymore. Okay? I can't even think straight."

They started toward the elevators. Daley felt as if his mind had shut down. He moved mechanically, barely aware of what he was doing.

"You must be exhausted," Rose said. "You've got to try to get some sleep. Do you think you can?"

"I don't know."

They stepped into the elevator. Daley knew he was exhausted, but the thought of being alone was suddenly intolerable. As the doors opened at their floor he turned to her.

"Will you stay with me tonight?" He paused, and for a moment the words seemed to stick in his throat. "I need you."

They lay close together, holding hands and not speaking. Daley's mind was in turmoil. Regardless of what Rose said, he blamed himself. Over and over, he replayed the scene on the street, as if in doing so it could be changed. If only he'd gotten there a moment earlier. If only the bus hadn't pulled up that moment, blocking his view. If . . . if . . . if. If's were an exercise in futility, he thought despairingly, remembering his father's saying, "If my grandmother had wheels, she'd be a bicycle."

"John, try to sleep," Rose said.

Daley turned to her, suddenly overwhelmed by a need so

fierce it startled him. He buried his lips in her hair and neck. Rose's arms held him tightly as he stroked the firm lines of her body.

Driven by a force almost beyond his control, he mounted her. He heard himself murmuring broken fragments of sentences, endearments he'd never thought himself capable of uttering. When at last they separated, spent and satisfied, he thought of Yoni, of Colleen, and felt ashamed.

"It doesn't seem right," he said.

Rose silenced him with a kiss.

"It's all right, John. Believe me."

She stroked his hair lovingly. He closed his eyes as the blessed relief of sleep claimed him.

He knew he was in a nightmare, but the knowledge couldn't stop it. The scene was familiar, but at the same time something was different. What, he didn't know.

He was marching under that incredibly blue sky. Fluffy white clouds drifted overhead. He was enchanted by the pristine loveliness of the sky and the lush forest all around. He knew he would see the little rabbit before it appeared, running out of the woods to stand frozen in the road before the line of marching men. He heard the rhythmic thumping of marching feet and waited for the other sound to begin. Like wind, the whisper swept through the column of men, growing stronger and clearer.

He willed himself to wake, but was firmly caught in the iron vise of the dream. All at once he knew what was different. Always before he had hovered outside the scene looking down at the marching men, who appeared no more real than plastic soldiers. This time he was one of them. They were real and life-sized.

The sound grew until it was thunder in his ears. Wake up! he screamed silently, but he was trapped. Nausea swept over him at the stench, which was suddenly everywhere. He heard sounds of retching and turned to see Vince throwing up by the side of the road.

"You won't believe it, you won't believe it." Over and over, the refrain was repeated as it passed down the line. I don't have to look, he told himself, I can go back. He pushed against the line of men. His feet were heavy. The ground had turned soggy with blood and he slid and slipped, desperate to get away from what lay ahead.

"Grandpa! Grandpa!"

At the sound of Yoni's voice, Daley whirled around. The camp loomed before him. Metal gates flung open to reveal mute, motionless figures, filthy, starving bags of bones, some half-clothed, others naked. They stood on a high platform. He wanted to escape, but the child's plaintive cry pulled him closer.

"Grandpa!"

Daley ran, then, at the gate, recoiled with horror. The "platform" was an immense heap of writhing skeletons.

Again he heard Yoni's cry. Knew he had to reach him before the boy became one of the skeletons. He searched the gruesome faces for Yoni, tried desperately to follow the sound of his voice, when the sound stopped. A deathly stillness fell over the camp.

Racing through the line of soldiers, he flew through the open gates. Hands reached for him, clawing at his sleeves, his pants.

"Yoni, where are you?" he shouted. "Yoni, I'm coming!"

A huge, stark black wall appeared in front of him. Daley knew he must somehow climb it. His hands bled as he scraped frantically at the hard stone. And then the sound of a shrill bell shattered the quiet.

"John!"

The bell was still ringing, only Daley realized it was the telephone. Rose was sitting up, her eyes wide with alarm as Daley reached for the phone, instantly awake.

"Mr. Daley."

Daley's heart leapt into his throat as he recognized the faint German accent.

"I apologize for the lateness of the hour. Someone wishes to speak to you."

"Sabba, it's me! Yoni."

"Yoni!" Daley shouted, but then Lobel was back on the other end.

"Listen to me, Mr. Daley. If you want to see your grandson

252

again, you will do exactly as I say. Go with your group tomorrow to Eilat. I will contact you there."

"Lobel!" Daley cried. "Don't hang up!"

He heard a click and then the steady drone of the dial tone.

FORTY-TWO

The older road through Beersheva and into the heart of the Negev was longer and more wearying than the more popular route through Dimona and the Arava. Lobel chose it not for the majestic landscape with its sprinkling of ancient ruins but for the measure of security he hoped the less-traveled, bleak desert route would provide. He experienced only one moment of panic, when a convoy of army trucks passed several miles outside the dry, flat Valley of Beersheva. He was certain by now that the entire law-enforcement organization of the country was mobilized. But the soldiers paid no attention to the elderly gentleman driving the inconspicuous Renault. And, of course, no one could have seen the small passenger sleeping on the backseat.

His anxiety lessened only after he had passed the orchards and vegetable fields of Ben-Gurion's home kibbutz, Sde Boker, and found himself in the vast wasteland of the Negev. Black-tented Bedouin camps began to appear on the deserted landscape. An occasional shepherd roamed with his flock. Few cars passed.

Lobel drove steadily, all his energy focused on the plan he had so carefully formulated, ignoring the tortured beauty of the valleys, the deep craters and burned-brown mountains. He stopped only once to relieve himself, staring in the distance at the craggy walls of limestone, mounds of sandstone, red and even green sand dunes strewn with great blocks of black volcanic silex.

He reached the mining town of Mitspe Ramon at sunset. The enormous panorama, a combination of the Grand Canyon and the surface of the moon, with its flat, twisting, and massive shapes, was drenched in reddish pastel hues. A quick glance convinced him his passenger still slept a drugged sleep. He knew he was operating on nervous energy. Fatigue was catching up and he was still far from his destination. He was tempted to stop for coffee, but dared not. He knew it was not advisable to drive the narrow road south by night, but he had no choice. He must push on.

A cold darkness fell quickly over the petrified desert world, plunging him into an eerie stillness in which nothing seemed to stir. He felt himself at the end of the world.

It was dark when he reached Eilat, Israel's combination military outpost-vacation center-shipping port at the southern tip of the Negev. The broad streets were quiet, the tourists having sought entertainment in the lounges of the luxury hotels after a day on the beach. Levi needed no directions. He drove south parallel to the Red Sea.

He allowed himself a wistful glance across the Gulf of Eilat at the rugged mountains of Saudi Arabia, Jordan, and the Sinai. In the distance, lights twinkled from the Jordanian port city of Aqaba. Jordan! He sighed. It might as well be a million miles away, for he saw the dark shapes of Israeli and Jordanian naval vessels patrolling the narrow straits.

He thought of Ernst living safely in Amman. It rankled him to realize he would need favors from such a simpleton. But then he hated receiving favors from anyone, even from Selim, who would gladly lay down his life for him.

This was no time for false pride, he told himself. Just past Coral Beach and the observatory, he slowed down, searching the dark landscape for the secondary road. It would be easy to miss at night. Braking suddenly, he swerved off the highway onto the cryptic path, which seemed to wind off into nowhere. He heard a moan from the backseat.

The boy began to stir as Lobel drove cautiously up the rocky, narrow road. Glancing at his watch, he knew the shot would be wearing off at any moment. He pulled over and stopped the car.

The boy sat up, looking around with a dazed expression. Lobel twisted around to face him and smiled.

"Shalom, Yoni," he said pleasantly. "You had a good rest."

"Where are we?"

"We are going to have an adventure," Lobel said. "Young boys like adventures, don't they?"

The boy emerged from his stupor.

"I want to go home."

"In good time. Of course you will go home. But first we are going to visit some friends. You will find them interesting, I am sure. Bedouins. Have you ever been in a Bedouin camp?"

"You tricked me. You're not a friend of my grandfather. Where's Sabba?"

"Oh, but I do know your grandfather. As for friends"— Lobel laughed shortly—"sometimes it is difficult to know who is a friend and who is not. Friends change. A person can be a friend one day and an enemy the next. Haven't you noticed that?"

The boy stared at him sullenly, then lunged at the door. Anticipating the move, Lobel reached over and seized his arm, forcing it from the handle. The child cried out, then slumped back against the seat.

"Don't try to get away," Lobel said coldly. It was time to stop the friendly, avuncular approach. As Lobel well knew, fear and intimidation were the safest means of ensuring cooperation. People responded to power. If one projected absolute power, thereby reducing the other to helplessness, one could do as he liked. It was easier with children. They were accustomed to obeying authority. He had cowed many a child into submission with trickery and then fear. And in the end he had always triumphed. Seeing the child completely at his mercy summoned forth the long-buried, heady sensation of power.

"My father has a gun," Yoni said defiantly.

"I know all about your father. I know all about you. Now

you listen to me. And listen very, very carefully. Are you listening?"

Lobel was pleased to see the boy's bravado disappear. He had not lost his touch. He nodded approvingly, as though the child had just given the right answer to a difficult problem.

"Good. Now, Yoni, do you remember hearing about the children who were kidnapped?"

"Yes."

"Tov. Good. Do you know what happened to them?"

"Are you the kidnapper?"

"Some of them were tortured," he said, ignoring the question. "Do you know what that means? They were cut with knives. They were burned. One child had his testicles cut off. They suffered very much. More than you can imagine. The pain was horrible. They screamed and cried. Some fainted."

He paused, allowing his words to sink in. He saw the boy's face pale.

"Have you ever been in pain? Think of the worst pain you have ever felt. Whatever that was, it was nothing compared to what those children endured. And it was only after they were tortured that they were killed."

He felt the boy's fear permeating the car. The child seemed to shrink back into the seat. His breathing was harsh and shallow. Good, Lobel thought. Now he had him. He would do as he was told.

"Now, Yoni. You must do exactly what I tell you to do. Those other children did not. And you can see what happened to them. You would not like to end up like them, cut and mutilated. Dead. But if you are cooperative, if you listen carefully and do as you are told, why then . . ." Lobel allowed himself a tight smile. "Why, then, we will call your grandfather. And you will be home with your parents in a day or two. And you will have an exciting story to tell. Do you understand?"

The boy nodded.

"Good." Lobel started the car. "Tell me, Yoni, have you ever met a Bedouin chief?" he asked pleasantly.

The Bedouin encampment was hidden in the shadow of the mountains of Eilat. Sheik Feisal and his tribe, unlike most of the approximately thirty thousand Bedouins in Israel, still lived in tents of black goat's hair in the wilderness. They were rugged people, preferring the ancient nomadic way of life. Lobel remembered well the time when all the Bedouins wandered, but in the 50's, under military law, they were prohibited from moving. They gave up their tents and began to live in huts and in the cities. Some, like Feisal, refused. As he had explained to Lobel once, "We come from Saudi Arabia, and our name, Bedouin, means 'Son of the Desert,' from the word *bedia*, desert. How can we turn our backs on our heritage?"

As far as Lobel could tell, they adhered to the ancient ways, living in the highly organized, military-like society of the tribe, with its strict laws.

Even before the tents began to appear, small boys materialized out of nowhere to run after the car. Although in recent years his visits had become more infrequent, Lobel was still known to them and they waved in greeting. He did not pause to talk, but drove directly to the largest tent.

Feisal stood by the entrance, an imposing figure in his burnoose, his dark, hawklike face framed by the flowing kaffiyeh.

Lobel stopped the car.

"Come with me and be quiet," he ordered the boy.

The sheik embraced him warmly, unperturbed by Lobel's unexpected appearance at their camp at this late hour. As Lobel had known, he was always welcome as an honored guest. To Feisal he was the miracle worker who had saved his son.

"My good friend," Feisal said, "I am honored."

Lobel returned the greeting, then drew Yoni forward. "This is my nephew," he said by way of introduction. "We are spending a little time together."

Lobel stooped to enter the tent, well aware that having crossed the threshold, his host would be obliged to go to almost fantastic lengths to provide for his comfort under desert law. Lobel also knew he was obliged to remain until he had partaken to the full of the feast that would be provided.

Inside the huge tent, they walked on rugs. Lobel sank down gratefully on the pile of soft cushions that were arranged for him. A servant appeared with the great brass coffeepot, which Lobel knew was always kept hot on the charcoal pit on the floor of the tent. He motioned the boy to sit by his side as he accepted a tiny china handleless cup and sipped the first of many bitter, thick coffees he would be expected to drink. Behind the hanging partitions along the length of the tent, he heard the women preparing the food.

He and Feisal talked . . . of hunting, of politics, of family. His oldest son was attending university, the sheik said with a hint of pride. He had a new grandchild.

"And Selim?" Lobel asked as the tiny coffee cup was refilled for him.

The sheik's forbidding features relaxed into an indulgent smile.

"He is to be married soon. But you shall see for yourself."

Lobel smiled. "I am happy. I look forward to seeing him."

Of all his former patients, Lobel had a soft spot for Selim, remembering the stoic little child who had submitted so bravely to his knife. He never forgot the child's expression of awed joy at the first sight of his reconstructed face after his accident. Yes, Selim held a special place in his heart.

At last the food was carried in by servants in a giant communal bowl, in the center of which Lobel saw the head of a sheep. The rest of the fragrant stew was steeped in a greenish sauce. According to custom, Lobel was expected to eat first. He turned to the boy.

"Watch what I do," he instructed. "You must use your right hand, never your left, and dip into the bowl as I do. And you must eat everything, even if it appears strange. Do you understand?"

The boy nodded.

Time, Lobel knew, was of no importance in the desert. The feast would go on and on. While he was impatient to move ahead with his plan, it would be considered an affront to stop eating first. Several other men had joined them. They ate slowly and no one seemed inclined to stop. When at last Feisal stopped eating, the hookah was brought out and passed around. Each man was given a puff. With a full stomach, Lobel was lulled into a feeling of security. He was among friends. Among people who would do anything for him. The shakiness had left him. True, difficulties remained, but he was confident he would prevail.

"Now I should like to see Selim," he said.

The youth was waiting for him at the entrance to his tent. In the moonlight Lobel was able to see his face clearly. Selim was truly one of his real successes. The scars had healed and he had grown into a good-looking young man. They embraced warmly.

"Selim," Lobel said, standing back, proudly admiring what his skill had accomplished, "I have a favor to ask of you."

The young man bowed his head. "You have only to ask."

FORTY-THREE

"The Red Sea isn't really red!" Daley heard Maureen Flanagan exclaim as the small Arkia Airlines plane touched down at Eilat, the southernmost city in Israel.

Daley couldn't resist exchanging amused looks with Rose. From the air the Red Sea was an incredible deep, transparent blue and Eilat a shimmering jewel resting on its shores. But peering out the window at the Red Mountains surrounding the city, and the Jordanian city of Aqaba clearly visible across the narrow tongue of water separating the Sinai from the Arabian Peninsula, Daley had only one thought. Yoni was there, somewhere. And so was Rudolf Lobel.

Only minutes after landing the group was registered at the Moriah Hotel. Daley immediately checked for messages. There were none.

The day's schedule included a morning tour of Coral World, with the afternoon free for the water sports for which Eilat was known . . . windsurfing, sailing, scuba diving, swimming. The next morning an all-day cruise to the Crusader fortress of Coral Island was planned. The tempta-

261

tion to stay behind and wait for Lobel to contact him was nearly overwhelming. Daley had to force himself to remember the policeman's instructions: "Go with your group."

The unique Coral World Observatory was on the outskirts of town. As the bus turned off the main street Daley surveyed the desert landscape on the right and the gulf on the left, as if Yoni might magically and suddenly materialize. And he wondered how and when Lobel would reach him. He told himself that whenever or however the contact was made, he would be ready. Ready to kill if necessary.

The observatory, with the only living coral reef reconstructed on land, was a major tourist attraction in a town of tourists. In the circular building they peered out of windows at the coral, which was kept alive and breathing by fresh ocean water and sunlight. From there Daley and Rose walked out over the water on the long wooden bridge to the underwater observatory and climbed down a spiral stairway to five meters below sea level.

Daley gazed out of a round porthole window at the coral, plants, and fish on the bottom of the sea. Next to him a small Israeli boy chattered excitedly to his parents as he pointed to a brightly striped, fluorescent fish. With a pang, Daley thought of Yoni. This was a place he was sure the boy would love. He wondered if Yoni had ever been here and realized suddenly that this fact was only one among hundreds of others he didn't know about his grandson. Things he might now never have the chance of knowing.

It occurred to him for the first time that he, not Colleen, had robbed himself of knowing his only grandson. He stared sightlessly at a school of slender, dark fish, sick with bitter anger at all those lonely, wasted years. Stupid, stubborn. That's what he was. All the things Colleen accused him of were true. And now it was too late.

Rose tried valiantly to keep his mind occupied as they toured the shark tank and aquarium and then wandered to the outdoor snack bar, where they drank filtered coffee at a table under a blue umbrella.

"There's nothing you can do except wait," she said, "but I feel he'll be fine. I just know it, John."

Daley nodded. He sipped his coffee, his attention riveted on the tourists, most of them young Europeans . . . English, German, Scandinavian. He searched the crowd for an elderly, white-haired man, knowing full well Lobel would hardly reveal himself in so public a place. But his heart lurched at the sight of every white-haired man, and when they were boarding the bus to return to town, and he heard childish voices chattering in Hebrew, he spun around, half expecting to see Yoni.

"Just beyond this point we are really in a no-man's-land," the guide said as the driver started back to town.

"Isn't that the Sinai? The territory that was returned to Egypt?" Rose asked. "What's there?"

"Nothing really but a strip of land called Taba at the border between Egypt and Israel. Now there is a dispute between us over this land. Before this problem the Egyptian Army was very friendly with us. Sometimes they would come on board Israeli pleasure yachts but now . . . they are not so friendly. Tomorrow, when we visit Coral Island, you will see Taba." She sighed. "Politics makes me so sad. Look . . ." She pointed across the channel where the mountains of Jordan and Saudi Arabia stretched endlessly, disappearing into haze. "You see Saudi Arabia. It is one of the richest countries in the world but needs technology, which Israel could easily provide. But because of stupid politics, the Saudis must import European technologists, scientists, and engineers at great expense. If there were peace, just think . . . Israeli experts could commute to work in Saudi Arabia on a daily or weekly basis. Both countries would benefit. Israel would boost its economy, Saudi Arabia would get much-needed technological help. It is as stupid as the Taba dispute." She sighed again. "Perhaps one day this will change."

As stupid, Daley thought, as his refusal to be part of his daughter's life. Realization, however, didn't change things—either on political or personal levels. Israelis and Arabs could fight forever over a useless strip of desert, knowing it was ridiculous; governments could help war criminals evade justice knowing full well it was immoral. Knowing he was to blame didn't mean he could ever be close to Colleen and Yoni.

There was no message at the hotel. At Rose's insistence they spent the afternoon on the beach. Daley checked the desk for messages every half hour. By late afternoon, when there was still no word, Daley placed a call to Tel Aviv.

Colleen answered on the first ring.

"No word," she said tersely before turning him over to Ilan.

"Rappaport says do what you normally would," Ilan said. "Behave exactly like a tourist."

"How's Colleen?" he asked.

There was a short pause on the other end. Then: "She's a strong woman. Like her father."

Daley hung up, wondering how strong he really was. There was a limit to anyone's emotional strength. He felt near the end of his.

The sunbathers had left the beach, and the seafront cafes were beginning to fill with tourists ready to relax over a drink and a glorious sunset. Only a windsurfer and a couple of teenagers standing on a *chasaka,* a long surfboard, remained in the water, although in the distance the ever-present naval patrol boats could be seen. The loud, infectious beat of the new oriental Israeli pop music blared from a radio as Daley and Rose strolled to a cafe near the marina within sight of the hotel.

Daley wondered which of the patrons were police. None looked likely in the mixture of nationalities, but he knew they were somewhere close. An English couple, their faces lobster-red and peeling, discussed the evening's entertainment at the next table. Two ebony-faced young men in colorful African garb drank beer at a table behind them. Sailors, probably. A group of slightly drunk young Germans was getting noisy.

"Yacht to Coral Island?"

Daley looked up. A slim young man, with the swarthy complexion of an Arab or Sephardic Jew, was standing over them. Daley noted the faint network of scars on the left side of his face.

"We're going tomorrow," Rose said.

"I have the best yacht," the young man said, "the best price. If you change your mind . . ."

Placing a white card on the table, he turned and walked away toward the dock.

"There's a persistent young man," Rose commented.

Daley didn't reply. He was staring at the crudely printed

words on the card: "Marina. 2:00 A.M. A boat will be waiting. Come alone."

Rose had made dinner reservations at a small, intimate fish restaurant called the Last Refuge near Coral World. Over grilled *locus,* she made small talk, trying to keep his mind off the ordeal ahead. Daley kept up the charade of normalcy, but by the time dessert and coffee came they both felt the strain of the artificial conversation and fell silent.

Rose stirred cream into her coffee.

"John, at least we know the police or the Mossad agents are watching. They'll get Yoni back."

"I know."

Along with his anxiety, Daley felt the crushing weight of responsibility. If it weren't for him, Yoni would be safe. And what that meant to Daley was that it was his responsibility to save the boy. He had done what he'd been told to do by telling the police about Lobel's call and then the message. What he hadn't told them was that he, too, had a weapon.

He set the alarm for one-thirty and stretched out on the bed, trying to catch some sleep. At one point he thought he dozed off, but it seemed he was wide awake moments later. At one-thirty he got up, splashed cold water on his face, made certain the gun was loaded and concealed, and slipped out of the room.

Daley crossed the empty lobby to the pool area and out to the boardwalk. Quickly he strode the short distance to the marina, where the cruise yachts were anchored. In the moonlight he could make out the dark shape of an Israeli patrol boat between the Jordanian and Israeli shores.

A prayer, the first in years, kept running through his head. Just let Yoni be safe. Let him be alive.

Daley looked around at the anchored yachts bobbing up and down. His watch said one-fifty. Ten minutes to go. He lit a cigarette and smoked nervously. Waiting. Wondering where the police were. Where Lobel was. Where Yoni was. Every nerve was raw, all his senses alert, his body tensed and expectant. Nothing happened. The full moon shone down on the water and empty beach. Maybe Lobel had changed his plan. Maybe something had gone wrong. Maybe he had misunderstood the message. Misread it. Or maybe the Nazi was sadistically playing with him. Daley's anxiety reached a peak.

Suddenly, seemingly out of nowhere, a low-slung skiff came into sight, skimming almost silently over the water. It was heading directly toward the shore where Daley was standing. Daley threw down his cigarette. Drew in his breath sharply. He felt he could hear his heart beating as the boat drew closer. He was comforted by the feeling of the cold metal against his ribs. Daley strained to see the pilot. He could make out nothing but the lone masculine figure that stood and beckoned to him.

FORTY-FOUR

Coral Island, with its craggy hills and Crusader ruins, stood out eerily in the moonlit night. Only three hundred meters from the disputed strip of land, Taba, its sensitive political situation heightened its appeal for Rudolf Lobel. The forbidding granite rock was the perfect place for his final meeting with John Daley, he told himself, as Selim steered his small fishing boat toward the dock.

Before Saladin captured the island in 1170, the Crusaders sailed from it to attack Arab ships in the Red Sea. Later the Mamluks and Turks fortified the island. Gradually it became deserted except for remains of the old Crusader fortress. Now controlled by the Egyptians, Coral Island was off limits to Israelis. Lobel was confident the Israelis would not risk an international incident by stepping foot on the island. And, he thought smugly, for their part the Egyptians would not risk touching an Israeli citizen, even one trespassing on their territory.

Selim dropped anchor and helped Lobel and Yoni from the boat.

"Many thanks," Lobel said.

Selim bowed his dark head.

"I will be back in one hour, maybe less."

Pushing the child ahead of him, Lobel jumped lightly from the rough wooden dock and set foot on the rocky shore. Yoni made no sound of protest.

He had succeeded where the boy was concerned. Yoni was thoroughly cowed into submission, terrified and compliant. He would do exactly as he was told. Lobel patted the child's head.

"Soon you will see your grandfather," he said cheerfully.

Yoni turned a tense face to him. He made no reply.

"Now we must climb a little," Lobel said, "up to the remains of the old fortress and we will wait. You remember everything I said to you, don't you?"

The boy was silent.

Lobel prodded him sharply with the butt of his gun. The boy jumped.

"You are being rude, Yoni. You must answer your elders. You remember everything I told you, yes?"

"Yes."

"Tov. Good. Now we must go."

It was an exceptionally clear night. A luminous moon shone down from a star-studded velvet sky. Lobel turned to look back at the Israeli shore, with its silhouette of the Sonesta Hotel. He was struck by the bizarre contrast of the ultramodern structure with the spartan Egyptian army camp just a few yards away, only flags between indicating the presence of the international border. And nothing else for miles around. From the Egyptian camp he saw the tiny red glow of cigarettes by the Quonset huts. It seemed to Lobel the last outpost of civilization.

A missile patrol boat, its two twenty-millimeter machine guns plainly visible in the moonlight, was docked near the Sonesta. Silently patrolling the Israeli waters were naval vessels, radar antennas constantly turning. Across the gulf, where Jordan and Saudi Arabia beckoned alluringly, Lobel made out the shapes of the Jordanian naval fleet. Amid all that power he was safe!

Lobel looked around. The three-hundred-meter granite

rock was formidable, barren but for a few palm trees by the water and a run-down thatched-roof hut. The hut was supposed to have been a restaurant, Lobel recalled, but the Egyptians ran out of money and abandoned the project midway. Now it was simply another ruin.

"Come," he ordered the boy. "Follow me."

The climb up the rocky slope was steeper than he had bargained for. Lobel was soon out of breath, his heart racing wildly. He stopped to catch his breath, taking huge gulps of the warm sea air. He wiped his perspiring brow with a handkerchief. He was grateful for the physical activity that had kept him spry. A more sedentary man his age would have been unable to make that climb, he told himself. Still, he felt his calf muscles aching, his shortness of breath. He must not stop, he warned himself. He must push on.

"Not too much farther," he said to Yoni, reassuring himself as much as the child. He pointed up to a portion of stone wall and pillar. "There. We will wait there."

When they reached it Lobel was pleased with what he saw. From the wall he could clearly see the dock below, but he would not be easily visible, protected as he was by the ruin. There was a large clearing by the remains. It was a good place in which to await his prey. All his hunting instincts emerged at the thought of his human quarry.

He turned to the boy.

"Sit down. We will wait here."

He reached into his pocket and withdrew a piece of chocolate. He gave it to the child, who accepted it silently.

The sense of isolation, of timelessness, lulled him as he waited. He felt his anxiety disappearing. He unwrapped a piece of chocolate for himself, savoring it contentedly. He was invincible. Everything had gone as planned. He had come this far, and he knew that nothing would stop him. He had nothing to fear from the authorities. Nothing to fear from John Daley. For the first time since he'd encountered the American detective, Lobel felt almost happy.

Ahead of him stretched a new life like a blank page in an open book. He had his health. Enough money to live comfortably. He had years ahead of him. He succumbed to a dreamlike fantasy in which he saw himself strolling down a street in

Damascus, well-tailored, distinguished. He saw himself entering a modern apartment, surrounded once more with books and art. Sitting with old friends over beer, speaking German. Ah, it would be good after so long.

Jerusalem, the hospital, Rivka, Buzz, Shlomo . . . even Frieda . . . everything that had made up his life for nearly forty years receded, becoming no more real than old photographs in an album. Recognizable but distant. He quite forgot the nostalgia leaving his apartment had caused.

Lobel had never been one to look back. A fortunate trait, he thought proudly. One must never look back. One must never have regrets. A profound waste of time and energy.

"Is that him?"

Lobel was jerked abruptly back to the present by the boy's voice. Lobel gripped the child's arm firmly. The unmistakable sound of footsteps on loose gravel seemed to echo in the night.

"Lobel! Where are you?"

"Your grandfather has come, just as I said he would."

Lobel heard the sharp intake of breath. He tightened his hold on the boy's arm.

"Keep on, Mr. Daley!" Lobel called.

Lobel gripped his gun tightly as he listened to Daley's slow progress up the steep, rocky hillside. Yoni was breathing rapidly. Lobel felt his tension and wondered if he had sufficiently frightened the child. It was crucial that the boy play his part. He turned to him and pointed the gun in his face.

"Remember, Yoni, if you disobey me, I will kill you and your grandfather."

What he did not say was that he intended to kill them both anyway after they had served their purpose. The child stared up at him. Lobel saw that he was trying to decide if he was being told the truth, trying to decide whether or not to believe him. Lobel held the gun to the child's head.

"I have killed more children than I can remember. And do you know something? To me it was no more important than stepping on an ant. Do you understand? Your life is no more important to me than that. But you are a good boy. I can see that. And so if you do as I say, you will not be hurt."

He saw the look of uncertainty turn into naked fear. It was a look he remembered well. It did not touch him.

Daley approached the clearing. Lobel readied himself.

"Mr. Daley!" he called.

His voice sounded strange in the stillness.

Daley stopped, looked around, but Lobel remained concealed behind the stone wall.

"Where's the boy?" Daley shouted.

Lobel nudged the boy with the gun.

"Come! And remember everything I have said."

Slowly Lobel led the boy into the clearing.

FORTY-FIVE

Daley stood immobilized, his mind feverishly racing for a way to save his grandson. The few yards separating them might well have been miles. The gun aimed at the child's temple had seen to that. Daley had no doubt Lobel would kill Yoni. Recognizing that fact rendered his own weapon useless.

"What do you want, Lobel?" Daley barked.

Lobel chuckled softly, and the sound intensified Daley's frustrated rage. The Nazi exhibited none of the nervousness appropriate to the situation. None of the typical behavioral signs Daley expected. If anything, that obscene chuckle told him Lobel was enjoying it, this playing with them. In a far corner of his mind Daley saw the jars of human organs lined up on shelves in the "hospital" of Mauthausen. All along he'd regarded Lobel as a criminal. He was used to dealing with criminals. With that unexpected chuckle, Daley's confidence was suddenly undermined by the chilling thought that Rudolf Lobel was not merely a criminal. He was insane.

Yoni stood motionless by the old man. He had obviously been thoroughly coached or frightened or both. Daley hoped to God that was all. He refused to think what other unspeakable things might have been done to the boy. The only thing he could do, Daley realized, was keep Lobel talking in hopes that the other man would provide an opportunity for Daley to make a move.

"What do you want?" he repeated.

"Look across the water to the far shore," Lobel replied. "Jordan. We are going to take a little trip, the three of us. I have always liked sea journeys. What about you?"

"Why don't you go alone? It shouldn't be difficult."

"I'm surprised at you, Mr. Daley," Lobel chided.

Again Daley heard that sadistic laugh.

"You are my insurance," Lobel continued. "You see, I have no more illusions that my life is of any value to anyone, least of all to my so-called friends. That is what it all comes down to eventually for all of us, doesn't it?"

Wondering if there might be a way he could catch the other man off guard, Daley strained forward, trying to see his grandson's face more clearly.

"What do you mean?"

"Only this. I am a doctor, you know. I have seen people die, and at that moment a person, no matter what his circumstances, is always and completely alone. As we all are. They used to call me the Hunter. Did you know that? I have hunted all my life and hunting has reinforced this view. Out there"— he waved his free hand toward the shore—"in the wild, animals fight for survival alone." He laughed again, this time a sharp bitter sound. "And we only believe we are different. We are all hunters in that sense."

"There's no way you can pull it off," Daley said in a reasonable, friendly tone. "You're an intelligent man, you can see that. So why not just give me the boy? You have less to be afraid of than you think. If you're tried and convicted, there will be legal appeals for years and you'll probably die in bed of old age." The scenario he was painting was probably accurate, Daley realized bitterly.

"I would never cage a wild creature," Lobel sneered, "and I will never be caged myself."

"But you can't pull it off. Look around, Lobel. The forces of three countries are around you."

273

The shadowy presence of Israeli patrol boats comforted Daley slightly. Still, Lobel was desperate.

"I am aware of that, Mr. Daley. However, you are an American citizen. No one will harm you, and as long as you are with me, I am secure."

"Then you don't know the Israelis," Daley responded. "You think they'll let you go off with the child? He's an Israeli! Do you think the country that kidnapped Eichmann will let you get away?"

"It is you who does not understand Israelis. I do. I have been one for half my life! Not long ago Israel released more than a thousand Palestinian and Lebanese guerrillas from prison, dozens of them convicted of murder, in exchange for three Israeli soldiers! And one of those guerrillas was involved in the Lod Airport massacre! All to save three Israelis! So you see, with an American citizen and an Israeli child, I have double insurance. They would prefer to see even someone like me get away than see harm come to the child."

With a sick feeling in the pit of his stomach, Daley recognized the truth of Lobel's words.

"Enough of this," Lobel said abruptly.

Daley saw him grip Yoni's arm rudely as they slowly approached, and the sudden blind anger at this sight almost caused him to lose control and lunge forward.

"You first, Mr. Daley," Lobel instructed. "There is a boat waiting. We shall see what sort of sailor you make."

Daley started down the steep, rocky hillside. He heard them behind him. He considered his options. He could turn suddenly, take a chance on overpowering Lobel. In a hand-to-hand contest Daley knew he would be the winner. But he knew just as surely, he couldn't take the chance. Lobel would kill instantly.

Somehow he must get Lobel, but it would have to be by means other than physical power. He would have to view Lobel as an animal he was stalking and use hunting instinct and hunting psychology . . . anticipate the other's moves, think as he did, while keeping all his senses alert.

The cold metal of the gun resting against his side comforted him as for the second time in his life Daley felt himself capable of cold-blooded murder.

FORTY-SIX

The Nazi had thought of everything, Daley thought with grudging admiration. Nearly hidden in a sheltered cove not far from the dock, a rubber craft with an outboard motor bobbed in the water.

"You will get your shoes wet here, I'm afraid," Lobel said. "I apologize for the inconvenience."

Daley was unnerved by the man's jocular, relaxed manner. Apparently out of touch with the reality of the situation, Lobel was, to Daley's way of thinking, even more dangerous.

"Get in, please. You first, Mr. Daley."

Daley waded into the shallow water and climbed into the boat. Lobel pushed Yoni forward. The boy clambered into the boat and stood uncertainly, looking from Daley to Lobel.

"You sit there, opposite your grandfather," Lobel instructed.

Yoni obeyed. Watching Lobel nimbly hoist himself over the side, Daley was struck by the old man's agility. Lobel sat next to Yoni, his gun nestled against the boy's ribs.

"You will row, Mr. Daley," Lobel said. "No point in using

the motor here. We don't want to disturb the guests at the Sonesta at this late hour, do we? On the other side of the island we can use the motor."

Daley picked up the oars from the floor of the boat and began to row. He looked at Yoni, trying to communicate silently, to reassure and comfort him. The boy's face remained frozen in fear.

"There are very swift currents between here and the shore," Lobel said, "but you needn't worry. My friend tells me this is a sturdy boat. Around the tip of the island, Mr. Daley, and then straight ahead."

As Daley rowed he scanned the dark waters for signs of help. It felt as if the three of them were cut off from the world. Where were the agents and police supposedly watching them? Israeli patrol boats?

As if reading his thoughts, Lobel spoke up: "The political situation here is working in our favor. Because of the dispute over Taba, everyone is on best behavior. No one will do anything. This boat, in case you are wondering, belongs to a Bedouin fisherman. It is familiar to the Israelis and Egyptians. They will pay it no mind. Row harder, Mr. Daley. Exercise is very good for men our age."

Daley forced his attention from the empty stretch of water to Lobel and the gun in his hand. His only chance was to get that gun away. If he could keep Lobel talking, he might be sufficiently distracted for Daley to risk it.

"Tell me something," Daley said. "Are you Ruven Levi?"

Although Daley was repulsed by Rudolf Lobel, at the same time he felt a genuine curiosity, the sort of fascination that compelled people to gawk at a gory traffic accident.

"I thought you already knew that," Lobel chided. "I'm disappointed in you."

One way of disarming Lobel emotionally was appealing to his ego. Daley had known few criminals who could resist bragging of their cleverness.

"I suspected, but I wanted to hear it from you. How did you do it? Pretty ingenious."

"It would make quite a story, wouldn't it?"

Lobel rose to the bait, nearly preening at what he took to be flattery.

"In your country I would write a book and go on television. I would be an instant celebrity and make a fortune!" he boasted. "If I were younger, I might be tempted to pursue such a path, but I think now I prefer the anonymity of the quiet life."

They were nearing the tip of the island. Only the Gulf of Aqaba separated Coral Island and Jordan. Daley saw no sign of Israeli military presence. He was further disheartened by knowing that even if they were following, once the little boat reached international waters, the Israelis would be forced to turn back. With the Egyptian Army only two hundred meters from shore, they would think twice before taking action that might be misinterpreted. Toward Lobel he felt the same admiration as for a cunning animal that had managed to outwit him.

"But how did you do it?" Daley pursued.

"Planning, Mr. Daley. Planning is everything." Lobel seemed relaxed, eager to talk, as if they were two old friends on a Sunday outing.

Daley studied Lobel's face as he rowed. He had been obsessed with Rudolf Lobel, the Hunter of Mauthausen. He realized that Lobel symbolized for him the evil loose in the world. To find himself now sitting across from him, listening to his voice, observing his mannerisms and the changing expressions on his face plunged Daley into turmoil. This personification of the devil was in reality an aging man, not much older than he. A human being, after all, who had been someone's son, someone's husband. For an instant Daley forgot his hatred. Then, just as swiftly as it had flared, the tiny spark of compassion died. The man who sat there with a gun aimed at a child had relinquished all claims to membership in the human race. God forgive me, Daley thought. I would kill him gladly.

"You may start the engine here," Lobel said.

Daley dropped the oars and started the motor.

"It was obvious to those whose eyes were open that Germany was finished," Lobel was saying over the soft put-put of the motor, "so I made certain I had money in safe places. Without money one cannot function. With it . . . anything is possible. I had in those days many wealthy, eager Jewish patients. You might even say they flocked to Mauthausen, and they paid well for my services. They did not even want a second opinion! My word was enough!" He laughed at his own joke. "I left two days before the Allies arrived, but was apprehended a short time later."

"I know," Daley said, unable to resist interrupting. "I was at your trial."

Lobel looked surprised. "You?"

"Military police guard."

"So that was how you knew me. Ah, I wouldn't have guessed. Yes, the trial was an unfortunate business. A total travesty of justice. Luckily, I had some friends or I would still be in prison."

"American friends," Daley said bitterly, thinking of Safehaven.

"Now I am talking of German friends. Fellow officers. You were in the military, Mr. Daley. You know how close war brings men. I often think the relationship between soldiers is stronger than between man and wife."

Daley thought of Vince. The experiences they had shared in the war had bound them together for nearly forty years. But that relationship was now changed, tainted with suspicion. He wondered if he would ever know the whole truth of Vince's involvement, of Lobel's connections to the Allied Forces.

"I didn't make my American friends until later. I spent some difficult weeks after Landsberg. However, as luck would have it, I found a valuable friend in one of your countrymen."

"You mean you provided information about the Russians in exchange for protection," Daley said, remembering all Goldschmidt had told him.

Lobel laughed. "I? What information could I have had? I am a physician. I was able to provide some notes regarding my research, which may have been of some small scientific value, but Russians?" He shook his head in amusement. "Nothing quite so glamorous, Mr. Daley. This very highly placed American was secretly experiencing some financial difficulties . . . a divorce, child-support payments, an ill father. In the true spirit of international cooperation, we helped each other."

Daley clenched his fists as the full significance of Lobel's words sunk in. He saw the bodies piled like cordwood at the entrance to the camp and felt the old rage burning inside.

"With his help I managed to get into a DP camp in the American Zone. I was quite thin at that point, and looked much like the others. Having been around so many Jews for so long, I had picked up some of their ways. Why, I even learned Yiddish. It was not difficult . . . a perversion of German. And believe it or not, I saw at least three other German officers there in that camp. I often wonder where they ended up. I would not be surprised if they are living in your country. Ah, well," he sighed.

"Who was Ruven Levi?"

"A former patient. Unfortunately, he expired. Even the best physician loses some patients, you know." Again he laughed at his own grim joke. "I had access to his records and knew that poor Dr. Levi was the only survivor of his family. We had many things in common . . . profession, age, similar appearance. In a way I like to feel I gave Dr. Levi a second life. And, pardon my boast, but very likely a more distinguished life than he would have lived himself."

The island was receding into the distance as the boat continued into the open sea. He wondered how much farther until they reached international waters. With every passing minute the lights on the Jordanian shore grew brighter. Part of his attention was focused on the dark, hulking shapes of Jordanian ships on the horizon while another part of him remained spellbound by Lobel's story.

"Why Israel, where you ran the greatest risk of discovery?"

"Once there, citizenship was automatic and no one asked for papers. I thought of emigrating to South America, but my wife had strong objections. Palestine was such a primitive place. You cannot imagine Tel Aviv then . . . so provincial. Donkeys in the streets. Still, I must admit, I was attracted by the professional opportunities and, to tell the truth, I quite enjoyed the idea of being one of the builders of the new state. I did play an important part."

"You weren't afraid of being discovered?"

Lobel seemed to consider the question. "Yes, at first, but by then, you see, I was Ruven Levi. I knew that former camp inmates would never look for Rudolf Lobel there. And I made quite certain I had the continued help of my American friends." He chuckled. "I let them know if anything should happen to me, my connection with my friend would be made public. Americans are such children. So afraid of scandal. As it turned out, ironically enough, of all the places in the world, I was safest in Israel. It was a good life."

For several minutes there was no sound but the rhythmic slap of water against the boat and the purring of the engine. Lobel had stopped talking. He seemed lost in a reverie.

"You had no right to change that!" Lobel's manner abruptly changed as he burst into a tirade. "Who appointed you my judge? You disgusting, vile excuse for a man! You had no right to interfere. How dare you! I am a pioneer of medicine! I saved hundreds, I rebuilt lives, faces! What have you done with your life? Who are you? Nothing, a piece of excrement!"

Something in Lobel had snapped. Daley felt the sweat trickling down his back as the torrent of abuse washed over him. Petrified, Yoni stared open-mouthed. Daley understood that once they reached Jordan, Lobel would kill them both. Had planned to kill them from the start. Their only salvation lay in disarming Lobel.

They were nearly halfway across the gulf and, for all Daley knew, might already have entered international waters. The Israelis might be watching, might even be somewhere close. Even if they dared chance an incident, they wouldn't shoot for fear of hitting Yoni. Daley felt everything resting on his shoulders.

Cutting the engine, Daley sprang forward and shoved Yoni to the floor.

"Stay down!" he shouted, lunging for Lobel.

Daley had the advantage of weight and training and surprise, but Lobel's desperation increased his strength. The violent rocking of the boat made Daley struggle to keep his balance. He heard Yoni's cries, his own labored breathing, Lobel's grunts. Lobel's knee came up, missing his testicles but jabbing his stomach. Daley threw himself on top of Lobel, pinning him against the wooden seat. His huge hand closed like a vise over Lobel's wrist. He squeezed, forcing the man's fist to open. The gun fell to the floor of the boat. Quickly Daley picked it up, flinging it over the side.

With an outraged scream, Lobel stretched out his arms toward the water. The boat capsized, hurling them into the sea. Daley saw Yoni, weighted down by clothes, struggling to stay afloat.

"Sabba!" he cried.

"Yoni, swim to the boat! Hold on!" he shouted. "It's okay. Don't panic!"

The boy paddled to the overturned boat, clinging to its side. Lobel was swimming away from the boat. Daley's powerful arms sliced through the water. He felt propelled by a superhuman strength, thinking only of overtaking the Nazi. The gap narrowed. Lobel was slowing. Daley pushed harder until he could reach out and touch him.

With his arm around Lobel's neck, Daley began to pull him back toward the boat. Lobel's energy seemed to have given out and he did not resist. They held on to the capsized craft, sputtering for air.

"There aren't any friends to help," Daley gasped. "I'll see you rotting in prison, or die trying."

In the moonlight, Lobel's face twisted with hatred.

"Guess again, Mr. Daley. I told you, I will never be caged."

Lobel reached into his shirt with one hand. For an instant Daley thought he might have a knife or a gun, but it was a small plastic bag with a capsule that Lobel held in his hand. Daley lunged for his bony wrist as Lobel brought the bag to his lips.

"I want you dead, but not that way," Daley shouted, but his words were lost in the roar of the two gunshots that shattered the air.

FORTY-SEVEN

Lights flickered on at the Sonesta as the kitchen staff set about preparing breakfast. Had he been looking, Daley would have seen stirrings at the Egyptian encampment. The curtain of night started to lift. The first pinnacled peaks on the Sinai side were suddenly lit up with an orange fire that then proceeded to diffuse to the purple massif below as fishing boats glided out across the gulf.

Daley, his arm around Yoni, was oblivious to the predawn activity around him. He held on to his grandson, his eyes drawn to the floor of the fast and silent naval command boat and the covered heap . . . all that remained of Rudolf Lobel. Ruven Levi.

He was not used to analyzing his emotions, but as the harbor came into sight Daley found himself trying to sort through his feelings.

He hated Rudolf Lobel as he'd never hated any human being. But he took no satisfaction in his death. He felt no relief, not even anger. He told himself Lobel should have stood trial before the world, his sins exposed. Judged by mankind.

Daley felt betrayed, as though Lobel had had the last word, after all. With Lobel dead, he thought in frustration, he'd probably never know the full story. Lobel claimed he'd bought somebody—an American—off. Left unclear was the question of whether U.S. Intelligence knowingly covered it up all these years, as Lobel had insinuated. Was that "friend" Lobel mentioned still alive, protecting his own sordid secret? And what of the Israelis? Had they known all these years that the respectable Dr. Levi was the Hunter of Mauthausen?

"Sabba, is he really dead?"

Daley lifted his eyes from Lobel to the upturned face of his grandson. The child's earnest, anxious expression filled him with tenderness.

"He's dead. You don't have to be afraid."

"I was afraid," the boy admitted.

Daley hugged him close.

"Yeah. Me, too."

The boat sliced through the water, throwing up a fine spray as the Israeli at the wheel headed for the marina. Two others, wet-suited, with infrared sniper guns at their feet, were smoking in a relaxed fashion.

"Where's my mother?" Yoni asked.

"You'll see her soon," Daley said.

Daley's thoughts shifted from Lobel to his daughter. He had brought Yoni back safely, he told himself. Colleen couldn't blame him. But something told him that while he could leave Israel with a clear conscience, he would not leave with a clear mind. It hit him suddenly that he had come to Israel not because he'd been given a ticket by his buddies, not because he was curious to see the Holy Land. He had come to see Colleen and to reclaim his share in her life. He wondered why he hadn't been able to admit it to himself. Why he had fought the idea. Maybe he'd been afraid she'd reject him after all these years.

He sensed that until he reestablished a relationship with Colleen, he'd never be able to really resume any kind of a life at home. He didn't understand exactly why that was so, but some instinct told him the unresolved situation between him and his daughter would stand in the way of any future relationship with Rose.

Some of the old resentment flared up. Hell, it was up to Colleen, he told himself, he'd done all he could. But for the first time the unspoken words sounded meaningless and empty.

"I'm cold," Yoni said, shivering in his wet clothes.

"We're almost there," Daley replied, pointing to a knot of men clustered together on the beach.

"Sabba, did he really kill children? He said he did."

"Yes."

"Then I'm glad he's dead. But who killed him?"

Daley didn't answer.

Five men waited on the dock as Daley and Yoni climbed out of the boat. One of the men wrapped blankets around them. Two others lifted the dead body of Lobel. The remaining two stood apart at a distance.

"I want to see my mother," Yoni said.

Daley took the boy's hand, curiously observing the men lay the body on the dock. He found himself wondering what procedures they would follow next, then caught himself as he remembered Colleen's accusation: "For once in your life, can't you stop being a cop?" Daley turned away, ashamed.

"I want to see my mother," Yoni said again.

"Me, too, Yoni," Daley said, and meant it.

The rising sun had turned the water golden pink. The faint sound of Arabic music from a radio drifted out from one of the fishing boats docked at the marina.

The Israelis ignored Daley and Yoni, speaking to each other in Hebrew. Taking Yoni's hand, Daley started forward toward the two who remained apart. He stopped in shock as he recognized, first, the "Englishman" from Hebron and then, right next to him, the stocky, blond Mossad agent.

The "Englishman" nodded in greeting.

"Mr. Daley," he said politely.

"Who are you?" Daley demanded.

"A friend."

Daley's temper flared. "Some friend! What was going on in Hebron? And in that car that almost killed us!"

The other man shook his head.

"None of this happened, Mr. Daley."

Daley turned to the others, unanswered questions bombarding his mind. The bombing in the hotel, the Englishman's appearance in Hebron, the car that nearly ran them down, the agent in the elevator, the missing photo of Lobel, the false photograph of Levi.

"I want some answers! What kind of crap is this 'None of this happened'?"

"I want some answers," he repeated when no one answered. "What the hell is going on?"

"It's over, Mr. Daley," one of the men said in an unmistakable American accent. "It doesn't matter. Your grandson looks cold and tired. Let's go in."

"The hell it doesn't matter!" Daley said. "I'm not going anyplace until I get some questions answered."

Despite the frustration and anger Daley sensed behind their steely silence, he felt he wouldn't get anything out of them. He thought how closely Yoni had come to dying, the agony Colleen and Ilan had been put through, the nightmares that had haunted his life for forty years, the tortured souls of Mauthausen. He looked from the dead body of the man who had evaded justice for forty years to the implacable faces of the five men, overwhelmed by rage.

"Goddammit, I have a right to know!"

"Things are complicated in the Middle East, Mr. Daley," one of the Israelis said quietly. "Sometimes one must make expedient choices."

"He was a Nazi," Daley spat out. "Or doesn't that mean anything anymore?"

The other man sighed. "Sometimes one must do things for a friend that one would rather not do. In the name of friendship and mutual need. You heard your countryman. It never happened."

Daley started to respond, to argue, but Yoni's sudden shout stopped him. The boy broke away from him, shedding the blanket as he raced down the dock. A dark blue police van had appeared on the beach along with an army Jeep. Uniformed men materialized, descending on the dock. The deserted marina suddenly buzzed with activity.

John Daley stopped mid-sentence, then he, too, started forward. Watching from the terrace of the Moriah Hotel, Rose Malloy noted he was not running, but neither was he exactly holding back. And not until he wrapped her in his arms did he once take his eyes off the red hair of his daughter.

"But if he smote him with a stone in the hand, whereby a man may die, and he died, he is a murderer; the murderer shall surely be put to death. Or if he smote him with a weapon of wood in the hand, whereby a man may die, and he died, he is a murderer. . . . The avenger of blood shall himself put the murderer to death . . . if the manslayer shall at any time go beyond the border of his city of refuge . . . and the avenger of blood find him without the border of his city of refuge, and the avenger of blood slay the manslayer; there shall be no blood-guiltiness for him. . . ."

 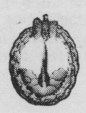